When I Think of You

CHERYL BARTON

Published by: Cheryl Barton Publishing, LLC

For printing and/or copying permission requests, write to the publisher, addressed to:
    "Attention: Permissions Coordinator," at the address below.

Cheryl Barton Publishing, LLC
P.O. Box 962
Reisterstown, Maryland 21136
www.crbarton.com
or
Email: prez@crbarton.com

Ordering Information:
Quantity sales.
Special discounts are available on quantity purchases by corporations, associations, and others. For details, contact the publisher at the address above.

Orders by U.S. trade bookstores and wholesalers.
Please contact prez@crbarton.com

ISBN:
ISBN-13:

Dedication

I dedicate this love story to every man who ever thought that his love wouldn't be enough to make a woman fall in love with him and not for what he could do for her. Walk in confidence in who you are and what you have to offer. It may not be silver and gold, but let your heart be made of platinum and diamonds and the woman who is supposed to return your love will embrace you with open arms.

To my sisters out here wondering if love is real – if that's what you want, let that be the defining factor in the man you choose to love.

Happy reading!
Cheryl

OTHER ROMANCE NOVELS BY CHERYL BARTON

WWW.CHERYLBARTON.NET

Prologue

A rainy morning was the last thing Leo Westmoreland needed on a day when he already felt as if he was isolated from the rest of the world. The pouring rain added to the sullen mood he woke up with which he contributed to exhaustion working three different jobs week after week. Nothing in particular had him down, just life itself. He was busy working all the time and didn't have a chance to actually enjoy the little time he had off. At twenty-nine, he had responsibilities and focusing on anything other than that wasn't a priority. He had a mother and brothers who depended on him. He'd made a promise and he was sticking to it.

Walking around his small, one-bedroom apartment in Harlem, New York, Leo took stock in what he saw from his favorite chocolate brown, silky velvet and plush cushioned L-shaped sofa to the accent chairs and tables all courtesy of his boss at one of his part time jobs where he staged houses for sale some evenings and weekends. His boss had surprised him a few years back after one of the houses he'd staged sold for more than the offer. Besides giving him a pretty large bonus because the buyer said their decision to buy was based on how well the house was staged, she also offered him any of the furniture from the house he wanted. In essence, his living room mirrored the room he'd staged from the lamps, to the chairs and just about everything else in the large room except the large flat-screen television that covered the wall in front of the sofa.

When he moved into the apartment five years ago, the only furniture he had was the bedroom set he'd bought after weeks of making payments on it. Leo looked around and saw his growth over the past few years and where he was brooding a few moments ago, he smiled knowing that despite where his life had been, he was still further than he thought he would be. He sat down on his sofa and reminded himself to never let himself get down because he wasn't where he wanted to be in life, but life sure could be a lot worse, including not even having a sofa in their apartment.

For anyone else, a sofa after a few years may have begun to deteriorate from use, but because he spent more of his time working than at home, his still looked brand new. Leo tried to remember the last time he'd enjoyed company on that same sofa. Had his last overnight female guest really been his ex, Misha, who'd dropped him six months ago as if he'd had the plague?

The worst part of being a single guy has to be the lonely nights along with the emptiness that was his apartment in the early morning hours. He had lived through quite a few of those lonely, empty nights and it wasn't because there wasn't a woman out in the world who could take the loneliness away. He found himself getting more particular about who he spent his time with. He thought Misha would fit the bill, but she'd shown him her true colors and he happily moved on and so far, that wasn't to anyone special. He'd had a few casual encounters, but knew better than to bring them to his place, preferring to let them entertain him in the comfortableness of their own place. He wasn't hiding anything or purposely keeping women from his space, but he preferred to let them decide what made them feel safest.

As he stood, he tried to shake off the softer side of himself especially since at one time in his life, he'd had a father who tried to raise him and his brothers to have strong he-man, caveman-like personalities which should always be stern and hard as rocks, no soft side at all. His father had poured and oftentimes beat into them that they were never to show a feminine side and if he caught them in their feelings, they would regret it. As a youngster, he took his advice to heart until he saw how his father treated their mother and then all bets were off. The last thing he wanted was to be like his father or be the kind of man his father wanted him to be, not if it meant he ended up treating another woman the way his father had done their mother.

Roland Westmoreland was a hard man, not just on his three sons, but also on their mother. As the oldest of three boys at the age of seventeen, Leo had come home one day to find his mother bruised and crying. She had a black eye and appeared to have a problem using her left arm. She winced every time he tried to help her up from the floor in the corner where his father had left her sitting, yet again, after one of his beatings. Where she should have been concerned about her own health, she was more concerned about him and his two brothers who were four and seven years old. She was scared that if their father returned home, he would take more anger out on them, something she had tried to avoid over the years by taking punches she knew he would have unleashed on her sons. She didn't prevent them all, but they received a lot less because of her standing in the gap for them. It wasn't until he'd become a grown man that he found out from family on his father's side that his father had been abused as a child. His abuse as a child wasn't an excuse for what he did to them, but he finally understood what plagued his father and a life of being abused continued with him and he became an abuser.

That day when he arrived home and saw his mother in the corner, he had been angrier than ever before and he vowed he would never lay his own hands on a woman in the way his father had. Unlike his brothers who had seen less than him, he'd seen enough hurt and pain on his mother face and in her eyes and enough was enough. Even at seventeen, he knew women were to be loved and cherished, something he had seen his father do a few times, but in those last few years, he'd become angry and his rage was directed at his family. Leo didn't know what had caused his temper to get out of control, but he hated to see his mother become a punching bag.

He'd tried to help her, but she begged and pleaded with him to take his brothers and go stay at their uncle Max's house, her only brother who lived in Brooklyn where they lived. Seeing his mother hurt wasn't the time to be hard and without feelings. He cried knowing if he left her, his father could return and do even more harm to her. He didn't want to leave her at the house alone, but he did as she asked and went to the house next door where his brothers were playing and took them to their uncle's house a few blocks away. What his mother didn't expect was that he had no intention of staying there after he took his brothers. He had to find a way to make the pain his father brought down on them stop. He ran the few blocks to his uncle's house and for the first time, he told him why they were there. With Leo in tow, his uncle jumped in his car and raced to the house.

By the time they got there, they could hear shouting coming from the inside of the small brownstone. That day, his life had changed forever. His uncle raced inside and from the car, Leo could hear more screaming and shouting. Unable to sit still any longer, he left the car and ran up the stairs to the house, breathing hard as he carefully looked inside. What he saw was his mother still cowering in the corner of the cluttered living room with furniture that had seen better days and his father and uncle were shouting and threatening each other in the kitchen. Feeling a need to protect his mother, he ran over and hugged her tight in his arms while she whispered how she told him not to come back. She kept asking him why did he return, saying it over and over again. He leaned close to her ear and told her because she was his mother and he would always protect her. He told her he may not have learned it from his father, but he knew that a man was supposed to be a protector, not the one that his wife should be afraid of. That day, he told her that if she left his father for good, he would always take care of her. He would get ten jobs if he had to in order to help her take care of his brothers. He didn't want to come home one day and his father had killed her. He cried and begged and cried more just as his father came into the room. That was a defining moment Leo would never forget. His father screamed at the top of his lungs telling him to be a man and stop crying and cowering in the corner with his mother.

Pulling himself together, Leo stood to his full height of six-foot-four inches tall, already five inches taller than his father. Holding his head up high and balling his fists into tight balls, he tried to use his height to intimidate his father away from his mother. They had words back and forth which shocked his father. He'd never heard Leo talk to him that way before. As Roland leaned back and was about to hit him, he grabbed his father's arm and held on tight. With a fear of God look on his face and through tightly clinched teeth, Leo told his father that if he ever raised his hand to his mother or any of them ever again, he would be willing to go to jail for them. He hadn't meant to threaten his father's life, but the state his mother was in and the weak man his father had become in his eyes, he'd had enough. He would never allow his father to attack any of them again, even if it meant he would receive the beating of his life.

He remembered his uncle coming into the room and telling his father that he needed to calm down, leave and never return again. He made it clear that if he ever showed up in his sister's life or his sons' lives again, he wouldn't have to worry about Leo going to jail because he would take that charge himself. Before Leo could react, he watched his uncle, who was well over six feet himself, pick his father up and walk with him literally over his head toward the front door which still stood open. When he reached the top of the four steps outside, he watched his father get summersaulted to the concrete sidewalk. As Roland Westmoreland screamed in pain, Leo didn't move to help him because as he glanced back at his mother, his first priority was to help her and not his father.

7

Evelyn Westmoreland had suffered enough and he and his brothers were no longer going to take a front seat to the abuse.

That had been the last day his father had ever walked into their house. A few months later, they moved from that house of bad memories and into a three-bedroom, two-floor apartment walk-up, leaving his father's things in the vacant house. From that day, they never looked back and he vowed he would never allow anyone to harm his mother again. His father may not have done his job of looking after the family the right way, but Leo never had a problem looking after them. They were his everything and they were all he had. He knew that day that he didn't want to be like his father and he didn't want his brothers, Trayvon and Major to think that how they saw their mother treated, was the way to treat a woman despite what their father told them a man's role is in the house and in a relationship.

Twelve years later, he was still looking after his mother and brothers, though he lived on his own. He'd made a lot of sacrifices and with the help of his uncle, his family was able to survive. His mother still carried the scars of the abuse, but thankfully, she still had love in her and showed it to him and his brothers every day. He kept his promise to her that he would look after them and he smiled thinking of his brothers who had thrived and were growing into positive young men. Major, at nineteen, was in his second year of community college while Trayvon, at sixteen, was a junior in high school and a star baseball and basketball player. His family was why he worked so hard every day and he never had a day of regret.

Time was getting away from him as his mind went down memory lane and with only a few minutes to get showered, dressed and off to his full-time job, Leo rushed around his apartment to get his day started. He thought again about the fact that he was alone after his last relationship because he hadn't been enough for Misha and so she moved on. There were a lot of sacrifices he was willing to make, but when it came to a relationship, he wanted love to rule over everything else and they weren't on the same page. He wanted them mutually thinking of each other the first thing in the morning and the last thing at night. He wanted his woman to feel his love even when she wasn't with him and to know that his love was for her and for her only. Shrugging off the thought of the past, he knew there was no need to dwell on the fact that some women wanted more than he was willing to give, but the woman for him was out there and he was a patient man. He already knew what was for him, would be for him.

1

Getting out of bed after a long night of working the day before, Leo stretched, trying to soothe the kinks that plagued his body which was tired, stressed and overworked as the result of working his third job as part of the late-night crew responsible for cleaning the Metropolitan Museum of Art of New York City. Tired, he still smiled knowing today was Wednesday, the only day off from all three of his jobs, but also, his busiest and most fulfilling day of the week.

Though he tirelessly worked himself with several jobs, what he enjoyed most was volunteering his time to teach digital graphic design to high school students. Doing so gave him the chance to low-key keep an eye on Trayvon, who had begun getting into trouble earlier in the school year. Things could have been worse if it wasn't for basketball keeping him semi-focused. It was mid-February and they were about to begin tryouts for the baseball team, something he already knew Trayvon would succeed at and hoped the path in the right direction he had been on lately would continue. He knew Trayvon's home life wasn't the best with some of the lasting affects their mother still suffered with after years of abuse from their now absent father, but he still expected him to stay on task.

Their mother was dealing with several lingering health problems and often had a hard time keeping Trayvon in line, which is where he stepped in. Once a week, he took the train into Brooklyn and spent the day volunteering at Trayvon's high school. He would love to add more than one day of teaching to his schedule, but his three jobs took up most of his time.

Monday through Saturday, except Wednesday, he worked for a small marketing firm in their digital art department. He loved the job and was lucky to have it considering he was the only member of the team who didn't have a college degree which was something the job description required. In spite of that, his talent had caught the eye of one of the firm's owners and he was now three years in. Monday and Tuesday and a few Fridays and Saturdays a month, after leaving his full-time job, he worked for a real-estate company where he helped design staging of houses, condos and apartments that were on the market to be sold. Some days he didn't have time to get more than a few hours' sleep, like last night, but he had things to do, so up and getting ready to head out was the priority of the day. Adding in the overnight cleaning job, he seemed to always be working.

Before heading out, he had a few minutes to look over the stack of bills that were laid out on the small table that was his make-shift kitchen table. The other space left in his apartment which could have been a bigger dining space was set up with various small television and computer equipment where he spent countless free time working on designing and development films he hoped to one day sell to a large production company or producer. For now, he plugged away and developing and continuing honing his skills.

The bills were separated into two stacks, his bills and the bills for his mother and two brothers that he helped pay. Each time he saw the two stacks, he was reminded of why he was working so many jobs to make ends meet. He was also able to save quite a bit of his money, making sure he had funds in case of a rainy situation, but he didn't get much of a chance to spend any of it on himself because if he wasn't working or checking in on his family, he was asleep.

Grabbing his checkbook, he wrote out the checks to cover their electric bill and their next month's rent to be sure they were done and his mother had no worries. Everything else was caught up and the only bill in the other stack for him was the cell phone bill which covered all four of their phones. He was appreciative of the discount he got on their phones since the marketing firm offered significant discounts to their employees. He couldn't imagine the size of the bill if he had to pay full price. Gathering what he needed to mail off the two bills, he dropped them in his backpack and rushed to get a shower to get to the school on time. His phone rang just before he reached the bathroom.

"Walt! What up dude?" Leo exclaimed, answering his best friend's call.

"I can't call it. What's happening in your world besides running off to volunteer on a day when you could be chilling and hanging with me at the gym," Walt shouted.

"Man, all you do is hang out at that gym. Shelly still paying that monthly gym fee for you? Man, where do you get these women who gladly pay your bills?" Leo laughed.

"Aye, don't knock a young brother's hustle. Yeah, she is and I can hook you up with one of her partners. I told you about that one chick who has a thing for you."

"You know my score on that. I'm not looking," Leo said shaking his head. He may not be looking for a woman to be involved with, but that didn't mean he didn't appreciate a good woman or that he didn't want one in his life. His problem was the women of this day and age didn't want a brother who was barely taking care of himself, didn't have a college degree and didn't have anything to offer her other than himself and it seems no woman really wanted that, though he often heard them complaining about that very thing. He relegated himself to his priorities and right now, it wasn't a woman.

"I know you keep saying that, but the ladies have their eyes on you. They want you, bro. Think about meeting a good woman and if you move in together, your two incomes could help you keep up on all those household bills you pay for two houses each month. You could have more money saved up to follow your own dreams."

"Man, cut that mess out. I do pretty good saving and just because I don't flaunt it with flashy clothes, cars and other material things, doesn't mean I don't have the money to get them. Using these women for their pockets is going to be the death of you. That's not how you treat a woman. You shouldn't see a woman as a means to your come-up and you know me better than that to think I'm about that at all," Leo explained.

He heard Walt sigh loudly through the phone.

"How long are you going to let what Misha did get to you? That woman was money hungry when you met her and still, you fell in love with her knowing you didn't have what she wanted most, which was large dollar bills flying through the air and haphazardly landing in her hands."

"Me not looking has nothing to do with Misha," Leo admitted.

"Come on, bro, I'm your best friend. I know you better than you know yourself and I know this mentality you have developed about not looking is all about her. Not all women think like her," Walt said.

Leo shook it off. He and Walt had been friends since elementary school and had lived in the same neighborhood. He may think he knew him, but the conversation alone told him Walt paid little attention.

"I know all women aren't like Misha, but I don't have time right now to devote to any woman."

"Yeah, I know you work three jobs and all you have time to do is eat, sleep and workout," Walt said snidely.

"Speaking of working out, I need to use your gym membership tonight, if you don't mind. I know you don't go on Wednesday evenings because of work. You down with that?" Leo asked.

Once a week, he got the chance to work out at an exclusive gym in Manhattan using Walt's membership. He would invest in his own if he didn't have to pay a monthly fee when he would only use it one day a week.

"Oh, you can scold a brother for having his girl pay for the membership, but you don't have any qualms about using it? Yeah, that's cool and only because you're the best friend a guy could have. Use the extra card tonight that I gave you. They wouldn't know it's not me coming back tonight after working out this morning. I'll be at work, doing a double shift tonight anyway."

"Cool. I need to get moving and get to the school for my first class."

"You're not tired of volunteering and not getting

paid? I thought you were going to try and take some classes of your own instead of teaching those high school kids," Walt said.

"I keep looking at the registration packet. I can't afford that right now. Maybe after a while when my mother has a few more months of working full-time under her belt. My schedule is hectic enough as it is."

"Look at how long you've been saying that. She's been working full-time for almost six months now and you told me she's doing much better with her medication. Is everybody cool? What about Trayvon and Major? They good?" Walt asked.

"Yeah, everybody is good. I get to keep an eye on Trayvon on Wednesdays. He had been acting up, but he seems to be back on track. Major is good, too. His first year of college kicked his butt last year and this year, he knows he needs to buckle down and focus on class and he's doing good. I wish I could afford to send him to a college out of state. I want to get him out of Brooklyn and into a dorm so that he can see that there is more to life than what he's always been exposed to. So far, he hasn't had many distractions other than women, but who hasn't at his age," Leo laughed.

"Your brothers are lucky to have you. You've sacrificed a lot so that they can have."

"That's called family, bro. You know they're what's important," Leo said and meant it.

"Right, but when do you make you a priority? I hear you and I'm here for you for whatever you need.

If you cut out one of those jobs and put more of an investment in you, you would find that their dreams aren't the only dreams that should be fulfilled. Look, I didn't call to tell you how to live your life. I called to see if you were off Saturday and if you want to come out to a launch party? I know you get two Saturday's off a month from the museum. There's a new rap artist who is blowing up and Shelly's company got the catering gig. She was able to snatch up a few V.I.P. tickets for me."

"Seriously? Yeah, I think I can swing that. I don't get out too often, so that would be a nice treat. What time?" Leo asked.

"About ten. I'll come through and snatch you up. I'm getting a town car for the night. Get ready for the party of your life!" Walt exclaimed.

"Good looking out and I'll see you Saturday. Thanks, as usual, for the use of the gym card."

"I got you," Walt said and hung up.

Leo rushed around knowing he only had a few moments to spare and with the little time he did have, his thoughts turned to Misha. Leave it to Walt to drum up an old memory of a time he'd rather not think about. He's tortured himself enough with memories. He tried not to give old relationships and breakups too much of his time and energy. After all, he was only twenty-nine and he still had a lot of relationships and most likely breakups ahead in his future and one thing he didn't want to do was live in the past.

Misha showed him a lot about himself, especially when it came to women. He'd tried too hard to make their relationship work even though he knew she was a money chaser. In the end, she told him she would have broken up with him a long time ago if he wasn't as good as he was in bed. Their sex life had been off the chain, but that couldn't sustain them and take the place of the love he offered her in place of the finer things in life she wanted him to provide her with. She loved him for the intimacy, but when it came to what he could do for her outside of the bedroom, she wasn't the woman to wait around for him to make it rich one day, if that day even came. She wanted the lifestyle of the rich and famous on his three salaries and that was never going to happen. It wasn't enough for her that he loved her unconditionally and would do anything for her within his power, but his pockets weren't deep enough and that mattered more to her than love.

One day, he hoped women would see that there was more to men like him than money. He was too young to be that serious about a woman anyway and so, when the relationship ended, he moved on with his life, but the experience made him more cautious when it came to getting involved for more than just a casual friendship. The kind of woman he wanted and needed in his life was out there and when they found each other, he would know it was right because she would be able to see who he was starting with his heart and not from his wallet.

"Game time," he said and pushed all thoughts of the past out of his head.

2

"Another pity party kind of day?"

Raquel Johnson looked back over her shoulder and tried to regain her composure after getting caught daydreaming while looking out of the window of the twelfth-floor office of the Mack Johnson Funds and Impact Solutions Firm, a funds management company named after her father, Melvin "Mack" Johnson who was also the company's chief operating officer. She loved her corner office, one held for company executives like herself. At thirty-two, she held a position not many women her age held and she was happy to let everyone know she didn't get it just because her father owned the company. As Vice-President of Finance as well as head of the Accounting department, she got her position, partly because her father wanted the top positions to stay in the family, but also because she'd obtained several degrees in accounting, including a PhD and therefore, she was more than qualified to hold the esteemed position. With it came great benefits which included her Manhattan apartment in a building her father owned and the car of her dreams, the brand-new red Jaguar which she loved getting out on the open road and testing the patience of state troopers with her speeding. She'd almost gotten a ticket a few days ago when she'd gotten out on the open highway and sped up a little faster than she should have. The only reason she got away without a ticket is because the officer who pulled her over was friends with her ex-boyfriend, Elijah and he felt sorry for her, clearly knowing that Elijah had moved on from her, but not before he'd ripped her heart to shreds with his infidelity. Guys and their wayward penises, she thought. Why was finding love so hard?

Even now, after what he'd done, he was on her mind, though it had been a few months since she'd last seen him. She wasn't thinking of him in terms of wanting him back, but more of how could she allow herself to be a fool for what she thought was love, but wasn't even in the ballpark of where love resided. Still, she didn't like getting caught in a vulnerable position of thinking about a man who meant her no good, not even by her best friend, Toni.

"Ugh, are you lurking?" she asked Toni without turning around to look at her.

"Not lurking, just observant as a best friend should be and from here, I sense a personal pity party," Toni said.

Raquel hated showing the vulnerable side of herself that may appear as if she's feeling sorry for yet another bad choice she'd made in life. She was once again feeling sorry for herself over a situation where she had no control, though the outcome was her eventual freedom from his drama. Still, it didn't make it hurt less. The pain was still very much alive in her, along with a small amount of embarrassment over who she had become for a man who had been cheating on her for the last six months of their relationship and she was blind to it all. She turned around with a fake smile on her face and greeted Toni who stood in the doorway to her office.

"Not a pity party. I was thinking and that's all," she lied.

"What? Thinking about Elijah, again? Really? After what that man did to you, you're still giving him space in your head?" Toni asked.

"It's not that easy to forget about. We were together for two years. My thoughts are not about love or even about wanting him back, but more about being so caught up in a man for what he has and not for who he was that I forgot about who I was supposed to be with him."

Toni came further into the office and closed the door behind her to be sure no one could hear their conversation.

"Correction, you were with him for two years – he was with you for about eighteen-months, taking away at least the last six months you were together where he cheated on you. That's only for the time we know about him cheating and I'm sure, knowing who Elijah is, that it was going on way before then. I'm not trying to be insulting, but I want you to live in reality. Even with all of his money, it didn't buy him any class or respect. He loved having his black princess on his arm to show how cool he was dating a black woman. Ugh, I never liked him and only tolerated him because you're like a sister to me, but I can't honestly say I'm upset he's no longer in the picture. Has he stopped trying to get you back?"

Raquel turned back to look out of one of the four large windows that overlooked the Manhattan skyline. She didn't want to lie, but wasn't in the mood for Toni's judgment if she told the truth that Elijah had sent her flowers every day for the first two months of their breakup and for the last few weeks, he had been calling incessantly, begging her to take him back. She wasn't even thinking about it and though her thoughts may turn to him occasionally, it didn't mean she was considering taking him back.

"Flowers, cards and calls and no, I'm not accepting any of those, nor am I considering seeing him or taking him back. Even if I did see him, which I have not, I don't hold any anger for what he did. It's water under the bridge, but that doesn't mean I can't think about what I allowed him to do to me. Besides that, I want you to know that I'm not a doormat and I don't care what race he is, I was not his arm candy or his proof that he was down because as a white man, he dated a black woman. As far as I know, he's always dated black women," she declared.

Toni sucked her teeth showing her annoyance and Raquel knew without her best friend saying so, in her head she was calling her naïve.

"Right, but the woman he cheated on you with and from what I hear, still seeing her, is blond, blue-eyed and white. I guess he's an equal opportunity cheater and he's still trying to get back with you? He's a snake of the worst kind. He knows he did wrong and still wants you to take him back after what he did."

Raquel turned back around and this time she straightened her red two-piece Versace suit with matching red Versace open toe pumps and sat behind her desk, shaking off any thoughts of her relationship that had gone bad and still bothered her at times. She waved off any thought of being consumed with Elijah Bohner for even one second more.

"Girl, I'm thirty-two and have plenty of time to make more mistakes with the men I choose to get involved with. It's all a part of life and just as I won't let future ups and downs distract me, I won't let him distract me now."

"So, you're fine, then?" Toni asked.

"I'm perfect. What brings you to the twelfth-floor?"

She and Toni both worked for her father's funds management company and while she served as an executive, Toni worked as an assistant in the marketing department, four floors below. The company occupied five floors in the thirty-story office building.

"Kelly needs the girls tonight. She and Clark are having some issues and she wants to get out of the house. I suggested a girl's night out for dinner since it's Wednesday, but you know where she wants to go," Toni said.

Raquel smirked.

"The gym?" she asked and laughed.

"Yup, the gym. She prefers the gym over going out to dinner and having a few drinks. Gotta love her workout ethic. She keeps us all in shape by dragging us with her to the gym," Toni said.

"That means a trip to New Rochelle in the middle of the week and that's a bit much. That's like forty minutes considering we all work right here in Manhattan."

"I know, but she's talking about some new gym right here in the city. Can we change at your place? You're the only one who lives close by and that'll save us all time with running home. I'm going to run out and pick up some workout gear over lunch. Kelly and Kenya already have workout clothes with them," she explained.

"You don't have your gym bag with you? I know you like to work out here in the building during lunch," Raquel said. Usually, she had her workout gear with her too, but she was planning on going home and relaxing for the evening, so she didn't bring her usual duffle bag with her.

"I wasn't planning on it today. I was planning on having a cheat day and pigging out over lunch. I keep hearing about that new deli that opened up down the street with those good Philly cheesesteak subs and hand-cut French fries."

Raquel shook her head in disgrace at the image of a juicy sub and crispy fries that danced in her head and then laughed at herself because she now wanted a greasy sub and over-salted fries.

"If you do, grab me the same and I'll share in your cheat day. I have meetings all morning and one will run through lunch. I can eat it after," Raquel said. "Oh, and yes, everyone can change at my place," she added.

She shook her head again when Toni began a ceremonious, jubilant clap.

"I love that you only live a few blocks from the office. Last week when I took that extra hour over lunch to run to your place and get that quick nap, it was the best sleep I've had in a long time."

"That was last week when your mother was in town, right?" Raquel tried to hide her sneaky grin knowing how the topic of Toni's over-the-top mother got under her skin.

Toni looked at her and rolled her eyes.

"Girl, you know I love my mother, but that woman is relentless when it came to spending every single hour together when I wasn't working while she was here. I needed that nap to keep up with her. I don't know how my father does it," she joked.

"I'm glad I'm close by, too. It saves on the commute time."

"Well, if I had big bucks like you, I'd live in Manhattan, too, in the same building where some of the biggest celebrities owned apartments."

"Yeah, well, I never see any of those powerful people. They aren't in them often and the private elevator is used for their floors which are the top four. The higher up you go, the more expensive they are. You know you can stay there anytime you need to. With three large bedrooms and all that space, we wouldn't know we were in there at the same time."

"I appreciate that. You know you my sister girl and I wouldn't trade you for anyone, except for maybe Rhianna because who wouldn't want to be sisters with a woman with that hot line of make-up? Can you imagine having access to everything she puts out and not having to pay for it? Now, I hear she has this hot, hot lingerie line and I'm hoping I can afford at least one piece."

Toni tried to stop Raquel with her hand before she could answer with a response about money.

"Really, Toni?" she questioned, looking at the hand in her face.

"Yes, really and before you say anything, I know we should support our sisters with our dollars and not look for a handout. I'm just saying, it would be nice.

Instead, I'll add some of her new products to my birthday list this year and make sure I haphazardly leave it on your desk by mistake," she laughed.

"Yeah, well, it's not like you don't do that every year. You know you could just give the list to me instead of trying to leave it by mistake for me to see it right smack in the middle of my desk on top of everything else. What time are we meeting up? I'll be here until at least six," Raquel said.

"I'm leaving at five today, so we'll be at your place when you get there. Maybe we'll run into some hunky men tonight. I know I could use some new blood and we all know you could. I hear there are some fine brothers who frequent this new spot."

"Here you go with penis on the brain, again. Do you ever think of anything else?" she asked.

Toni waved her off with a hand and her middle finger as they both fell into a fit of laughter at the gesture that only two good friends could share and smile about.

"Admittedly, no I don't and neither should you. It's been what, six or seven months since you and he who shall remain nameless broke up and I haven't heard about any horizontal activities happening in your life since then. It's time you gave that hot spot some real meat for a change and not that itsy bitsy, teeny weenie…"

Toni didn't get a chance to finish because Raquel's laugh nearly shattered her eardrum.

"I told you to stop calling him that and it wasn't teeny – just not as long and thick as I would have liked. Why am I explaining this to you? It's not about that for me and you know it. I enjoy a fine man as much as the next woman, but hopping from bed to bed is not my thing."

"Right, that's because money, power and respect are," Toni said.

Raquel sucked her teeth.

"Now, you're making me sound shallow and I'm not that at all," she said, trying to defend her character. It was true that the last two men she had been in a so-called relationship with were well off financially and she didn't see anything wrong with wanting that.

"Girl, you have never gone out with a man who wasn't wealthy and running some company or having some other high-profile, high-paying career. Didn't Elijah's marketing firm breach the ten-million-dollar mark in profits last year? The guy before him was a broker and had more money than Elijah, living in that top floor, penthouse apartment overlooking Central Park. You have had your share of millionaires. I'm not saying there is anything wrong with that, but don't tell me you don't check how deep the pockets go first, so be honest."

Raquel rolled her eyes and tried to act like she was reading something on top of the stack of papers in the center of her desk.

"I'm not saying I'm a woman who doesn't have

expectations because I do and so do you."

"Damn right I do! Those things are important. I expect to have the chair opposite me at the table be occupied by someone who brings big dollars. A girl can dream, can't she?" Toni said confidently.

"I hear you, but you know what, that's not all a man is and even though I'm one to talk after the last two boyfriends I had, it's still not the most important thing and I've never been caught up in that."

"Girl, that's because you have your own money and trust fund and you and your sister don't have to work. Your father is a multi-millionaire several times over and he gives both of you anything you want or need. There is nothing wrong with that, but that means you're privy to a certain type of man because of who your father is and that's all good. It's a shame that's all they seem to bring to the table when I know you want and deserve more," Toni said.

"Before all of that, and I'm not saying it's not important, I want a man who respects me enough to treat me like a queen and honor his commitment to me. That's so rare these days and I'm tired of being mistreated. I want love and not the kind I've been getting. I'm talking about a man whose focus is on loving me and me loving him. Someone I can cuddle up with and watch my favorite movies while pigging out on wings and pizza, my favorite foods and not tune his nose up when he wonders if I'm going to gain weight and destroy his perfect image of me. One where we can tune out the entire world and just be about us. I've been wanting that and missing that. He can have or not have money, that doesn't matter. Yes, I have money and I attract money because of the circle I'm in, but that doesn't mean every guy with money is a jerk and every guy without money isn't. I'm only hoping to find a comfortable middle where the focus is on us and not money or status. I'm learning to prioritize and how I'm treated is top on my list. Everything else is a plus," Raquel said.

"I'm going for the money," Toni laughed and walked toward the door.

"I know you are."

"I'll drop your lunch with your assistant and then I'll see you at six or so. I'll call Kelly and Kenya to let them know we're in. I can't wait to hear how Clark messed up again. Whatever it is has Kelly pissed off. I don't understand how she could ever get upset with that blond, blue-eyed hunk of a husband she has who looks like a clone of that actor who died in that car crash, Paul Walker. Those two with their blond hair and blue eyes making those three gorgeous clones they call kids should be happy just by being them."

"Hey, men of every race mess up, not just white men," Raquel added.

"True, even the brothers have issues. You never did tell me if Elijah was the first white man you've ever dated?"

"That's because you've never asked me before and

yes, he was. You know I don't see color. Snakes come in all shapes and origins and has nothing to do with race. Thankfully, in today's society, no one cares about race anymore. He was the perfect boyfriend in the beginning and then his money began buying him new bed partners and I'm not here for that," Raquel declared with a fist pump in the air.

"I hear that. Let's keep hope alive then! I have a meeting I need to get to. I'll catch you later!" Toni said and left.

Raquel turned her chair around and within seconds was deep in thought. People thought that because of who she was and who her father was that she shouldn't have an issue in the world. Having money and a high paying job doesn't buy happiness and love, though it was easy to rent. She wanted more and expected more when it came to love. She was a post-graduate, career woman who was a whiz when it came to numbers, a gift her father noticed and offered her a job in his company the minute she received her doctorate degree in accounting and corporate finance. She had a great job, money, condo and the best friends in the world, but her love life could use a serious boost and not just with any man.

She longed for a man whose biggest quality is his love and respect for women. Too many men lack that and she seemed to keep running into those type of men. True, she wanted a man who was about something because he needed to be her equal, but where was that code of honor where men should treat a woman like they would want their mother or sister treated? Did she even really understand what having her equal was? She thought it was about money, but now she knows different.

With Elijah, she could see that he never learned how to truly respect and love a woman since he didn't have any sisters and he hasn't talked to his own mother in years. That should have been her first clue, but she ignored it because he was the caliber of man she'd desired. He wined and dined her, they went to the hottest, most high-profile parties in New York and they had lots of fun, but she'd turned a blind eye to his womanizing thinking in the end, she would be enough for him. He had started out treating her well, but then she realized it was so that she wouldn't question his actions when they weren't together. Now, all she wished for was that her desire for a good man would lead her to his heart where once she was there, he would treat her with love and care and know the importance of handling her heart. She had been asleep on desiring that, but not anymore. She didn't care if she was single for the rest of her life and she would happily be so if it meant she was protecting herself from being disrespected.

She and her sister, Tyra, watched their father's devotion to their mother until the day she died from breast cancer three years ago. In just the past year, he'd begun dating again and she knew that any woman who captured his heart would be the luckiest in the world. There needed to be more men like her father.

Of her closest friends, Kelly was the only one who was married and though they had their issues, Clark was a good man who loved and cherished Kelly and their three kids. Every now and then, they went through ups and downs like most, but it was never due to a lack of respect on either of their parts. She was looking forward to their girl's night out and she already had a feeling that whatever Kelly was going through, it would all be worked out before they even got to the gym. She was use to that with her and her husband and she has always loved their love – the kind of deep-seated, deep-rooted love from the heart that they shared.

There other friend, Kenya, was single like her and Toni and the vote was still out on whether she preferred men or women. She smiled as she thought about how Toni was another story completely. She was the serial dater in their group of friends and though that wasn't for her, Raquel knew it was all Toni and she lived happily in that role. She didn't want to date around like Toni did. She wanted her *Mr. Right* and not a *Mr. Right Now*. She wanted the kind of love her parents shared until the day her mother took her last breath. Seeing her father's commitment showed her what she longed for, but didn't fight to get. No longer would she settle for anything less than what she wanted and deserved. She wanted to love freely, placing more on the feeling than the tangible whether he had or didn't have.

"One day," she said out loud before remembering she was about to be late for her first meeting of the day. Grabbing her laptop and cell phone, she rushed off to her meeting and happy that she was temporarily distracted from how she allowed Elijah to treat her. No one, not just women, should ever settle for being a doormat. Real love was better than that.

3

Leo walked with Trayvon out of the school and headed toward the subway. After his day of teaching each week, he and Trayvon met up after and walked to the subway together and talked before they went their separate ways. He wanted his brother to know he would always be there for him and the thirty minutes or so after school one day a week where they got the chance to chat face to face was one of the many highlights of his week.

"How's mom doing?" Leo asked as they walked.

"She's better and she loves her new job. I don't think she's ever had an office position before. She told me the people are nice and she's about to get a raise later this month. Maybe then you can quit one of your jobs," Trayvon said.

Leo grabbed him playfully around the neck as they walked.

"Don't worry about me. I'll stop by one day this week to see her. I don't want her to think I forgot about her," he said.

"She doesn't think that. She talks to you by phone every day and that makes her happy. She knows you work hard. In my opinion, you work too hard to take care of all of us and no one is taking care of you. You stepped in as a father when you should be out here chasing your dreams. I think you should be working in Hollywood or in New York city with your digital illustrations and all that stuff you create on all that equipment in your apartment. You actually wrote and digitally produced your own science fiction movie. Who does that and is not living the Hollywood dream? You should be trying to sell that movie to some big producer or something. I mean you wrote an entire movie and digitally produced it like it was nothing. I can see you being the next George Lucas, creating your own science fiction movies with the newest digital graphics ever seen before or maybe the next Stephen Spielberg. I feel like we're holding you back because you're taking care of us," Trayvon said with a hint of sadness to his voice.

Leo stopped walking and turned so that he was facing Trayvon.

"Listen to me when I tell you that I love you guys and you are what makes me happy. Seeing you and Major become successful is all the dream chasing I need right now. I will have my day, but right now, my purpose is to make sure you both get college degrees and I don't care how many jobs I have to work to make that happen."

Trayvon huffed as he listened. His brother was his hero, but he still wanted him to take time and focus on himself as much as he focuses on the rest of them.

"Still, Major and I know you want to go to college, too. You've put it off to send him to college and to keep an eye on me. I promise you I'm back on track and no more slipping. That was a temporary act of me exerting some independence and I get it now. Let me get a job to help out. I can work after school," he pleaded.

Leo turned and walked ahead of Trayvon. He didn't want to have a conversation about him getting a job. School was his job.

"No, Tray. You need money for something? Tell me what it is and we'll work it out, but I don't want you losing focus by getting a job after school and besides you're about to start baseball season. You don't need a job. Is there something you want? You need some new kicks or gear or something?" Leo asked.

Every spare dime he got went to making sure Trayvon and Major didn't want for anything. He would do what his father was supposed to do, but didn't. He would give his last to his mother and his brothers before any of them tried to find their own way to make ends meet. He was surprised that he was able to save up some money for a rainy day or maybe take a few classes himself soon, but for now, nothing else was on his list of priorities besides his two brothers and his mother.

"I don't have to play baseball," he said softly.

"Oh, yeah you do. You're good at it and I still think

one day you'll go pro, but you have to stay focused and I'm here to be sure you're doing that. Now, again, is there something you need?" he asked.

"No, I'm good. You know I'm not about all that flashy stuff. I want to get a job to help with some of the bills so you don't have to do it all. You started working and helping out when you were seventeen and that's only one year older than I am right now. You still finished high school," Trayvon said.

"I don't do it all. Mom is working now and making pretty good money. I'm only helping where I'm needed. Major got a scholarship, so all I had to pay for was books and other fees. I'm working this hard because I want him to be able to go away to school to finish his last two years and when you get to college, I want you to apply out of state, too. I know it costs more, but if you keep those grades up and continue with the extra-curricular activities that colleges like, you'll do fine, too. We'll make it work," he said.

Trayvon stopped walking and waited for Leo to notice he was no longer beside him. When Leo turned and walked back to him, Trayvon stood his ground.

"Promise me you'll do somethings for you. Major and I love you for everything you've done for us. We want to see you succeed as much as you want to see us succeed. Promise me you'll do something for you. Maybe take a trip, go to a ball game, take one of those classes I see you looking at on the internet all the time – something," he pleaded.

"I promise. Now, let's get you home," Leo said and started walking toward the station Trayvon needed to take. He was going in the opposite direction to get home and then to the gym.

"Can I stay at your place tonight? I can get up extra early to get to school. I don't get to stay with you as much as I did before and I know you're off tonight."

"I'm going to the gym later this evening for a little while," Leo said.

"I can hang out at your place until you get back. Maybe I can cook us something good to eat. Mom is working late this evening anyway. I miss hanging with you," Trayvon said and looked way.

Leo knew Trayvon hated expressing his feelings, but he taught him to not shy away from what he was feeling, good or bad. He also told him to always look a person in the eye.

"You know better than to look away. When you ask someone for something, you look them right in the eye," he declared in a serious tone.

Trayvon looked him dead in the eye.

"You know you'll be hungry when you get back from the gym. I have a lot of homework to keep me busy and we're the same size, so I can wear some of your fly gear tomorrow. Plus, I want to talk to you about girls," he said shyly.

Leo looked him over. They'd had several talks about girls and what he should and should not be doing. In a just in case situation, he provided both of his brothers with condoms and stayed on them about using them. The three of them were close and he asked that they stay honest and open with him. He answered all their questions on any topic especially when it came to girls and women and from the few words Tray had said, he needed some time with his big brother to talk.

"Girls or one girl in particular?" he asked.

"One girl in particular. Her name is Tammy and she goes to my school."

"Is there something that you and Tammy have been doing that you want to tell me about?" he asked and held his breath. He remembered his conversation with Major the first time he'd had sex and it was more of a scolding than anything else because Major had forgotten all the warnings he'd given him about being safe. Luckily, nothing rose from that encounter and since then, Major assured him he was always safe.

"Oh, we haven't done anything and I'm not going to do anything. She's not like that. She's really a nice girl and she's about her books."

"Ah, is that why you're now getting back to being about the books? If so, I like her already."

"Yeah, well, you told me to tell you when I really, really liked a girl and I really like her. Can we talk after you get home from the gym? Maybe by phone if you don't want me to spend the night?" he asked.

"Okay, you can stay as long as mom is good with it and we can talk when I get in. Call her and make sure and we can head toward my station."

Seeing Trayvon perk up made him smile as he watched him excitedly dial their mother. As they talked, he thought about how lucky he was that despite how their life had been years ago, they were all in a better place now. He had to remember to give Trayvon more of his time especially with Major in school well into the evening most days.

"Mom said that's fine and she said to call her later. She has the money for her rent this month and didn't need you to pay it. I told her you probably already did and she said she'll give that back to you."

"Really? I didn't pay it yet. The check is still in my backpack. I'll text Major and let him know you're with me tonight, so that he won't worry when he gets in and you're not there."

They turned and headed in the opposite direction.

"Now, about dinner. What should I make us?" Trayvon asked.

"Nothing. I'll bring us some pizza and subs on my way back from the gym. You get your homework done and then when I get home, we can talk more about college and definitely about Tammy. I also want to start talking about college for you."

"You know I would love to go out of state, but if we can't afford it, I can do what Major did and go to school locally and then transfer later."

"No, you're not. I'm making more money now than I was two years ago when Major started college. We'll make it happen. I don't want you focused on the money part, I want you focusing on the grades."

"My counselor already said if I stay on track, she knew of several scholarships I could get and you know coach is already talking about helping me secure athletic scholarships!" Trayvon said excitedly.

"That's what's up. That's what I'm talking about."

"Don't forget your promise to me. Your dreams matter, too."

Leo smiled and playfully punched him.

"All lives matter, right?" Leo asked.

"In this family they do. So, are you seeing any hot women these days? After that girl, Misha, who kicked you to the curb, I haven't heard you say much about any other women."

"Yeah, she did drop kick your brother, didn't she? Trust me, it was for the better. Now, I know the kind of woman I was dealing with and she's the kind I want to always avoid. You can't chase a dollar and love at the same time, equally."

"Did you love her?"

Leo had no problem admitting his vulnerabilities if it meant his brothers would learn from him and make better choices when it came to matters of the heart.

"I did. I loved her very much, but she wanted fame and fortune, something I couldn't give her."

"You could if you went to school and graduated so that you can make the big bucks."

"Money is not everything, Tray. I know we see the

glitz and glamour of the high life, but a lot of those people aren't happy either. Happiness is not found in money and a lot of times, it brings more problems than it cures."

"Do you think you'll fall in love again?"

"I know I will and she'll be someone who will appreciate me for me and for the heart of a gentleman that I have. You know what I've always taught you and Major, right?" Leo asked.

"Yeah. Girls and women are all precious jewels and should be treated like rare diamonds. We're never to use or abuse them, never to lift our hands in anger at them and when we say we love them, we better mean it by the words we say and in the actions we convey."

"That's right and the right woman will appreciate that. Now, let's get home so that I can get to the gym and get back home. I'm proud of you and Major," Leo said as they entered the subway station.

"We're proud of you, too."

4

Raquel wiped down the treadmill she'd finished using after the allowed sixty minutes and rather than head to the next machine, she walked toward the entrance of the gym and sat at one of the available tables to take a break and think about what she'd hop on next. Kelly, Kenya and Toni were in different parts of the gym and she had to admit, she'd never been to a nicer one. This one even topped the on-the-spot gym her father had added to their office building where she worked out when she wasn't using the gym in the building where she lived.

Fitness was important to her and it helped with her obsession with junk food. Working out as much as she did, she still allowed herself to indulge in her favorite pepperoni, sausage and extra cheese pizza. With her love for parmesan garlic wings, she would add in an extra thirty minutes to her usual workout.

As she gulped down her water and swayed to the sounds of Mary J. Blige in her headset, she looked toward the door when it opened and in walked a man who made her forget her own name. He was slim, but muscular, showing that this wasn't his first time in a gym by how toned and in shape he was. His strides were long and confident and his electric smile lit up the room as he greeted the receptionist at the desk. His skin color was a delicious milk chocolate and she loved his fresh cut with new twists. The mustache and trimmed goatee added to his strikingly handsome, yet rugged features. He wore knee length black and red basketball shorts and a black muscled shirt that accentuated his toned abs and muscled chest. Her eyes followed him along with the eyes of other women who stood around gawking at him as she was doing. Before she had a chance to look away, the mystery man turned and their eyes met. Out of nowhere, her heart began beating faster as his piercing, black as coal eyes landed on her and stayed there. When he nodded a hello at her, she could barely move. What kind of animal magnetism is this? The confidence the man exuded rang loud in her ears and made her eyes bulge with delight. He was definitely fine. She smiled back with a slight nod of hello and when he turned and walked toward the men's locker room, her eyes followed him until he was out of sight.

"Are you in there or should I come back after you wipe up the drool?"

Raquel snapped out of her trance and turned toward Toni's voice.

"What?"

"Did you just say what after you practically had

your way with that man who just walked in? I wish you could have seen the look on your face. Too bad I didn't think to take a picture as I walked up. I was afraid to interrupt the moment. Did you know him or is it that you want to know him?" Toni asked.

"He was fine."

"Yes, he was and I see we're not the only ones who think so. Look at how those ladies over there are still watching the locker room doorway as if they're expecting him to reemerge any moment. It's not like there aren't handsome men all over this place tonight."

"I know, but there was something about all of him, not just his handsome face. The way he walked and that sure of himself kind of way was intoxicating. That's why we're all looking at the locker room door. I don't blame them for wanting another look."

"Well, damn. I see you're no longer walking around with Elijah on the brain. I can't think of the last time I've heard you refer to a man like that. In fact, I don't think I have ever heard you talk like that before."

"I don't think I ever have."

Toni sat at the table with her.

"Then when he comes out, you need to say something."

Raquel turned to her with fear on her face.

"What? I can't do that. He came here to work out, not be hounded. Besides, we're here for a girl's night out to be here for Kelly."

"Really, because Kelly has been on her cell with Clark pretty much the whole time and Kenya has already found her something to squeeze on."

"Who? I don't see her talking to a guy."

Toni pointed in another direction.

"That's because she's macking on that woman over there."

"Oh, that's right. She's gender- equal when it comes to dating."

"That she is. Now, what about you? He is probably some high-priced lawyer or other business executive with a high six or seven figure salary, the kind you like."

"How do you know the kind of money he has just from seeing him for a few seconds?" Raquel said and on the sly, looked toward the locker room door again.

"Uh huh, look at you. I saw you look again. I'm just saying, this club is quite exclusive. The monthly fee is more than I can afford and if it wasn't for Kelly's rich father, we wouldn't be here either, well, except for you. He must have a boat-load of money," Toni said.

"You're so shallow."

"So are you and it's why we get along so well. We think alike."

"Is that why? I'm still trying to figure that out," Raquel joked.

"Real funny. Anyway, I'm heading back to the machines. We're meeting at the gym's smoothie bar in thirty minutes to wrap up our evening and get some girl chat in."

"I'm going to do a few small weights and I'll meet you there," Raquel said as Toni got up to leave. Her eyes wandered to the locker room door one last time before heading back to finish her workout. She wondered who the man was because unlike any other time when she's met a handsome man, this time everything about him lingered after he had been out of sight for a few minutes.

Standing and turning, she grabbed a bottle of cleaner and paper towels to wipe off the equipment before using it. When she reached the weight area, she first stretched and was about to sit on the closest bench when she turned and bumped into the man she'd watched come in.

"I'm sorry," he said. "I didn't realize you were going to use this bench."

"Oh, it's okay. You can go ahead and use it. I was still trying to figure out what I was going to do. I can wait."

"No, I insist that you go first. All of the others are being used and this place is packed tonight."

Raquel wasn't nervous or jumpy the way she tended to react to a man she found attractive. His pleasant personality and demeanor made her feel comfortable.

"Are you sure? I can go do something else and come back to the weights," she said.

"Ladies first," he said. "Maybe I can spot you while

I wait for an open bench. I'm Leo, by the way," he said and extended his hand toward her.

"I'm Raquel and if you're sure I'm not keeping you from anything, I could use a spotter. I assume you're an expert with the weights," she said and then felt ridiculous since her comment was referring to his gorgeous muscles. `

"I'm no expert, but I do work out with weights once a week."

"It shows."

Raquel wanted to slap herself. When did she start saying the first thing that came into her head.

"Thank you. I can tell you work out, too, though I've never seen you in here before. I'm typically here on Wednesdays."

"I've never been here before. I'm here with some friends who are all scattered about."

"How many pounds did you want to start with. I'll put it together for you," Leo said. He turned around and took a moment to pull himself together. He was nervous and knew he had to be if he offered to help someone workout. He'd been coming to the gym for months and not once has he even said more than hello to anyone. He tried to be low-key since he was using Walt's gym pass.

"I don't do much with weights, something very light," Raquel said and waited.

For the next twenty minutes, they took turns using the weight bench. By the time they were done, she was intrigued enough to want to know more. She'd never been forward with a man before and as soon as she was about to do something she'd never done before, someone called his name and he thanked her and walked away. Her window of opportunity was over. Perhaps he didn't find her interesting enough to even ask for her phone number. Disappointed, she wiped the bench down, grabbed her towel and water and walked away.

"Where have you been?" Toni said walking up to her.

"Looking for you and ready for my smoothie. The girls ready yet?" she asked, temporarily taking her mind off of Leo.

"I saw you at one point working out with the good-looking guy. Was he as nice as he looked?" Toni asked.

"Even better. We didn't really talk other than exchange names, but he was so helpful and patient with me."

"Ah, you like him."

Raquel ignored her to end the conversation.

"Come on, let's go find Kenya and Kelly."

**

Leo finished his workout and was able to get rid of the stress of the work week so far. Where he would usually shower before leaving, he decided to wait until he got home where Trayvon was waiting for him. With his water bottle empty, he headed for the smoothie bar to get a new bottle of water for his train ride home. The moment he rounded the corner, his eyes laid on Raquel, the woman he'd helped with the weights.

She was beautiful and where he thought he'd lost his chance to ask her out for coffee or even dinner, he was called away by one of the trainers who he chatted with whenever he came to the gym. She was sitting at the smoothie bar talking with three other women and he became enthralled the minute she threw her head back and laughed. She was beyond beautiful and the way her long hair swung around and back and forth, he couldn't stop looking at her. He could barely keep his eyes off of her gorgeous body as they worked out. Keeping his eyes on her, he walked over to the bar and ordered two bottles of water. When their eyes connected, he smiled, hoping to not be caught gawking at her. He had a feeling she was use to the attention. She had to be. He wasn't the only man who found her beautiful enough to approach. He struggled with walking up to her and not walking up to her. He had already decided no more women for a minute, though there was something about Raquel. He could tell she was probably a business woman from Wall Street or something along that line, way out of his league. Still, he liked her and going against his decision to stay hands off, he decided to talk to her anyway. He didn't think much would come out of it especially if they talked any at all about what they did for a living. If she were like most women he tried to connect with over the years, she would run and hide when he told her about his three jobs and not having much else. Perhaps, he'd just made a new friend, if nothing else. She was pleasant and seemed interested in talking to him.

Wanting to and then not wanting to keep his eyes on her, after receiving his waters, he put them in his duffle bag and walked over to her.

"Hello," he said as all of the women turned around.

"Hello," they said in unison.

"Uh, this is Leo. He helped me with weights tonight. These are my friends, Kenya, Kelly and Toni."

"Ah, the ladies from the girl's night out tonight. I hope you enjoyed your evening," he said.

"We did and it's nice to meet you," Toni said.

"Say, Raquel, do you mind if I speak to you for a minute?" he asked.

"Not at all," Raquel said getting up from her stool and joining him at one of the small round tables.

"I don't want to take you away from your friends for long. I wanted to apologize for rudely walking away after the workout. Charlie, one of the trainers around here wanted to ask me some questions not related to working out and he knows I'm only here once a week."

"Oh, don't worry about it. I know you were only helping me out with the weights. I didn't mean to take up all of your time."

"Well, actually, I was hoping I could get you to take

up a little of my time perhaps over coffee one day soon?" he asked.

There it was, he thought. He'd put himself out there and prepared to be shot down. After practically swearing off women in order to not set himself up for failure, the first beautiful woman he'd seen tonight, he was drawn to and he knew she wasn't just any woman. There was something about her that he felt a level of comfort with that he'd never felt before and it was one that he couldn't ignore. His sixth sense told him they probably were as different as night and day, but for some reason, he didn't care. He liked her and wanted to see her again.

"I would love, too."

Without trying to show how excited she was that he was interested, Raquel read her number off as he typed it into his phone. She took the few seconds to check him out again and her heart skipped a beat at all his gorgeousness. He wasn't just in shape athletically, but he was handsome and the one thing she was good at peeping out when it came to men, she didn't see in him. She didn't see arrogance and that alone was a major turn-on for her. He seemed genuine in his approach and like him, she wanted to know more.

"I'll give you a call, Raquel."

"I look forward to it, Leo."

As he waved and turned to leave, she watched him until he was out of sight.

"Yes," she mumbled to herself and turned to go back to her friends.

**

"Tray, I'm here!" Leo called out the minute he entered his apartment. He didn't immediately see Trayvon and assumed he was in the bedroom watching television. As he put their food in the kitchen, Trayvon came out from the bedroom.

"How was your workout?" he asked.

Leo smiled thinking about Raquel, the favorite part of his workout session.

"It was great. I look forward to it as often as I can make time for it. Plus, I met a beautiful woman."

"Oh, that's why you're smiling all crazy like. Who is she?"

"Just a woman I met. Her name is Raquel."

"Did you get her number?"

"This is your big brother you're talking to. What do you think?"

"I think it's about time. Maybe now you can do some things with her that are about you and not about us."

"We'll see, we'll see. Let's sit down and eat and you can tell me about this girl you like. Tammy, huh?" Leo asked.

"Yeah and like you, when I think about her, I can't help but smile."

"You noticed that, huh?"

"Yeah. All I did was ask about your workout and

you were thinking about this woman. She must be something really special to have you thinking about her and smiling like that," Trayvon said as he gathered plates and started dividing up the pizza.

"I only talked to her for a little bit, but that was enough for me to know that I think I like her already."

"Nothing wrong with that, right?"

"That's right. Now, about Tammy," Leo said and sat down to eat as they talked.

"Okay, I'll start from the beginning."

5

Raquel was having an uncomfortable evening. After meeting a guy as fine as Leo in the gym, she was surprised that he still had yet to call or text her and it was now Saturday evening, three days later. She thought she felt a connection especially after he asked for her number. Her eyes had been on him throughout her time at the gym and something about him connected with her and her hopes that he was remotely interested in her was solidified the moment he asked for her number. Now, here she was on a Saturday night with no plans and watching her sister go through one outfit after another in her closet.

Tyra, who was two years older than her, had called earlier in the day to ask if she could borrow a specific dress and even though she'd laid that dress out to keep her sister from rummaging even more through her closet, here they were.

"I pulled out the dress you asked for and I still don't know why you couldn't go out and buy a dress or even this same dress. You know where I got it from," she said as she let her eyes follow Tyra as she moved from the huge walk-in closet to the bed and back again.

"I know, but I didn't want to spend that kind of money for a dress I would only wear once. Unlike you, I prefer sweats and sneakers over high-priced dresses, suits, gowns and shoes. For the few occasions when I need that, I prefer to shop in your closet where I can borrow without buying."

"Yeah, well I'm going to start adding a cash register at the exit to my closet because lately, you've been borrowing a lot of fancy stuff. What gives?"

Tyra temporarily stopped walking and turned to face her as she laid across the top of her bed in sweats and a t-shirt, attire she only wore at home. Seldom did she venture out without her usual heels and killer designer outfit.

"I met a guy and I'm still trying to see if things are going to work out. If so, I'll invest in a better wardrobe like my runway model looking baby sister. If not, I won't have to worry about trying to impress him more."

"You're trying to impress a guy with my clothes? That's crazy. You make as much as I do at the company and you also have a trust fund like I do that you can access any time you want and yet, you are going through my closet like it's the discount rack. You're crazy!" she yelled and flopped back on her king-sized bed, covered in navy-blue, one-thousand thread count solid Sateen fitted sheets from Niemann

Marcus. She laughed at herself as she focused on the thread count of her sheets. She and Tyra were complete opposites.

"Crazy or not, I'm not all wild about expensive clothes like you are."

"I know, you prefer to spend your money on trips."

"Well, being the executive over marketing, travel is a large part of my job and I love visiting places around the world. You prefer having the world come to you in the form of expensive designer clothes from around the world. Now, which looks better?" Tyra asked as she held up one black dress and then the other.

"They're both black dresses with bling and both will look amazing on you."

Tyra smile. "Yeah, you're right. I'll take them both and figure it out when I get home. What are you up to tonight?"

Raquel's smile disappeared. She didn't have any exciting plans and as the hour grew later, she doubted she was going out any place for the evening. She was opting to stay home and either catch up on reading one of the many hot, steamy romance novels she'd recently purchased or catching up on a few of her favorite shows on cable she'd been missing lately.

"Nothing, just hanging around. It's been a busy week and with tomorrow being Sunday, I'm going to stay up late and sleep in even later in the morning," she offered.

"No hot date?"

"None."

"No signs of Elijah?" Tyra asked without looking her way.

Knowing Elijah wasn't a good conversation piece between them, she started to brush it off, but didn't.

"You hated him, so why would you bring him up knowing we split up?" she asked as Tyra loaded the dresses and a few pair of shoes into a garment bag.

"I'm trying to see where your head is. That man was trash in an expensive suit, tie and car. I couldn't stand him and you know I always told you he was too slick."

"I know and that's old history. That thing with him is dead, I've buried it and the body is decomposing as we speak. I'm done with him."

"Ah, good for you. Ready to move on I see. Are you moving on with anyone in particular?"

Raquel knew she would love to say yes, but that wasn't the situation.

"No, just trying to keep my options open for now," she acknowledged.

"I'm happy to hear that. Well, I'll let you get to your night in. Thanks for letting me borrow stuff again."

"Anytime. That's what sisters who wear the same size are for. Listen, before you leave, can I ask you something?"

Raquel loved that they were close enough that she could share from the heart and get an honest answer.

"Absolutely. What's up?" Tyra asked moving to sit at the foot of the large bed.

"Have you ever met a guy who you thought was really into you and you gave him your number only to have him not call you?"

"What? Did that happen to you? You've met someone?" Tyra asked curiously.

"Can you answer my question with a statement responding to my request and not hit me with more questions first?" she asked.

"You're so bossy," Tyra joked. "Okay, yes, I have back when I was in high school. I'm thirty-four years old and I expect better from men at my age. Now, tell me what happened? You gave your number to a guy who you thought liked you?" she asked.

"I don't know what it was. I thought we connected earlier this week at the gym. You know who I'm talking about. Remember?" Raquel asked. She knew Tyra would remember when she mentioned the gym.

"Wait? That hot guy from the gym you told me about the other day didn't call you? Even Toni told me about him and said he seemed to really be into you. She spotted the two of you a few times that night and thought there was a vibe."

"I thought so too, but he didn't call or text after I gave him my number on Wednesday. He was fine and seemed really cool and not arrogant as if I would be lucky if he asked for my number and actually called me."

"In other words, he wasn't like Elijah the day you met him and you fell for him anyway kind of arrogance?" Tyra said and then held her hands up in surrender. "Okay, that was my last dig about him, but you know I hated him. Good riddance to that dead weight," she added.

"Well, tell me how you really feel then," Raquel said flippantly.

"Well what do you think happened?"

"Maybe after he left, he ended up not being as interested in me as he thought he was."

"That can't be it. Maybe something happened to him," she said.

Raquel huffed.

"That's a horrible way to look at it."

"Sis, what else can it be? The two of you had some serious eyes for each other, according to Toni and you're fine, he's gorgeous, there was something happening between you and yet three days later and not even a text?" Tyra asked.

"No contact at all. Maybe I was too interested and he was turned off."

"Yeah, you can come off as aggressive."

Raquel threw a pillow at her and Tyra ducked before it hit her in the head.

"I am not aggressive, especially when it comes to men. I have to be aggressive in the office all day and when I'm not walking around with my work hat on, the last thing I am and try to be is aggressive. There was something about him that I liked immediately besides the fact that he's handsome."

"It's only been a few days and perhaps he's busy. Maybe he's another Elijah or some other Wall Street brother who is more focused on work than on a personal life. He could be involved with a woman and he hasn't been able to sneak in a call with you yet. You know how crusty these brothers can be."

"I know I can't know for sure, but I didn't sense that in him. I haven't had the best of luck when it comes to reading men, but there was something honest and genuine about him or I wouldn't have given him my number."

"Don't worry about it too much. Your last relationship left you vulnerable and I know you've been hesitant about dating, but I don't want you reading too much into that. I'm declaring nothing bad happened to him, but he, instead, got wrapped up in a work thing or something, not even knowing what he does. You should have gotten his number and you wouldn't be in this predicament. You know it's okay for women to call a man these days. It's twenty-eighteen!" Tyra exclaimed.

"I know and I didn't think about it because I assumed he would call. I'm not going to worry about it. Have fun at your shindig tonight and don't get anything on my dress. If you do, don't take it to any of those corner places you go to dry-clean your clothes. Bring it back and I'll get it cleaned. I'm glad to see you going out and really doing it up. I knew there was a girly-girl in you somewhere besides the one around the office who dresses up because she has to."

Tyra stood to leave.

"Yeah, yeah. I hope your guy calls you soon and that he is the man of your dreams because as your big sister, I want everything in this world for you that's good. I'll call you tomorrow."

"Okay. Put the alarm on as you're leaving out. I'm not getting out of this bed for anything," Raquel said, sliding lower under the comforter while reaching for the television remote. "And cut the overhead light out and then I know I won't have to get up," she added.

"I got you!" Tyra said leaving the bedroom and heading for the front door.

6

All black was the attire for the night. Having reservations about attending the celebrity event still resonated within him, but Leo put that to the side and prepared to enjoy the night out surrounded by a bunch of celebrities. When Walt first mentioned the party, he was all for it and then he came back down to earth and knew that wasn't really his crowd, but he didn't want to disappoint his friend. They didn't get to hang often and definitely not at some swanky event. What he should be doing is going through the list of contests he was thinking about entering. One in particular had drawn his attention and winning could mean the next step up for him.

It wasn't until after his talk with Trayvon a few nights ago that he actually thought about entering the competitive Black Film Festival contest where contestants were asked to submit their best science fiction short film, either animated or with live actors. The contest was sponsored by one of the largest entertainment companies in the world, Sky High Hill Entertainment out of Los Angeles and the judges were a local New York City marketing firm looking to help new talent bridge the gap into the entertainment business. The winner not only had the chance to win the chance of a lifetime to have their film produced by the major entertainment label, but the winner would also get a one hundred-thousand-dollar prize for the top submission.

He had passed over a few contests over the past few years, but after he and Trayvon talked in depth about a girl he liked at his school that he was now sort of dating, they again talked about the dreams Leo had that he had put to the side for the sake of family. The next day, he'd spent some time on the internet looking up contests and was happy to come across the one he was currently considering entering. Rather than going out tonight with Walt, he should be spending his time fine-tuning his submission of a futuristic sci-fi film, digitally created from beginning to end. Even without a college degree, he knew that he was well-versed in everything when it came to digital technology and stayed up on the latest when it came to creativity.

Winning the contest could mean something big for his family, something he had not thought about before because his only thought was on making sure they had what they needed in the present to get them to their future. Winning could mean Major going to a good school away from Brooklyn and moving his mother from the small brownstone into something a little nicer. Winning the contest could mean a move out of

New York for him and that was the biggest challenge. According to the contest rules, the winner would be flown to Los Angeles where the short film would be turned into a feature film all produced on the west coast. He'd seen the story of the winner from the year before and didn't like how things had turned out for him. That guy had won and moved to California where he let the lights, camera and action get the best of him. His movie never got made due to some legality stuff and the fact that he tried to swindle Tyrus Hill, the owner of Sky High Hill Entertainment, out of more and more money over the rights to the movie. He had no plans of becoming all Hollywood. That same guy had gotten so caught up in the Hollywood scene that he turned to drugs and drank heavily while his dreams of stardom tanked.

Leo had lived in New York his entire life and had only ventured outside of it on a few occasions and never to the west coast. He was a simpler kind of guy who didn't need the limelight, but Trayvon was right, he could take care of them and find a way to pursue his own dreams. He still wanted to go to college because he knew how important it was and it was hard to keep drilling that into his brothers if he wasn't willing to go that route himself. First, he needed to think about what entering the contest would mean. That, he would leave for another day. His cell phone beeped with a text that Walt was outside in the town car. He was dressed and ready to leave and had already said he would go. Locking up, he rushed outside.

"Looking good, Leo!"

He waved at the teenagers who were sitting on the steps next door to his apartment building. He'd developed a great friendship with them – he looked out for them and they looked out and looked up to him.

"Thanks guys. Don't hang out here too late. You know how wild things could get out here," he advised.

"We hear you and we won't. The recreation center is taking a bunch of kids to midnight bowling on a bus trip and we're all going, so we'll be safe. Looks like you're in for a night of fun looking like a GQ model!"

Leo fist bumped Troy, one of the kids who lived in his building.

"I appreciate the compliment, now get going to the recreation center so that you're not walking there too late!" he said and wave back as he got into the town car.

"You ready for tonight?" Walt exclaimed as the car pulled out onto the narrow Harlem streets.

"Yeah, I'm good. I was close to changing my mind, but then you showed up."

"Well, it's a good thing I did. You spend enough time doing everything except having a good time and your best friend got you the hookup tonight. Tell me a little more about this honey you met at the gym the other night while we're riding. Traffic will be crazy so it'll be a few before we get there."

Once again, the thought of Raquel made him smile, but then he frowned. He'd been hesitant about calling her for the past few days, not sure he was ready for another letdown when it came to yet another woman. He did tell Walt a little about her and to his surprise, he talked as if they were already dating because he was that interested in her before reality set in. Was he ready to be turned down again because of his status in life?

As the days went by, she probably thought he only asked for her number because they had been watching each other throughout the evening and him asking her was the right thing to do. He knew that wasn't the case and that he really was interested in her. The reservations were all on him. Still, he loved talking about her and Walt was the perfect audience. He laid it all out again, this time adding in details he'd left out the first time like how bright and beautiful her smile was and how sexy she looked when she tilted her head to the side when they talked. Some men may not have noticed small things like that, but he took pride in taking in everything about a woman he enjoyed looking at. He felt even worse, now, about not calling her after he said he would. He was doing the very thing he hated that men did when they met a woman.

**

Leo had to admit the party drew some of the most famous celebrities from around the country and he found himself right in the middle of it all. Alcohol flowed, music rocked and people partied in every corner. After the announcement of one celebrity after another, the crowd cheered as if they were at a New York Yankees ballgame. As he watched Walt move throughout the room as if he was use to walking amongst the most elite, he smiled and shook his head. Walt had that kind of electric personality while he, himself, preferred to stay out of the spotlight and work behind the scenes, the same position he was hoping his career would lead to.

What he should be doing was enjoying the party like everyone else, but his mind was always in work mode and having an evening off, he still couldn't seem to shut it off. He was at one of the biggest events of the year in New York City and he was standing against the wall watching everyone else have a great time. He wasn't usually the person on the side holding up the wall, but tonight, his thoughts were in several directions.

Besides work, he was still thinking about Raquel, now even more than he had two hours ago when he and Walt talked about her on the way to the party. Walt had chastised him for not calling Raquel since it was clear he was interested in her and from what he could tell, she was just as interested in him. His friend had been right to call him out on his mess. He didn't do women like that and he felt ashamed that he allowed his negative feelings about women keep him from enjoying the good woman he felt he'd sensed in Raquel.

His biggest reservation was that deep down, she was most likely out of his league. Her beauty and the way she smiled at him had him acting out of character and approaching her. He had already relegated himself to the fact that he wasn't financially in a place to date a woman like her who he was sure wanted and expected more from a man than to hear he's working three low paying jobs to support not only himself, but his mother and two brothers.

"Leo, you're still standing where I left you an hour ago!" Walt hollered when he walked up.

"Oh, yeah, I'm just taking everything in. It's a nice crowd," Leo said.

"Nice crowd? That's all you have to say? Have you seen the women up in here, up in here!" Walt exclaimed.

"Yeah, I see."

"Tell me you're not going to stick with this no women thing, even tonight? You can have your pick, I'm sure. Get out there and get you some. Not every woman is after what's not in your pockets. Some just want a good roll in the hay and won't even care what your name is. Come on, get out there and enjoy the night."

"I am enjoying it. Just because I don't enjoy it the way you do, doesn't mean I'm not enjoying it. I'm a little distracted at the moment."

"Yeah, well, that distraction better not be about work. I'm good if it's about the woman you told me about. I still want you to have some fun tonight," he said.

"I'm working up to it."

"You are thinking about her."

"I can't stop thinking about her. Whenever I think about her, I smile and can't stop."

"She got you like that after a few hours of glancing at each other at the gym? What did you ask for her number for if you weren't going to call her? I'm not liking this new Leo. I'm serious, you're too serious these days and you have no idea how to have fun anymore. From what you told me, she sounds like a cool person. You'll never know if you don't call her. Get over what you don't have and be about who you are and what you do have. I'm getting back out there. I've got my eye on a cutie who was all over me on the dance floor. I promised her a drink and I better back before another dude snatches her up. You good?" Walt asked.

"Yeah, I'm good. I'll join you in a few."

After Walt disappeared into the crowd, Leo's thoughts turned to Raquel and what she must think of the fact that he asked for her number and never used it.

As the crowd grew larger and louder around him, he pulled out his phone. Knowing a conversation wouldn't work with the noise in the background, he sent her a text to say hello and apologized for the late hour. The time was just at eleven at night and he hoped she would at least respond in the morning. Besides saying hello, he apologized for not calling her earlier and wanted her to know he had been thinking about her. Putting his phone back in his pocket, he moved away from the wall after finally deciding to get out on the dance floor to become part of the crowd. He was there so he may as well enjoy the party. He hadn't walked two steps when his phone vibrated in his pocket. Taking it out, he was surprised to see that Raquel had sent a text back. He smiled when he read her message telling him that she was glad he had finally reached out and told him she didn't mind him reaching out days later as long as he eventually reached out. He laughed out loud, though it couldn't be heard over the noise, when she texted she didn't haphazardly give out her number and hoped he understood how special he was to get it. When she followed up the words with a bunch of funny emojis, he laughed even harder. He already liked her whit. He moved back against the wall and preferred texting with her over being in the midst of the crowd.

'You're up late. Did I catch you at a bad time?' he texted.

'Not at all. I was up binge-watching Suits, one of my favorite shows on television. What are you up to at this hour?' she texted back.

'At some celebrity party I allowed my best friend

to talk me into accompanying him to. It's nice, but not really my scene.'

'Well, if you had texted or called earlier in the week, we could both be enjoying a better evening at a movie or over dinner or something,' she texted.

'Is it still too late? I know an all-night diner that serves the world's best double cheeseburger and hand-cut French fries if you don't mind eating this late.'

Leo sent his last text and waited. He didn't know what possessed him to even suggest they meet up especially at this time of night, but he'd had enough of the party and was ready to leave anyway. If she agreed, and he hoped she would, he could easily get a taxi or other transportation that he already knew was outside of the club waiting for patrons to leave. He waited and waited and when he didn't receive a response, he figured it wasn't a good idea to ask since he'd waited to contact her and other than their chat at the gym, they hadn't spoken to really learn anything about each other. He began typing in an apology for being presumptuous when her response came through.

'I love burgers. If you're sure I'm not taking you away from anything or anyone if you leave your party, I'd like to grab something to eat. Where is this diner?'

Deleting what he'd started typing, Leo told her where the diner was located which was about thirty minutes outside of the city. He told her if that was too far and she knew of a place more convenient for her, he was up for that, too. The minute she replied she would meet him at the diner at midnight, he moved away from the wall and looked for Walt. Finding him on the dance floor, he pulled him to the side.

"Look, I'm going to head out."

"What? The night is just beginning. Most of the celebrities aren't even here yet," Walt proclaimed.

He leaned closer to Walt's ear.

"I'm meeting Raquel at a diner for burgers. I was here and the party is nice, but you know I'm already over it. I'll catch up with you later," he said.

"Definitely, go see that woman. She needs to cut you down for waiting days to reach out to her. There may be hope for you yet," Walt said and laughed.

Leo waved as he turned and made his way through the crowd. As soon as he stepped outside of the club, he noticed the long line of people still waiting to get in and saw the long line of cabs dropping people off. Running over to one, he found a cabbie willing to take him thirty minutes out and hopped in. He didn't care how far it was or how much the ride would be, he was looking forward to sitting across from Raquel.

7

Raquel rummaged through her closet to find something to change into. When she received the text from Leo, she was already in bed lounging in attire that was not proper for meeting a man out on a date for the first time.

"Is this really a date?" she said out loud, talking to herself.

Date or not, her favorite worn gray sweatpants and her favorite black and white t-shirt were not her usual attire when she stepped out. Pulling dress after dress out of the closet, she looked at what she was choosing from and decided against a dress. The time was drawing close to midnight and they were meeting at a diner for burgers, not a five-star restaurant in Manhattan. Going back into her closet, she found a pair of her favorite Dolce & Gabbana Embellished jeans and a shirt that tied at her waist. She did pull out a pair of heels knowing that even if she was running to the corner store, she always had on heels. At five-foot-seven, the heels gave her a little extra height.

She'd already taken a shower and sprayed on a

little of her favorite perfume before quickly dressing as she grabbed her wallet from her purse knowing she didn't need to carry too much at that hour. She ran into the bathroom and checked herself in the mirror, adding a touch of makeup and pulling her long hair up and off of her neck before she headed for the door. Once it shut and she locked it behind her, she waited for the elevator to arrive to her tenth-floor condo to take her down to the underground garage. She thought about calling for a car service, but it wasn't often that she got the chance to drive her Jaguar around New York because of the gridlocked traffic. At this hour, it wouldn't be as bad and since she was heading out of the city, she would be fine.

As she finally made her way through the light traffic and got on the expressway, she was at the diner sooner than she thought.

Pulling into the parking lot, she looked around and was surprised at the number of people at the diner at midnight. It wasn't often she ventured out this far and had never been to this diner before. Usually when she ate, it was at some fancy restaurant in the city and most were closed by now. After finding a parking space near the door, she exited her car and looked toward the entrance and there stood Leo waiting for her. She smiled as she nervously walked toward him and took in how handsome he was. He appeared to be even more so than the first time she'd seen him at the gym. He looked like a sexy member of the secret service in his all black attire with his full set of gleaming white teeth greeting her, showing how happy he was to see her.

"Hi there," he said as she walked up to the entrance.

"Hi. I hope I didn't have you standing out here waiting too long. Traffic wasn't too heavy, but it took me a while to get dressed and get on the road," she explained.

"Don't worry about it. I would have waited all night for you. I was actually inside and when I saw you get out of your car, I came out so that you weren't out here alone. I didn't know if you would change your mind because of the hour of the night."

"What, and pass up on a burger and fries? Never. I know I don't look like it, but I love junk food and burgers are at the top of my list."

After going inside Leo escorted her to their booth and sat down after she took her seat across from where he would sit.

"I'm glad you like burgers. I don't know if you've ever been here, but this place has the best burgers. I love coming here to think and I do that best with my favorite burger or a big stack of fries in front of me."

They quieted while looking over the menu. He looked up when she cleared her throat and he saw her looking right at him.

"So, what took you so long to call me?" Raquel asked, not beating around the bush. She thought it best to get that part of the conversation over with.

Leo coughed and almost spit out the water he was drinking.

"Right to it, huh?" he laughed.

"Yup. I'm that in your face, right to the point kind of woman."

"Well, it wasn't that I wasn't feeling you, that's for sure. You are beautiful."

"Then?" she pushed.

"Well, I'm usually one of the most secure people you'll ever want to meet when it comes to having confidence in myself. There was something about you that immediately caught my interest which led to me asking you for your number. Being truthful with you, I had doubts the minute I walked out of the gym and it wasn't a doubt about you, but about myself."

"Doubts?" she asked.

"I've had my share of getting to know women and the fact that I'm single now gives you an idea that those didn't work out. I wasn't looking to meet anyone when we met at the club, but your beauty radiated throughout the place and every time I looked over at you, you were smiling and laughing and just enjoying yourself. I liked that, so I asked. I didn't mean to wait three days to call you. I wanted to call you that night, but besides the fact I promised my little brother he'd have my undivided attention that night, I didn't know what I was going to expect from a conversation with you."

"So, you're saying you've had some bad experiences and were willing to not call thinking that getting to know me would be another of those experiences?" she asked.

"Not that I think of you as a bad experience, but I've found that women don't really want what they say they want and again, not saying that is you at all, but I had to search within myself to find out if I was ready to experience you. You are lovely and I was and still am intrigued. I apologize for any presumptions I may have made, but we're here and I want to get to know you."

"Okay, so, why don't you start by telling me about you," Raquel said and only looked away briefly when the waitress came to take their orders. After she walked away, she turned her attention back to Leo.

"Okay, well, in a nutshell, I'm twenty-nine, I live in Harlem in a one-bedroom apartment. I have two younger brothers, Trayvon and Major and I help take care of them. They live with our mother and I work three jobs right now to help with whatever they need. I spend all of my time either working or with them giving and getting quality time because they are what's most important to me and when I can, sleeping because a brother is tired after all that working. I volunteer at my brother's high school one day a week teaching creative and digital design and one day, I'd like to write, direct and produce my own sci-fi movies or perhaps television series. For now, family is first until I'm able to focus on me. I love life, I enjoy working out, as you saw at the gym and the highlight of my week was meeting you. I'll give you more, but first, give me who Raquel is in sixty seconds or less," he joked.

"Okay, I'm thirty-two, which makes me an older woman, whoo-hoo!" she cheered.

"I like your sense of humor," Leo chimed in.

"That's a good thing because I have more," she quipped. "I work as an executive at my father's funds management company where I started working after college. I have an older sister, Tyra, who also works for the company. Our mother passed away a few years ago from cancer and my sister and I are pretty overprotective when it comes to our father, so I understand when you speak of how important your family is. I live in Manhattan which I love because I'm a few blocks from where I work which works well for nights when I'm working late. I liked you from the moment we first met and I hoped you would call me. Thanks for finally reaching out and inviting me out for burgers because I love to eat, though I may not look like it. Like you, I love to work out, though that was my first time at that particular gym and it's a good thing because you asked for my number," she smiled.

"Yes, I did and that was one of the best decisions I've ever made. Did I tell you how beautiful you are?" he asked.

"Yes, you did and I thank you for saying it. You look

really good yourself. You said you were coming from a party?" she asked.

"Yes. My best friend, Walt, is dating a woman whose company catered a big-time event for an up and coming rap artist and she was able to get him passes for it. It was nice, but I was thinking about you."

"You were? At the party?" she asked.

"Yes. When I think of you, I smile, from what my brother and Walt tell me."

"You told them about me?"

"I told them that I'd met a beautiful woman that I wanted to get to know."

"Did you tell them you left me hanging and didn't call?"

Leo had to laugh out loud because when she smiled over at him, he knew she was joking.

"Actually, I told Walt that very thing on the ride to the party and he called me a fool for not contacting you and he was right. I guess I had fallen and bumped my head or something. I'm glad you didn't hold it against me and came out anyway."

"Again, burgers and fries work every time and I wanted you to have a chance to redeem yourself."

Leo was enamored with the banter between them as if they had known each other for a long time. She was as beautiful inside as he knew she would be.

"You are refreshing," he said.

"Again, more good stuff! Now, tell me about these

reservations you had. What was going to keep you from contacting me?"

Leo was about to respond when their food arrived.

"Saved by the burger," he said.

"Not for long and this looks delicious. Even without tasting it, I know I'll be coming back here again."

"I hope you invite me next time."

Raquel looked over at him.

"Will there be a next time?" she asked.

"I sure hope so. More than you could ever know, I sure hope so. I like you."

"I like you too, now about those doubts?" she asked again.

"Okay, okay. Well, I made a bad mistake in categorizing you based on my last girlfriend."

"Was she that bad?"

"No, I would never say that. People are who they are. She wasn't the right person for me which didn't make either one of us bad people. I wasn't what she wanted when we really got deep in the relationship. She wanted more than I could provide for her when what I had most to give her was my love. That wasn't enough to sustain her because she was more material and I wasn't in a place to provide that for her, nor would I. No one should be used for that sole purpose. I told you I work three jobs and that's because my brothers and my mother are a priority and making sure they have what they need is all that matters to me right now. If I have, they get it first and she couldn't understand that. One of the issues was she is estranged from her own family and so having that kind of connection meant nothing to her. Again, I'm not saying she was a bad person because she wasn't. We were simply not on the same page at the same time and eventually, she moved on and it left me bothered by the things she felt would make her happy. In the end, it wasn't meant to be and for a second, I looked at all women the way I saw her and decided to give my dating life a rest and then I met you."

"Well, not all women are like her though I will admit, I've had my share of being in and staying in a relationship for the wrong reasons and some of those reasons were for material things."

"From what I've learned about you already, I'm sure you can get your own material things and I saw the Jaguar you drove up in. Very nice car," he said.

"Thank you and I hope that doesn't deter you. I can be as shallow as the next person and I think we all can be. I have learned that things like my car, where I live or what's in my bank account don't matter when it comes to what I really want from a man. It's true, that I've been drawn to men who could provide those things in spite of the fact I can provide them for myself, but what was missing was the immaterial which is what all women want if they look deep inside themselves. It's fine to want to have the finer things in life, but I'll take a good, honest man over that any day of the week. I hope you know I mean that and I want to also state that the moment I began liking you even more than I did the night at the gym was a few moments ago when you explained how important your mother and brothers are to you. Family means everything and they should come first. I respect that more than I can tell you."

Leo started to respond, but couldn't. He took a moment to enjoy his burger as he delighted in realizing how wrong he could have been and what he would have missed out on if he hadn't called her.

"How do you like the burger?" he asked after watching Raquel practically devour the two burgers, bacon, lettuce, tomato and mayonnaise between a sour dough bun.

"This is the best burger I have ever had."

"So, if I asked for a second date, you wouldn't mind coming here?" he asked.

"You should ask for a second date and coming here is top on my list!" Raquel exclaimed before going back in on her burger.

"What's it like working for your father?"

Not having a relationship with his father, he knew he was missing out on that kind of connection, but was willing to forgo it if it meant his family's safety.

"I love it. After college, and there were a lot of years of that, he invited my sister and me to join the company wanting to keep it as much about family as he could. He was all about business until my mother got sick. He spent time focusing on her and when she passed away and he eventually came back to work, I had been there a few years and he was already a different person. He was still about his business, but it wasn't as important as my sister and me. He knows we're good at what we do, me at numbers and money and my sister is a wiz at marketing and promotion, bringing in new business all the time. She has the personality that draws people to her."

"Sort of like you? I'm drawn to you."

"Yeah, sort of like me. I love her, though we are very much different. I'm more of a girly-girl and she loves all things rough and athletic. I prefer heels and designer clothes and she prefers sneakers and sweats and would wear them to the office if my dad allowed it. She's good people and the loss of our mother brought us even closer together. Now, we band to make sure our father is still living his best life. He's dating a nice woman now, so we've backed off a bit, but he is our priority."

"Clearly, we have some things in common, but we also live different lives. Do you see that as a problem?"

That was a question he should always ask and hope to get an honest answer. He liked Raquel and would love to see more of her, but only if they could focus on who they each were and not what they each had or did not have.

"I don't see a problem at all. I respect a man who does what he has to do to look after his family. What you have or don't have doesn't matter to me because in the few minutes we talked at the gym and since sitting here across from you, I can see that you are well worth getting to know if that's what you want."

"I definitely want that."

"Me, too. You mentioned writing, directing and producing movies. Did I tell you I love sci-fi? It's my favorite genre of movies."

"I've had a knack for drawing and creative writing since I was a kid. Back in high school, I would draw these off the wall characters that no one understood but me. As I grew older, I turned that into more digital designs with my love for all things computers. You would understand if you ever see my place. I have more electronic equipment than I should have in my small apartment, but it's all needed for me to continue plugging away at my dream and one day, it will be a reality. One day a few years back, I started working on my own fantasy sci-fi short film. Recently, I came across a contest for short film creators of sci-fi and I've been thinking about entering. It could mean a lot for my family if I won, but could also take me away from them if I won because it would mean a trip to the west coast while the film is being developed for the big screen. That's a lot to think through even if I'm thinking ahead of the game over a contest I have yet to enter and may not even win."

"You know you can do it all and your family will thrive whether you are here in New York or on the west coast. You can all have your dreams fulfilled, not just your family," Raquel said.

"My little brother said the same thing which is why I decided to at least look into it. I haven't made a decision yet, but I will."

"Well, if you want to bounce any ideas off on me, let me know. I'm all ears."

"Beautiful ears and I appreciate that. Thanks for coming out tonight," he said.

"Thanks for inviting me. I hope I give you more to think about when you think of me."

"Trust me, I'm already there. You sure you want to hear more about this contest?" he asked.

"I sure do because after this burger and fries, I intend to get a large piece of cheesecake I saw when I walked in here. Tell me about it and before you do, I'm already going to spend the evening convincing you to apply for the contest. I say, just do it."

"See, I knew you were the kind of woman every man should have in his corner. Let me tell you what I know about it so far."

Leo felt better about everything in life and it was all because of the woman who sat across from him.

8

"Raquel, you have another delivery. Would you like me to bring it in?" her assistant asked.

"Of course," she said smiling the moment Aisha walked into her office with a huge bouquet in her hands. She already knew who they were from, her second in the past two weeks.

"Someone has a serious admirer. Are you going to tell me about this mysterious guy?" she asked.

"Not yet. For now, I want to keep him all to myself."

"He must be special."

"That he is. Never have I ever met a man and in three weeks, has shown me what it means to be adored."

"So, is this some rich guy you're keeping a secret?" Aisha asked.

"Oh, he's rich, but not in the way you're thinking. He's intelligent, kind, considerate, asks me about my day each and every day we speak and does sweet things like send me flowers like this. The other day we had dinner at my place and he brought over Chinese food and it was delicious."

"Wait? You ate take out Chinese food on a date?"

"Yes, and it was one of the best nights of my life."

"Oh, I see. It was that kind of date, huh?"

"No, not at all. We haven't gotten that close yet. We've been having fun going out doing things I haven't done with a guy in a long time like bowling, something I had never done before. I even went ice skating at the Rink at Rockefeller Center. Last week, he took me roller skating, another first and though I fell most of the night, he caught me every time. When we're together, we dream together and talk about our love for sci-fi movies and shows. We pig out on ice cream, chicken wings and my favorite pizza. We also work out together and overall, just have fun together."

"All this in three weeks?"

"Yes, can you believe it?"

"I can because you've been leaving work on time lately and not working too many late nights. I love it and I love who you are since meeting this guy and not like before," Aisha said and then regretted the words.

"Oh, really?" Raquel asked.

"I'm sorry, I didn't mean to say that."

"Yes, you did because it's true and you know what, you're right. I feel different. I'm having fun and not fake fun, but real fun. It feels great."

"Okay, so what company does he run or what family money does he come from?" Aisha asked.

"He doesn't come from money and he's got my best

friend sprung!" Toni said entering the office as Aisha and Raquel turned to her.

"Eavesdropping?" Raquel asked.

"I sure was and I got an earful."

"I'll leave you two to share all the details. I'm happy for your Raquel. It's good to see you this happy," Aisha said and left the office, closing the door behind her.

"She's right, you know. I've never, ever seen you this happy. Leo must be something."

Raquel danced around and leaned down to get a whiff of the gorgeous bouquet of flowers in various colors.

"I've never been this happy. I am having the time of my life with Leo."

"No hang-ups about your different lifestyles?" Toni asked.

"None and after three weeks, don't admonish me, but I think I'm falling in love with him and get this, we haven't even slept together yet."

"What!" Toni yelled.

"You heard me. We've kissed and cuddled and all that type stuff, but no actual sex. We agreed to wait and get to know each other first because we decided we didn't want to go there unless we were looking to take the relationship to the next level, too. He is a wonderful man and he does small things like send me flowers and brings me the best fried chicken wings after I've had a long day. The other night at my place, he massaged my feet while we watched a movie. We fell asleep in my family room and woke up in each other's arms on the sofa, relaxed as if we'd spent the night making love. I've never been in this kind of a relationship that doesn't start out jumping each other's bones."

"You've wanted this kind of love and it looks like you've found it."

"I have. Now, there is one thing that I need to tell him and I haven't yet, hoping it won't ruin things."

Toni walked over and sat on the leather sofa across from Raquel's desk and waited for the other shoe to drop.

"What is it?"

"Okay, here it is. Leo has been thinking about applying for a Black Film Festival contest, where he has created and designed his own short digital film. He did everything from the cinematography to the sound, design quality, color, graphics, you name it, he did it all himself on computers. He showed it to me the other night at my place when he brought his laptop over and it was incredible. I've been pushing him to submit for the contest because I think he could win it. I had no idea he was that talented. All of the colors and characters, setting, movements, it was all amazing and digitally done," she said.

"Raquel, this all sounds good. So, what's the big problem?"

Raquel huffed and paused before continuing.

"The contest he is thinking of applying for ends in a few weeks and the company backing it is Sky High Hill Entertainment, Tyrus Hill's company out of Los Angeles."

"That womanizer?" Tyra exclaimed loudly.

"Shhh – Yes, that very one, but that's not the issue. Last Wednesday, I left work early and Leo came over so that we could work on finalizing the paperwork which was the first time I was able to look at the full registration packet. As I was looking over everything to be sure we didn't leave anything out, guess who I discovered the marketing firm is that has been selected to judge and decide on the winner? They will also be the company responsible for marketing and promoting the contest, it's contestants and then the winner. They were contracted by Tyrus Hill himself. Go ahead and take guess of whose marketing firm it is – just guess."

Raquel waited while the wheels turned in Toni's head. She had no doubt she'd figure it out. That moment didn't take long as a look of pure shock graced her face.

"No!" she exasperated loudly.

"Yes."

"No!" Toni said again.

"Yes! Elijah Bohner's marketing firm will decide on the winner. What happens when Elijah finds out about Leo? What if he finds out I'm dating Leo?" Raquel asked worried.

"Then Leo can count himself out because Elijah is an unforgiving you know what. I'm trying to hold to the company's policy of no cursing in the office, but you know I want to."

Raquel nervously held her bottom lip between her teeth as she played with twirling one of the rings on her finger, a habit she picked up when things around her were crashing.

"I know you do and so do I. I haven't told Leo yet."

"Why not?"

"When he told me about it a few weeks back when we first met at the diner, I didn't know about all of this. It wasn't until I've already gotten him all hyped about applying for it and supporting him knowing he really could win, that I found out about the judging. It's right on the website, someplace I hadn't looked. Leo knew so much about it, I let him tell me about it. Without giving anything away, I reached to Hazel who works for Elijah and she told me that last year when they had that contest, Elijah's firm didn't win the contract, but this year they did. She told me about how he schmoozed Tyrus and she believes what got him the contract was all of the women he was able to hook Tyrus up with every time he comes to New York."

"Isn't Tyrus Hill still married?" Toni asked.

"He is, but you know the gossip about him is real and as long as there is a woman around, his zipper is permanently stuck in the down position," Raquel said sharply.

"Yeah, I heard about that. I saw him a few times and though he is handsome, he's used his elite status to treat women worse than Elijah does. I guess that's why they get along so well," Toni said.

"This isn't about either one of them, this is about Leo. I've been supporting his decisions since day one and now that he's ready to submit, I think I need to tell him what he's getting into if Elijah finds out he and I are seeing each other."

"When is Leo sending everything in?"

"In a few weeks. He still has some time and wants to check and double check until the very end."

"Is Elijah still after you to take him back?"

"Yes, he is, but I ignore him like I have been doing since we broke up. I haven't even thought much about him until I start thinking about that contest. Should I tell him that I know?"

Raquel had been torn for days about what to do. She didn't want to bring an old situation into her new situation with Leo especially after the wonderful times they'd been having. She didn't want him at a disadvantage because of her history with Elijah. Leo deserved as much of a chance as any other contestant.

"You have to tell him. Don't let him walk into that contest blind. If he makes it to the final round, he'll want you there with him for support and then what happens when Elijah sees the two of you together? You know he is malicious enough to try and ruin Leo's chance at winning even if he is the best contestant."

"I know and that's what I'm afraid of. I'll tell Leo and let him decide if he still wants to enter. He may not want to."

"Raquel, there are tons of contests all the time. If he doesn't want to enter this one, he'll find another one."

"I know, but I think he really has a chance to win this one. His specialty is science fiction and it's perfect for what he created. I hate that this could turn out bad. Maybe he could win it anyway."

"Even with Elijah on the team of judges?" Toni asked.

Raquel knew she had a lot to think about, but she knew her first move had to be to tell Leo to clear the air. They were getting together later in the week. Something she hadn't told Toni was that she had a feeling their night of lovemaking was coming up soon. They were getting closer and closer and the kissing and fondling was getting hotter and hotter. He was planning to finally spend the night with her after teaching his next Wednesday class. As much as they wanted each other, they waited and now to her, they'd waited long enough and she wanted to be in his arms, making love until the sun came up. She was ready, but first, they needed to talk about the contest. She couldn't let him go into it blind.

"I'll tell him," she said.

9

Leo made his way from the subway closest to Raquel's condo and walk through the brisk night air that chilled him to the bone, but nothing was going to keep him from spending time with her after the last few busy work days. Even though they were in March, the weather was still wintery with blustering cold temperatures.

He was running later than he had planned after taking some time after he left the school with Trayvon to stop and also see his mother and Major. He wanted to finally tell them about Raquel, the woman he was in love with. One thing about him was that he didn't fall in love easily, though he had been known to fall in lust. With her, he was dying to take his relationship with her to the next level, but he opted instead to listen to his head and not his body when it came to her. He had never met a woman quite like her before, one who cared for him deeply from her heart and not from a place that he couldn't feel. He felt her falling for him as hard as he had fallen for her and it was time his family knew about her.

Since the day they shared burgers and fries at his

favorite all-night diner, they had been pretty much inseparable. At times when he was thinking about her but was away from her, he would send her little things as a way of letting her know she was on his mind. He had sent flowers and cards that he hoped made her smile and think about him. A few times, he'd even sent her favorite candy bar or her favorite bag of popcorn letting her know he had been listening when she mentioned something she liked. When he really liked a woman, he paid attention to everything about her. He may not have a lot of things to offer or give her, but his attention was something he loved giving freely and he'd come to love the smile he saw on Raquel's face whenever they were together. That showed him he was not only showing her the kind of man he was, but he was giving her what she wanted and needed.

When he arrived at his mother's house, he went right into telling them about Raquel and Trayvon even inserted his own opinion of her, telling how much he'd already come to really like her. The few times he was able to meet her when he and Trayvon ventured into Manhattan to meet up with Raquel, she had been pleasantly nice to him and showed genuine interest in getting to know him. Leo loved hearing Trayvon talk about her which was a surprise to them all because Trayvon never liked any of the women he introduced them to over the years. Now that they were getting closer, it was time to share with those closest to him that what they shared was honest and true.

After an hour or so with them, he finally found his way home to get work clothes for the next morning because he would have to get up extra early to get on the train. He also had a small gift for her, a scarf he thought she would love. It wasn't designer, but it was beautiful just like her and he knew that each time they'd been out, she'd had a different scarf around her neck. He loved doing small things for her and she reminded him that she loved small gestures and all she needed to know was that he was thinking about her because he was always on her mind. There was no semblance of doubt on his part when it came to his love and desire for her.

What was happening between them grew fast and deep and where he would usually question if he was enough for a woman, Raquel never let him forget he was what she wanted and needed. Like him, she'd had her share of hits and misses when it came to relationships when the focus was on the wrong thing.

Tonight, he would not pressure her, but he wanted her in his arms where he could love her until their bodies tired with exhaustion. He was more than ready for her and from her reaction to his every touch and kiss, she was ready for him. Always prepared, in his overnight bag, he packed a box of condoms he'd purchased the day before. The few he did have at his place, he'd given to Major earlier in the week, reminding him that the time for slip ups and babies would come later. The name of the game right now was safety and that applied to him, too.

After checking to make sure he had everything he needed, he locked his apartment up and headed for the subway after texting Raquel to let her know he was on his way. When she replied back with a sexy kiss, he replied that he was ready for her and asked if she was ready for him. Though they had yet to venture into being intimate with each other, that didn't stop them from having sexy chats via text and conversations that drove his body's temperature into the stratosphere. After Raquel replied that she had been ready for him for a while now, he quickened his steps to get to her.

The subway ride seemed to take forever and that was because he loved enjoying his downtime with her. Out of the subway station and with her building in view and the cold air hitting his face like small shards of ice shavings, he rushed to get to the entrance and into some heat. The guard knew him and waved him in through the locked door that led to the bank of elevators to her floor. Knowing she was waiting excited him on a level that was reserved only for her. He had a lot to share tonight, including the fact that he had finished reviewing and re-reviewing the short film and wanted her to see the completed product he was ready to submit for the contest. They had looked at it together a week ago, but he'd made a few small changes he wanted her to see. He also wanted to do something nice for her for being in his corner and encouraging him along the way. The idea had been planted by Trayvon who reminded him that he needed to do more for himself, but it was Raquel who gave her support, reassuring him that he was as talented as any of the other contestants. He was thinking of planning a quick getaway where they could spend time together outside of New York and away from any thoughts of work or contests. He hoped she was up to getting away. He knew how busy work was for her, but hoped she needed a getaway as much as he did. Once he reached her door, it opened before he had a chance to knock or ring the bell.

"Hi, beautiful, he said the minute he saw her standing before him looking like a goddess.

Raquel beamed.

"Hey baby. You are a beautiful sight after a busy work day," she said immediately going into his outstretched arms.

"That bad?" he asked as he removed his coat and denim jacket underneath. After placing his backpack on the floor near the door, he pulled her back into an even tighter hug and this time added a deep, passionate kiss, the kind he'd been thinking about sharing with her since he'd woke up that morning.

The kiss which started out slow and exploratory was now wild and untamed as he licked and sucked on her lips, first the top one and then the lower before tracing the seam from one side to the other with his tongue, wetting a path blazoned with his love and desire for her. Leo was so lost in the sensual dueling of their tongues that he was ready to take this action straight to the bedroom and talk later, but he slowed things down. There would be time for that later.

"You know you're killing me with these kisses, right?" he finally said after catching his breath.

When Raquel reached to wipe her lip gloss from his lips, he took the opportunity to kiss each of her fingers, the back of her hand and her palm. She may not have realized he noticed, but he saw a slight tremble in her body and got his confirmation that tonight was their night.

"Anytime you want more, I got you," she said.

"Hold on to that thought until after dinner because I don't want any interruptions like food or anything else in my way of giving us both more. How about that?" he laughed.

Excitement like nothing she'd ever felt simmering in her body filled her head with all kinds of images of them together, pleasuring and loving each other the way they had been putting off for far too long. Her mind and body craved him, but she would wait, perhaps not patiently, but she would wait.

"Yeah, let's eat now," she said and pulled him toward the kitchen where she had cooked dinner after leaving the office earlier than usual.

Leo laughed through her exuberance knowing what she was feeling. He was right there with her.

"You know I could have brought us something to

eat. I know you're exhausted after a day of meetings. I read your texts to me throughout the day and I felt sorry that you barely had a chance to grab a bite to eat because you were so busy running from one meeting to the next. You, my sweet, need a vacation."

Leo walked up behind her and pulled her body back against his, holding her tight.

"If I do, I hope that vacation includes you and I wasn't too tired to cook for my man. You do so much for me all the time and I wanted to do something nice for you. I made some of your favorites. See, I listen when you talk too."

"Really? What are we eating?" he asked while placing a sweet kiss on her bare shoulder before leaning forward to wash his hands as they stood in front of the kitchen sink.

"I hope you're hungry," she said and moved out of his embrace over to the stove to show off her cooking skills.

Leo looked her over from head to toe, taking in the white tank top and red and white shorts as his body hardened with the thought of removing them and feeling her soft, luscious body against his.

In a voice laced with the ultimate desire for her, he said, "You have no idea how hungry I am, but let's talk about food," he grinned at her with a devilish look.

Raquel moaned when she saw the heated gaze from his eyes as they covered her all over. As she did before they entered the kitchen, her body trembled seeing the look of want staring back at her.

"I'm right there with you. First, I made rice pilaf with sautéed onions and red and green peppers and then we have braised short ribs of beef, I skewered some jumbo shrimp on my indoor grill and to top it off, we have your favorite veggie, seasoned green beans."

"Smells delicious. You really got your cooking on, huh? You made all of this yourself? I appreciate you and I love you," he said for the first time to her. Never had the words held as much meaning as they did when he said them to her knowing she adored him for who he was, which was enough for him. He hoped he was being enough for her.

"I made every bit of it. I don't do much cooking, but when I do, the internet has everything you need and..." pausing, she walked over, leaned up on the tips of her sock covered toes and planted a sweet kiss square on his lips. "I love you, too. I never dreamed I would be this happy. Being with you is so comfortable and I feel so wanted and loved. It's not even about the word love as much as it is about the action of love. I'm glad you're you and I wouldn't change a thing – nothing at all. You are perfect for me."

Leo again pulled her close.

"Us, together is not what I thought it would be, but I am happy that we are who we are together. I didn't realize what I was missing out on backing away from relationships until I met you. Even if you never said it,

I know that you love me for me, the me that I've shown you from the start. Your love is what matters the most," he admitted.

"I'm glad because I want to make you as happy as you make me every single day and when I got that Hershey's chocolate bar with almonds at work today, I was crazy excited. You know exactly what I need when I need it and for the first time in my life, I see that happiness is tied to the heart and nothing else. You lead with your heart and I want to thank you for trusting me with it," she said.

"Just for you, baby," he said and when they began kissing again, neither were able to stop as he leaned down and lifted Raquel up and wrapped her legs around his waist. If there was any vestige of doubt about their love left anywhere, it was small enough to be unnoticeable.

"Ready to eat?" she asked with her lips close enough to his but not touching. The heated, minty fresh breath that escaped through his lips caressed her face like a loving glove and she wanted nothing more than to feel it all over her body, but she promised him a meal and then they would be free to explore other things, starting with each other.

"I am and we can talk while we eat," he said placing her back down on her feet while adjusting that part of his body that grew with unwavering yearning for her. "Also, I have some news for you about the contest. What can I do to help get dinner on the table?" he asked.

As soon as she heard the word contest, her mind drifted to what she had to tell him and hoped it wouldn't ruin their night together. She had been anticipating a loving night with him all day and had prepared with a trip to her favorite spa on her lunch hour. Throughout the day, they'd shared how much they wanted each other and how deep desire flowed between them that she had no doubt, the night would be a memorable one. She was nervous about the conversation, but the way she felt about him, she didn't want any secrets between them.

"Why don't you get us some plates and the bottle of wine from the fridge."

"I can do that," Leo said going into action.

"Listen, I know you have news for me about the contest and I have something about it I want to share with you that may impact your desire to compete," she acknowledged. Raquel tried to tamper down her uneasiness, but couldn't and when she looked over at Leo, she could tell he sensed it. After sitting the wine, glasses and plates on the table in the other room, he returned to the kitchen and leaned against the black and gray marble-topped counter.

"What's up, baby? Talk to me. We share it all - whatever is on our minds."

Gripping the edge of the counter to brace and conceal her level of discomfort, she exhaled and then told him everything she should have told him when she first discovered Elijah's connection.

"The night you told me about the contest weeks ago at the diner, I was excited for you and I wanted to push and support you to submit for it because I believed in your talent even before I saw it. Your love for creativity showed through your words. Recently, I found out something about the contest that could hurt your chances and I struggled with how to tell you and now that you're ready to submit, I want to share something with you."

In the same tone he always used when they talked, Leo gave her his full attention knowing whatever it was, they were still going to be fine.

"Okay, hit me with it."

Moving the food to the table, they finished setting up in silence and then sat across from each other.

"Remember when I told you about my ex and how things didn't end well with him because he cheated on me and had been doing it for a long time without me knowing? After that, he's spent the months since we broke up trying to get me back, but of course when I said I was done, I was done and I meant it when I said I loved you."

"I know and I don't doubt that at all, no matter what you have to tell me. Okay?"

If nothing else, he wanted her to know that they can always talk about any and everything and work through whatever the issue was and this was one of those times. No matter what, he wasn't walking away because he loved her, too.

"Okay. I would never go back to a cheater anyway. His name Elijah Bohner and his company is the marketing firm that represents Sky High Hill Entertainment's interest in the contest. Elijah is one of the judges of the contest. If he finds out about you and me, and he will, he may purposely hurt your chances of winning the contest. He can be and is that spiteful. I wanted to tell you, but I didn't want you to second guess sending your movie through. The parts I've seen were incredible and I know you were planning to show me the rest tonight and I want to see it. I want to support you in any way I can with this project and anything else going on in your life. I thought about talking to Elijah, but then I knew that would be wrong. I don't want to sway him one way or the other, but I want the selection to be fair."

Leo reached across the table when he could see how upset she was making herself.

"Baby, don't you worry about a thing. Despite him being one of the judges, I'm still going to send my short film in because I believe it's good, too. It wasn't until I really started to believe I could win that I knew there was no turning back and there still isn't, no matter what. If this contest is meant for me to be a finalist or to even win, that's what will happen even if he finds out about us and I hope he does. I don't want him out here trying to win you back, though he's no competition for me. If he cheated on you, he's already out of the running for your heart. No woman wants a cheater unless she's a glutton for punishment. I'm not worried about him and neither should you. I'm glad you told me about it and I want you to always talk to me. Communication is key in any relationship. Now, shake it off and let's enjoy our night, starting with this wonderful dinner you cooked. My stomach is growling and this food is calling my name," he proclaimed.

Raquel looked for any signs that Leo was hiding any worry that he wasn't sharing, but she didn't see any. His confidence was all she saw and it was one of the many things she loved about him. He looked at life on the positive side and as refreshing as it was, she still had concern over what Elijah could do given the chance. She would trust Leo's feelings about it and let it go.

10

"That dinner was everything and then some," Leo said as they put away the last of the dishes they'd washed together.

"Thanks for helping me clean up," Raquel said.

"We're partners in everything, including cleaning up after dinner. Do you want to relax and watch a movie or something?" he asked knowing it was the farthest thing from his mind, but he wasn't in any rush.

The look he saw on Raquel's face gave him his answer. They had survived dinner without ripping each other's clothes off, but now that dinner was over, everything was fair game.

"Come with me," she said, taking his hand and walking from the kitchen toward the bedroom.

"Are you sure?" he asked.

"I'm more than sure."

As they walked past the front door, he grabbed his backpack and entered her bedroom. He had been in her room before when she'd first given him a tour and another time when they fell asleep in each other's arms after watching a late-night movie. They woke fully dressed, refreshed and feeling closer to each other than they had before they fell asleep. Love didn't need to be rushed, but relished and savored. Now, here they were more than ready to seal their love in the most primal way.

When Raquel stopped and turned to him in the dimly lit room, his eyes focused on her mouth. From the start, he'd been fascinated by how sexy her lips were and the fact that they melded perfectly with his every chance they got let him know they were perfectly created for him to love and adore like he was about to do.

As her mouth tempted him to come closer and closer, he slowly reached for her body and after using one arm to bring her flush against his body, he dipped his head and nibbled then sampled the shape of her mouth. He kissed her with all the passion he could draw from his body and the moan he thought was coming from her, had actually come from him. His excitement was ramped up when he felt her arms reach up and enclose around his neck.

"I love you," he whispered against her lips before kissing her again, holding on to her tight as she reached for his shirt and pulled it up over his head and tossed it to the floor. As their eyes locked, the moment between them would forever be branded on his mind whenever he thought of her. Thinking about her everyday was like the feeling of waking and having the sun greet him when he looked out of the window. His love for a brand-new day matched his love for her as it felt brand new every day.

When Raquel's soft hands caressed his bare chest, his knees felt weak, but he stood strong, never wanting to let her go. No words were needed or exchanged as their eyes did all the talking. He was about to kiss her again, when she felt a long, raised area of skin on his chest that stood out. Looking, she could see it was about the length of a long middle finger and could have been the result of a deep wound.

"What's this?" she asked allowing her fingers to run across it over and over.

Leo unconsciously jumped when she focused on it. Even though he knew it was there, unless it became a topic of conversation, he'd rather forget about it. With Raquel, he knew he could share everything and he wanted to.

"I never told you about my father."

"No, you didn't. Is it bad and am I going to be really upset?" she asked.

"Possibly. He left my family when I was about seventeen years old after years of abusing us, mainly my mother. There were times when he took things out on me and my brothers and to protect them, I would get in his way of getting his hands on them and I suffered because of that defiance when he would yell for me to move. My brothers were little, about three and six at that time when it started. To punish me since my mother wasn't home that day to take a whipping, he beat me with a belt so severe that the one welp across my chest was so deep, it never healed correctly and left this mark across my chest. No one ever knew about this until I was almost a grown man. I would hide it from everyone. A year after this, he was gone after beating my mother to the point that I had to finally tell someone. My uncle threw him out of our house and a few months later, we moved into a new place and we never saw him again."

When Raquel looked up at him from the scar, he saw unshed tears in her eyes.

"Oh, my god. He did this to you?" she cried softly.

"Don't. Don't cry. It was a long time ago and the pain went away."

"You mentioned once that he was abusive to your mother, but you never said he was abusive to you and your brothers."

"He was, but we all survived and the pain has gone away."

Raquel didn't know what to do, but she wanted to take away all thoughts of the scar on his chest being about pain. She leaned forward and kissed his scar again and again while whispering how much she loved him and would always want to help take his pain away.

Leo lightly grasped her face in his hands.

"Loving me unconditionally is all I need – that and

you. Already my scar has new meaning, one not associated with pain and abuse. Now, I'll see it and remember how beautiful you looked giving it a loving kiss," he said leaning down for another searing kiss.

"That's what love is," she said.

"Yes, it is."

Walking them backward toward the bed, they kissed fervently as their lips trembled with love and need for one another. His love for her was so great, he could hear his heart beating in his chest. He was already on the edge and wanted to be as close to her as he could get. No love had ever felt as good as it did when he was with Raquel and he already knew none ever would.

Kicking off his shoes, he reached for her and moved them to the bed where they rolled around in heat with a zest that proved they were both holding on by a thread.

In between kisses, there were caresses as hands explored here and there, each touching every bit of skin they could reach.

Leo surged his hands through her long, natural hair and while lightly gripping her head, he pulled her mouth tightly against his, making sure not even air could get between them.

Needing to feel more of her, he pulled her top over her head and off and without missing a beat, he slid her shorts down her legs, leaving her naked and bare for his perusal.

"You are even more beautiful than I imagined you would be," he said taking a moment to remove the rest of his own clothes. With them both naked, there was nothing holding them back from each other. As his tongue again plundered her mouth over and over, sharing his love with her, he felt every bit of her love for him in the way she looked at him and communicated her love with her eyes.

His pulse quickened as his body hardened. When he moved closer, allowing her to feel him, he saw her inhale deeply as the craziness of the moment filled them with a need only surfaced when love was as real as theirs was.

"You make me feel wonderful," Raquel uttered.

"I want to kiss you everywhere – I want to worship you and your body," he pleaded.

"Do you, baby," she whispered.

Leo drew back and climbed up over her body, allowing Raquel to get a good look at him.

"I've been waiting to make love to you," he said.

"Oh, my. You are definitely worth waiting for," she quipped. "I'd say you're more than worth waiting for. I have protection, but none that will fit you. Your body is beautiful and I do mean every part of you," she admitted.

When Raquel's eyes landed on his manhood and he watched her tongue slip from her mouth to caress her lips as if she'd landed her eyes on a feast, he felt his flesh grow longer and harder from her admiration.

"All for you," he said.

Raquel felt her body tremble with an intense need as his deep sexy voice floated through the air straight to her womanhood which jumped in anticipation of what was to come.

Going first for where his eyes landed, Leo leaned down and kissed around her breasts, tempting her by not going directly for the center, puckered nipple. When Raquel squirmed under him, he couldn't tease her for long. The moment his mouth covered first one hardened peak and then the other, he knew this was the kind of intimate kiss he'd been planning to give her all along. He made love to her body with his mouth and his hands and as he allowed them to roam all over, his desire for her increased the more she moved around with her hips going in sexy circles while she moaned his name on a whisper.

Leo savored the softness and hardness, both in his mouth and hands at the same time. He licked and sucked as the feeling he knew zinged through her, zapped through him at the same time.

"I love you," Raquel said over and over.

Going lower, Leo took his time discovering every delicious part of her body. Every part of him was in dire need of her and the more he touched and kissed, the more he wanted. His heart overflowed with love knowing that this is what he had been desiring in a relationship with a woman – nothing but pure, unadulterated love. It made intimacy between two lovers more powerful.

Reaching down with his hand, he caressed the area between her legs, coaxing her to open wider for him. As Raquel flung her head back and forth, overtaken by the sheer magnitude of not just the feel of him touching her, but also from knowing their love was rare, she felt like she was experiencing an out of body experience. There was swift and what was unleashed was the kind of joining she's always wanted, but only now discovered with Leo.

As Raquel's legs slid further open for him, his caress coaxed the slippery essence from her body he needed in order to know her readiness for him – her want and need for him. As his fingers moved around, stroking her, bringing her to the edge, his eyes watched her drowning in the tantalizing moment, enjoying the feel of him giving her everything she needed. He didn't just want her to know he was there, he wanted her to feel him all around her.

"God, you're so beautiful laid out before me like this. Absolutely gorgeous!" he proclaimed.

"I'm close," she muttered as her hips moved faster and faster while her sex throbbed with the need to let go.

"I know you are baby," Leo said kissing around her stomach before moving so that his mouth took over where his fingers had just been, giving her pleasure. The taste of her was sweet like strawberries and slippery and soft like the dew in the morning.

Raquel was dizzy with a thirst for Leo she didn't know existed. Never had her body felt so good or climbed to a peak this high so fast. Her eagerness to let go was out of her control as she moved about wildly on the bed.

"More!" she screamed and as his mouth centered on her hardened nub, her body finally let go as a burning fire seared through her, causing her hips to rise off of the bed. Her orgasm was powerful as her brain tried to wrap around what was happening to her body. She drew in a sharp breath as Leo pleasured her with his tongue more and faster. Her body rose higher and higher as if she were floating on a cloud. She tried to muffle her own scream by putting her arm across her mouth, but it didn't help. The feeling was too intense to be restrained. She let go as her mind and body exploded again and again.

In the few moments it took for her to regain some control, she watched through hooded eyes as Leo reached for his backpack and retrieved a condom. With shaky hands, he covered himself and rejoined her on the bed.

"You are amazing! That was as good for me as it was for you and trust me when I tell you I speak the truth. You may have been the only one experiencing that release, but I enjoyed watching you in the throes of it. It was beyond erotic," Leo said as he kissed her face from one side to the other, taking his time as her body continued to calm.

"I've never felt an orgasm that deep inside of me before," Raquel admitted.

"Really? If that's the case, I want to see and feel you experience another one. I want to be sure you and I will always remember our first time together like this," he said while kissing her lips once, twice, three times.

Moving in between her legs, the moment he took her lips in a fiery kiss, he used his hand to enter her body, giving her a little at a time. He knew his size could be uncomfortable and his goal was pleasure, not pain.

"Ah, yes," Raquel moaned into his shoulder as she widened her legs even more, delighting in the feel of him as he went deeper and deeper inside of her, stretching her wider than her womanhood had ever been stretched before.

"You good?" he asked even while his body fought the urge to drive forward. Once he'd felt her moistened walls, he knew it would take every bit of strength to keep from powerfully moving into her.

"Yes. You feel good. You feel better than good," she groaned out and then joined in with the slow pace to their love making that he'd set.

"Oh, baby," Leo grunted as his teeth clinched.

"Love me," was all Raquel could get out as her body took control of her mind. As Leo quickened the pace and increased the speed of his movements in and out of her body, she matched his demanding strokes. She again felt her body chasing her next orgasm as their tongues wrestled and their desire grew.

"I with you baby. I'm with you," he groaned out.

"Mmmm, I can't hold out any longer. What's happening? I can feel it and it feels amazing!" she yelled.

"Let go baby. I'm right with you."

Leo meant it. He tried to prolong the moment, but the way his body connected with hers was too great of a pull to resist giving her every part of him including his release.

With their bodies moving faster, writhing about, deliciously and furiously loving each other, together they surged into a heavenly bliss as they screamed through their pleasure, calling each other's names. Leo saw white stars as his body surged forward again and again with powerful strokes driven on by Raquel's squeals of delight and encouraging words to never stop. He already knew he never would. He never wanted to stop loving her.

As their bodies finally calmed, the sight of watching Raquel come down from her powerful release was as exciting as watching the beginnings of it. Their breaths were ragged as their bodies still moved together as one, in sync on all levels.

"Okay, I don't know if I can move even one muscle in my body," Leo joked. "You wiped me out," he added breathlessly while his body fought to calm.

"I don't know what to say, but that was incredible.

I've never felt like that before. That's never, ever happened to me."

"What's never happened to you?" he asked, not sure what she was referencing.

"I..I..I." Raquel tried to put her feelings into words, but none would come out. She didn't know how to tell him what she really meant. At her age, it would be an embarrassment.

"Don't do that. Don't shut down on me," he said when he sensed her hesitation.

Leo rolled so that he was no longer on top of her, moving to the side and turning so that they were facing each other. "What's going on? Am I missing something?" he asked.

"No, nothing. That feeling from you being inside of me has never happened before."

Raquel tried to hold his gaze as she watched his eyes search for clarification. She looked away only to have him turn her head back toward him with a finger under her chin.

"Talk to me. What are you saying? We share everything, remember? Now that we've shared our bodies with each other, there should be nothing you can't tell me."

"I've never had an orgasm from penetration before. I've been able to give them to myself, of course, and from oral stimulation, but you are my first when it comes to coming with you inside of me. I've never been able to achieve that before," she admitted.

"Really? I know we haven't talked much about partners in our past, but I have to ask, what happened when you've shared that in the past?"

"I never have. I let them believe I had," she said as the words stammered out.

Leo kissed her. "Oh, baby. Never, ever do that with me. Promise me that if you are not getting satisfied, you tell me. I never want our coming together to be about me only. It's a shared experience and I don't know what others have been doing, but making love to you, for me, is all about you first and me second and that is always the case. I'm glad I could do that for you. It may have been the first, but absolutely not the last. I love you."

"I love you, too."

This has to be what real love is like, Raquel thought as Leo pulled her close to cuddle as they usually do, but this time they were naked. In the quietness of the moment following her revelation about never having an orgasm by way of intercourse, she knew their hearts really were now one. She held on tight to him as sleep consumed her.

11

"Leo? Is that you? Is that my long-lost brother from another mother that I haven't seen in weeks?" Walt said, walking up behind Leo as he stood outside of their favorite pool hall.

"Oh, now you want to be Kevin Hart, telling jokes."

"Man, I was going to send out an S.O.S. to find you if you hadn't answered my call today. If I hadn't decided to call you today, I never would have known you were off and had time for a brother. What gives? Raquel has your balls in her grip or what?"

"Crass, Walt. That's even a bit much for you," Leo said flippantly.

"I speak the truth. How is that beautiful lady of yours?"

"She's great and this has been the best two months of my entire life, man. I'm serious," he admitted as they walked inside to play a few games and catch up.

"Look at you all in love and happy. I'm happy for you and her. I thought we would have double-dated or something by now, but you're treating me like the black sheep of the family," Walt kidded.

"We can definitely do that. I've been working extra

hours lately and Raquel has been busy with a new acquisition."

"So, things with you two are really good?"

"Are you going to rack 'em up or dive deeper into my love life?" Leo joked.

"Both and you're up first this time."

Leo grabbed his favorite cue.

"As an answer to your question, yes things are really good. I think we're in a place where we know that we're meant to be together. Raquel is an amazing woman."

Leo smiled just thinking about her.

"There's that silly grin I've seen a few times since you've started dating her. Man, I've never seen you this happy before and I've been through a few of your relationships with you. I thought when you told me about who she was that she would turn out to be like Misha, expecting you to be someone you aren't. I wasn't trying to bring her down or anything, but I was a little worried in the beginning, but now, I guess she really was a woman who was out for the same thing you were in search of. The fact that she's from a rich family hasn't come in between you?" Walt asked.

"Not at all. I know she has money and power and I'm not intimidated by it. All I want to know is that I make her happy. She knows I don't have much and how important it is that I take care of my family."

"How's the family?"

"Much better and getting better every day. My

mom is really coming into her own. She loves her job and they love her. She's making decent money and my brothers are both rocking the school thing. Trayvon had a good basketball season and now is gearing up for baseball. I'm still focused on sending Major to a four-year college if I can swing it. Life is good."

"Yeah, I can see that. What happened with that contest?"

"Oh, yeah, I'm sending everything in this week. I'm all set."

"You're really doing it, huh? You've been working on developing that film for a long time. You're a master at digital characters and I can't wait to see what happens. How long will you have to wait to find out if you're a finalist?"

"The five finalists will be announced in thirty days. After that, it's a matter of the judges agreeing on who the winner is. If I make it as a finalist, there's a big, fancy event where the winner will be announced. I get five free tickets and the other five people at the table have to pay a hundred dollars, all proceeds going to a charity."

"Count me in for a free ticket!" Walt laughed and took his shot.

"I kind of figured that already."

"Who's at your table when you get that far because I already know you will?"

"I don't know yet. Right now, I'm trying to make sure I get everything in on time. I haven't told you the crazy part," Leo said. Ever since Raquel told him about Elijah, he hadn't told anyone else about the bad link in the chain.

"What's that?"

"One of the judges is Raquel's ex. He owns the marketing company who's judging the contest. Can you believe that?"

"Was it a bad breakup and does he know that you're seeing her now?"

"It was a really bad breakup and he's been wanting her back, but she has never been interested in taking him back, not even before I came along. If I get to the final round, he will know because I'd want her with me at my table. She's my lady and I would never hide her, not even for a contest."

"I hear that. What will you do when that hits the fan?"

Leo hadn't thought about that, but he wasn't one to chase fame and fortune. If luck were in his corner and things panned out, he wouldn't turn away from it, but if he had to decide, he would choose family and Raquel every time without a doubt.

"I love her, man and I don't give two shakes about her ex or the fact that he could hold my future in his hands. If it's meant to be for me to win, then I will. If not, it won't stop me. There are other contests. My family deserves my best and some of these contests can go a long way to getting my foot in the door."

"I hear that. Who is this guy anyway?"

"His name is Elijah Bohner."

Leo shrugged when Walt looked at him sideways.

"I've heard of him and I think I actually met him before at an event. He's a white dude. Did you know that? She used to be involved with him?"

"She was and I know he's white. She mentioned that to me. She was into him and race doesn't matter. What matters is love and she thought he loved her until she found out he'd been cheating on her."

"Ah, yeah, that's the same guy. He loves the sisters, but he's not known for being faithful."

"He couldn't make her happy and despite all his wealth, prestige and status, it didn't buy the kind of love she and I share. Thinking about her and having her in my arms is like heaven on earth. We've shared our past and we've both been through some good and bad, but now we're greater because we found each other. We've been talking about meeting the parents now that things are getting pretty serious."

"You're meeting her parents? That is serious. I don't think I've ever heard you say you were meeting someone parents before."

"It's parent, just her father. Her mother passed away from cancer a few years ago. You've never heard me say it before because I was the naughty secret only to be seen and heard from in bed. I'm telling you, Raquel and I are in love and she loves me for me, the Leo who works himself crazy and lives in a small one-bedroom apartment, a stark contrast to her life, living in a Manhattan condo, driving an expensive car and having a job that pays her a high six-figure salary. We've learned that none of that matters if the heart isn't right and connected to the right love. When I think of her, I think about forever."

"Does Raquel see forever?"

"Yes."

"You're sure about that? I'm only asking as your best friend."

"I know and I appreciate it. I have had my doubts about women before, but not with her. We bring out the best in each other and we like what we see."

"That's what's up! Now that you're back out from under your rock and this woman is letting you out for air, I want to meet her and shake the hand of the woman who has brought life back into you."

"You're going to really like her. Trayvon loves her. He's the only one who has met her so far since he spends time at my place and we've gone into the city to hang with her. She's that big sister he never had and between the two of them, pizza joints will always be in business. My woman can eat and I love it. She doesn't try to be fake to impress me and I've already told you she's beautiful."

"You're a lost cause brother!"

Leo tried not to laugh, but couldn't hold it in.

"I'm a happy lost cause. Now, let's finish this game so that I can get to my woman. I took this whole day off so that I could hang with you this morning and relax with her all evening."

"Whipped like never before," Walt yelled.

"Happily whipped!" Leo replied.

**

"Hazel, I'm finally catching up on my messages and you have one there that says Raquel called a few weeks ago? What was that about? Was I supposed to call her back? I've been calling her for months and I've gotten nothing. She didn't leave a message?" Elijah asked.

"Elijah settled in behind his desk and looked through the stack of messages and mail left for him over the past two weeks that he'd been in California meeting with new clients.

"Oh, that was a note for me, not one for you. She had called for me that day and I was on the phone. I wrote a note to call her back and forgot to throw it away."

Elijah got up from his desk and walked out of his office and stood in front of Hazel's desk which was right outside of his office.

"Why did she call you?" he asked, confused. He hoped Raquel had been calling to say she was finally ready to give him another chance. Since they broke up, he hadn't been able to fully explain why he'd been cheating on her. He wanted her back if for no other reason than the one that she was his in when it came through making business connections through her father's company. That was how he had met Tyrus

Hill and Tyrus had been throwing work his way ever since. Raquel was nice and he enjoyed being with her, but he missed the parties and events her father's company threw where he could hobnob with the best in the business. Word had gotten out about what he'd done to Raquel and he'd lost a few clients out of the loyalty they had to Raquel's father. He had to find a way to make things right and get not only those clients back, but possibly some new ones.

"Don't worry, it wasn't anything about you. She wanted to say hello to me. Even though you were a bad boyfriend to her, she always liked me and wanted to say hello."

"She must have known I was out of town. I guess she's still keeping up with my whereabouts. That's a good thing," he said.

Hazel sucked her teeth at him. Elijah wasn't one of her favorite people, but he paid her extremely well and she'd worked too long for him to leave and go someplace else. At fifty, she would have to compete with millennials for a job and she wasn't trying to do that. She was quite comfortable where she was.

Elijah's personal life was a mess and she often had to lie for him when it came to women, but he was good at what he does when it comes to running the marketing firm.

"That woman is not checking for you and you know it. If she was, she knows how to reach you directly."

"Did she ask about me when she called?" he asked.

"Not even once. You need to let that go."

"I would, but I'm not going to. The fact that she called here at all was a good sign. She'll come to her senses soon enough. I wonder if she's been seeing anyone? Did she say anything about a new man when you talked to her?"

"I'm not telling you what we talked about. That was between me and Raquel. You need to focus on all of those submissions that are coming in for the contest. We've received about two hundred of them so far and we're expecting a lot more as the deadline gets closer."

"Right. We need to start assembling the review team who are going to do the first-round applications. Can you call a meeting with the team and reach to a few of our temporary employees to help with this? I want to know who the top fifteen potentials are. This is a big opportunity for our company and could lead to more opportunities like this one. Working with Tyrus was the best decision I've ever made."

Hazel looked at him superficially.

"Is that so? So, the fact that he's married and you're pretty much his pimp doesn't bother you at all?"

"What Tyrus Hill does in his free time is no concern of mine or yours. If his wife lets him cheat and trust me she has to because it's not a well-guarded secret that he does, then I'm good with it. I'm doing what I need to do in order to stay out front in this competitive world of marketing."

"You were doing well even before Tyrus Hill came

along with him and his cheating penis."

Elijah laughed so hard, he almost choked.

"You have a way with words. I'm in this for the business and I leave the personal out."

"Well, speaking of personal, he called and left you a message that he's in town at his usual spot and wants you to call him. I guess that means he needs a hookup," she said.

"Yeah, he called while I was on the plane. I didn't get the message until after I had landed. I'll give him a call. Let me know if Raquel calls again. Why don't you send her some flowers from me again and maybe this time she won't send them back?"

"I got you, but I think she's moved on."

"Maybe or maybe not. She'll come around and when she does, I'll be here waiting with an arm full of flowers."

"Flowers that I'll pick out and order, right?" Hazel asked, slyly.

"Yeah, yeah!" Elijah said going into his office and shutting the door.

12

Raquel drove up to her father's house in Teaneck, New Jersey for their family's usual family night in for dinner and board games. She already spotted her sister's car and knew she was the last to arrive. With Tyra's new house being remodeled, she sometimes stayed with their father, some with her and a few times at a small apartment she rented by the month if she really wanted to give their father his privacy since he now had a love life.

She would explain her lateness due to the detour to Leo's place in Harlem to be there with him when he emailed his application for the contest in and then they rode to the post office together to send, by certified mail, his short film. They were excited and a little apprehensive knowing about the Elijah connection. After their talk about her ex, she was happy to see that Leo wasn't hesitant about taking part in the contest despite her history with Elijah. He had every confidence in what he was submitting and if it was meant to be for him to win, he would. If not, he would apply for other contests. He'd waited a long time to take part in something that could secure a future for him and he didn't want to back down from the challenge, even one as big as her rich and powerful ex-boyfriend who knew media mogul Tyrus Hill on a first name basis.

After taking him back to his place, she got on the road to her father's house, not wanting to disappoint them. She and her sister were supposed to spend the weekend and really make a family gathering out of it since they'd all been busy with work. She loved their time together, but what she really wanted to do was spend time with Leo and his brother.

Trayvon had an assignment for school which required him to go to the museum. After meeting Trayvon several times, she liked him right away. He was a handsome, kind, young man and she saw a lot of Leo in him. Leo had invited her to go with them the next day and she was hoping her father would understand if she only stayed the evening so that she could get back to New York to get up early to join Leo and his brother.

Making her way into the house, she called out for anyone who was within ear-range in the large six-bedroom, eight-bathroom house, the same home she'd been raised in.

"We're in the family room."

Following the sound of her father's voice, she walked into the family room where he and her sister were already sitting around the card table talking.

"Glad you could finally make it, sis. How did everything go?" Tyra asked.

"He got it all sent out and now we wait."

"Who got what?" Melvin asked.

"Oh, daddy, her boyfriend is going to be a contestant in that big Black Film Festival contest held by Sky-High Hill Entertainment. You know, that company owned by Tyrus Hill, the snake," Tyra said glumly.

"Tyra!" Melvin said.

"I know and I'm sorry, but he is. He's slipping and sliding all over the place. You know it's true, daddy," she said.

"I know it is, but the name calling is not necessary," Melvin said sternly.

"You're right and I'm sorry."

"You have a boyfriend?" Melvin asked, directing his question to Raquel.

"Speaking of Leo, is it okay if I leave tonight and not stay the whole weekend?" Raquel inquired.

"Hot date sis?"

"Actually, yes I do. I'm going to the museum with Leo and his brother," she explained.

"Museum? Do uneven know where the museum is," Tyra joked.

"Who is Leo?" Melvin asked.

"Yes, I know where the museum is and you're already starting with jokes, I see," Raquel said.

"Who's Leo?" Melvin asked again, this time a little

louder.

"This guy must really be something if he has you going to museums and not he hottest clubs or parties. I think I go to more celebrity parties than you do these days," Tyra said.

"Who is Leo!" Melvin finally shouted, drawing the attention of both of his daughter who looked at him, eyes wide and mouths open.

"Okay, pop, you're going to blow a vessel in your neck. He's a guy I met a few months ago and I really like him," Raquel finally answered.

"That doesn't tell me who he is and what does he do? I hope he's not another moron like your last boyfriend. I still want to hurt him," Melvin said, causing both girls to laugh out loud.

"Stop it, daddy. He works as an advertising designer, for his first job. He also cleans the museum at night and at his third job, he does staging of houses to be sold. He also volunteers at his brother's high school teaching digital computer design to students."

Melvin looked at his daughter as if he didn't hear a word she'd said.

"I'm sorry what did you say? You mean he's not some banker, executive, actor or other high-flying type of guy driving around in a fancy car to impress you or to impress me?" he asked.

"No and he doesn't even have a car."

Raquel looked over at her father who couldn't stop staring at her. She waved her hand in front of his face to be sure he was still with them.

"You still in there?" she asked. "I know, you're shocked, right? You expect better from me, right? A guy who can take care of me and all that stuff, but I really like him. In fact, I'm in love with him."

"You're in love with a guy that I haven't even met? When did you meet him?" he asked.

"A few months ago at the gym."

Tyra reached over and pinched him.

"Ouch! What's the matter with you?" he asked her.

"I'm making sure you're okay. My sister who has never dated anyone who made less than a million dollars a year just told you she's dating a regular, run of the mill guy and you're not having a heart attack."

"Don't do that again," he admonished, yet in a joking manner.

Melvin turned back to Raquel who appeared to now be uncomfortable.

"I would have told you, but I didn't think you would understand my falling for Leo when he's not who you would probably expect me to be with, but he's a really great guy and he treats me better than any man I've ever dated. I see a lot of you in him and that's what made it easy to fall for him. He has a heart as big as yours," she explained.

Melvin leaned forward and then leaned back in his chair and crossed his legs at the knee while resting his head on his knuckles.

"Is that what you think of me? That I wouldn't

understand you falling for a man who isn't flashing money, cars and jewelry at you to buy your affection and loyalty? If so, then I'm not doing a good job of setting an example of what your mother and I set out to do when you saw us since you were born. I didn't raise you to have money that wasn't your own. I didn't raise you to go after a man because he had money and power. I have always told you to follow your heart and you never have unto now. I don't care if he was the guy who took out the trash every day as long as he loves, honors, respects and cherishes you. I want to know that even if you lived in a shack, you did it together and worked as a team to better yourselves. I've never placed any expectations on you girls to go after money. I've made money so that you don't have to chase it. I made sure you both had the best education so that you could pursue whatever dreams you had to make your own way in the world. I have always wanted you to follow you heart when it came to love. I want you to find the kind of love I shared with your mother. I know you saw that and it wasn't fake."

"We know, daddy," Tyra said.

"Your mother was my life and I was hers. I loved her unconditionally and likewise from her. I made sure each and every day she felt like the most beautiful woman in the world. I made sure every day she knew I loved her and never had a doubt about that love. If this young man does that for you, then I'm the happiest father alive and I expect to meet him soon."

Raquel couldn't stop the tears from flowing if she tried. She jumped up and hugged him so tight, he had to ask for room to breathe, causing them all to break out in laughter.

"I love you, daddy," she said.

"I love you, too and remember to always chase love and happiness. If you need a dollar, I got you," he joked and they all laughed again. "Let's get dinner and you get back to New York before the hour gets too late so that you can get up in the morning and meet up with your young man. Perhaps we can have him over for dinner next week."

"I will ask him tonight. Thanks, daddy."

"I'm happy to see you happy," he said. "You both make me a very happy father and your mother would be proud of who you both turned out to be."

"We miss her," Tyra said.

"I miss her, too."

"How is Ms. Helen doing?" Raquel asked.

Their father had finally begun dating again, a few years after their mother died and they could tell he was happier than he'd been in a long time.

"She's fine. When we have Leo over for dinner, I'm going to invite her. I want you both to spend more time getting to know her."

"You really like her?" Tyra asked.

"I do and that feeling is mutual. We've gotten pretty close and she'll be spending more time here with me and I'll be spending less time around the office. I want to travel more and with the company as much of a success as it is, I will eventually turn it over to the two of you to run."

"You're retiring?" Raquel asked. "Say it isn't so?" she added.

"Not today, but when I decide to, it will be because I think you're ready to run things with the help of the board, of course, but we don't need to worry with that right now. Let's eat and talk some more and then we'll let Raquel get back home to her young man."

"Well, what about me?" Tyra asked. "I have a life, too!" she exclaimed.

"True, but I need to talk to you about yours. I've heard some things about you partying like crazy lately and I'm a little concerned. Nothing big, but I want to talk about it."

Tyra folded her arms across her chest like a child who had just been chastised.

"I guess I'm not thirty-four anymore, huh?"

"You are and if you want to see thirty-five, you'll slow the limelight down a bit. Now, dinner?" he asked as they stood.

"Dinner!" Raquel hollered and led the way into the dining room.

13

Raquel drove through the streets of Harlem, racing to not be late picking up Leo and his brother for a trip to a local museum. Trayvon had an assignment for school and she was happy they allowed her to include herself into their outing. The original plan was for her to meet them at the museum, but after hanging out with Toni doing a few errands, she was already on the road and when she called Leo, she offered to drive them and hoped they could take Trayvon to their favorite diner which would require her car.

Checking the GPS, she knew she was less than ten minutes from his place. She was about to change the satellite radio station when her cell phone rang and since she had yet to program her car with her contacts, she answered without thinking about checking to see who it was. She needed to keep her eyes on the road. Her assumption is that it was Leo calling to check on her.

"Baby, I'm a few minutes away," she said answering.

"That's good to know, but you're a few minutes

away from where and I love hearing you call me baby."

Elijah! She screamed in her head. Why did she not look before answering?

"That comment wasn't meant for you and why are you calling, Elijah?"

She wasn't in the mood for his shenanigans.

"I was calling to see if you wanted to go to Amour, our favorite French restaurant or The Modern in the city tonight. I know you love expensive restaurants with your expensive tastes. You know I love spoiling you. It's been long enough that you've kept me in the doghouse and we need to talk. I've apologized for my little slip up and I'm sorrier than you can imagine."

"Oh, I can imagine it because I lived it. I'm not going out with you and you may have unnecessarily spoiled me, but you forgot that a key part of a relationship is treating me with respect. You forgot that part. The fact that I've made no effort to reach back out to you after the calls, flowers and invitations out should give you a clue that when I said I was done, I meant it. I'm seeing someone and I'm happy. You should do that same thing."

"You are? Who? I know he can't hold a candle to me, so why don't you save him the heartache when you break up with him and come back to me like you've done before. We've wasted enough time."

"You're not hearing me. When I said I was through, I meant it. I'm seeing someone and I'm in love. There is no hope for you and I and I recommend you move on because I have."

"You know you always say that. Every time we've broken up, you say you're not going to forgive me and you eventually do, so cut through the chase, forgive me now, put on one of those expensive, sexy dresses and meet me for dinner."

Raquel huffed out of frustration, angrier at herself for continuing the conversation than at Elijah's arrogance.

"Goodbye, Elijah and please lose my number."

After disconnecting the call, Raquel shook off the encounter and wondered how she ever settled for a man like Elijah even for a brief amount of time, though what they shared wasn't brief or brief enough. How desperate had she been for someone to give her attention, spoil her or even take her to the hottest, most elite events around the country, all things she could have done for herself. Until she met Leo, she didn't know that what she needed the most was the love of a good man – the kind of love that she was able to carry with her throughout the day and when things may have turned sour with work or in a personal situation, just the mere thought of a man who loved her as deeply as Leo did is what would sustain her.

She now understood the love between her parents. As she made her way through the last few streets to Leo's place, she thought about all of the times her father would gaze at her mother for no reason and he would be smiling. He wasn't just looking her way – he was wondering how lucky he had been to have loved her and to have her love in return. She would sometimes find her mother, even when she was heavily sedated with pain medication, smiling with her eyes closed and saying thank you for no apparent reason. One time she asked her what was she always smiling about and saying thank you for. Her mother replied that she had been thinking about the love of her life, her husband and how blessed her entire life had been because of his love for her which resonated in every part of their life, deep down in her soul. She said thank you even when he wasn't around, thanking God for giving her the best man, husband, father, friend, confidant in the entire world.

Before her mother died, she'd asked to speak to her and Tyra alone and in that moment, she told them that she hoped and prayed that one day, they would find the kind of love she shared with her husband. She didn't want them wasting time on material things because they come and go. She didn't want them wasting their efforts on men who didn't love and appreciate who they were inside and not just the life their father was able to provide for them when it came to wealth. On her deathbed, Veronica Johnson told her daughters about love and what real, true love would look and feel like and she told them to never forget her words, don't get caught up in being well off and be careful who they trusted their love, heart and life to. It will matter when all else fails.

A tear slid down Raquel's face as the memory of watching her mother take her last breath surfaced and she wondered how could she forget her mother's last words to her. Feeling sad was immediately replaced with the sensation of being overjoyed, ecstatic, delightful and most importantly, grateful that Leo entered her life when he did. As she smiled with thoughts of him, she understood all her mother tried to tell her and now that she had that kind of love for herself and gave that love in return, her life was filled with the joy her mother always told her to chase. Feeling giddy just thinking about Leo had her beaming from ear to ear.

As she waited for the light to change, she glanced at the car next to her and the driver smiled after having caught her smiling for no reason. When the woman, who appeared to be in her sixties signaled for her to roll the window down, she obliged.

"I know that smile," she hollered at Raquel. "I've been married for forty years after meeting my husband at a movie theater and there are times when all I have to do is think about him and I smile like you're smiling. Stay that lucky in love and you will never, ever want for anything else in life."

Raquel placed her hand over her heart, overwhelmed that a complete stranger would pour into her all because she caught her smiling.

"Thank you and yes, this smile you see is love," she

replied. She waved as the light changed and she said a quiet thanks to her mother for reminding her of what was important even through the eyes of a stranger.

**

Leo opened the door to Raquel who was talking a mile a minute on her cell phone. He pulled he phone away for a second and kissed her sweetly on the lips and mouthed, 'hi baby'.

"Sorry," she said. "Tyra, I have to go. I just wanted to tell you about the encounter. She was a sweet older woman and all it took was one look at me. I'll call you later. Love you, sis. My love is standing in front of me looking like a delicious afternoon and evening snack!" she laughed. "My sister says hello," she shared with Leo.

"Tell her I said hello."

"Leo says hello. I'll call you tomorrow about the party," she said and hung up.

Having her full attention, Leo pulled her securely into his embrace and kissed her deeply the way he loved doing whenever he saw her.

"Party?" he asked when he allowed them to come up for air.

"I needed that," Raquel uttered and gave him another quick kiss on the lips. "My sister wants to use my place for a girl's night out lingerie and body oils party. She just sold her condo and bought a house that needed rehabbing. She's waiting for the updates to be completed and she goes between my place and my dad's house. She wants to use my place for some party she wants to have."

"Mmmm, lingerie and body oils? Nice, I hope you get something sweet and sexy looking and smelling that you can model for me," he crooned against her now thoroughly kissed and puckered lips.

"I got you, baby. I think I've become addicted to making love to you now that I can...well, you know," she said looking around the apartment. She wanted to say now that she was experiencing orgasms through intercourse and Leo had released the beast, but she knew that Trayvon was there somewhere and that would be too much information to share in front of him.

Leo chuckled. "I know what you mean and you can say it. Tray isn't here," he said.

"Where is Trayvon? Isn't this a trip to the museum for a school project or something?" she asked.

"Yeah. He and his friend are helping my neighbor put her groceries away. She's eighty and her son and daughter live out of town. I try to look out for her. We went to the store and I picked up a lot of stuff she needed. This was my first time meeting his friend or should I say his girlfriend, Tammy. Her father dropped her off earlier and she's been hanging out with us today."

"Wait, now you're helping the elderly with grocery shopping? Goodness, will I wake up and you're not real? I've never met a man as caring for others as you are."

Leo laughed again. "What you see is what you get, baby. How was the time with your family last night?"

"It was great. My dad wants to meet you. He asked if you could come for dinner soon. Is that too soon? I'm sorry if that was presumptuous of me to tell him all about you. I know we talked about meeting the family, but we didn't decide when."

"Baby, you could have told him about me on the first day and it would have been fine. You know my work schedule, so any of my days off is fine for me and I look forward to it. Before we get to that dinner with your father, let me tell you what I plan to tell him. I want him to know that though we've only been going out a few months, I love you, something you already know. I'm not looking for anything from you other than your love and respect. I'll leave the sex part out, but I want you to know that's pretty damn good!" he joked.

Raquel playfully swatted at him.

"That part is off the charts and if we weren't going to the museum and your younger brother wasn't here, I would recommend we stay in and indulge," she swooned.

"With the exception of right now, I'm yours whenever you want or need me. Being near you or even just thinking about you always has me ready for whatever," he crooned lovingly.

"Happy to hear that and as for my father, not that I

want to talk about him in the same breath as you and I doing it, but he already knows you love me and he knows that I love you. You should have heard the speech he gave me about finding love and being happy and not chasing a dollar and a dream that someone else has. He knows all about you and he's excited that I'm happy which means he will love you."

"No one could hate on the kind of love we share, but I'm not oblivious to the fact that our lives are different and a man in your father's position would be concerned about any motive. It's natural and it's okay if he feels that way. I can handle it because people who meet me and get to know me find that everything about me is genuine. I don't come from a mean-spirited place in my life or in my heart. It is important that your family knows that."

"As much as I talk about you to them and all the fun things we do together, I think they already like you better than they like me. My sister was mad I didn't tell her about the Harlem Festival you took me to because she would have loved going. I told her that was part of the, you and me getting to know each other time."

Leo pulled her close again. "I love our getting to know you time," he said and kissed her again, wrapping his arms around her waist and when her arms held him tight, he forgot everything except for the feel of her.

"Really, bro? You told me no affection with Tammy,

but you get to lay it on heavy with your woman in front of me?" Trayvon exclaimed as he and Tammy entered the apartment.

After one last quick kiss, Leo separated them and turned to Trayvon.

"My house, my rules," he said.

"Yeah, yeah, I got you. Hey, Raquel. This is my girlfriend, Tammy," he said.

"Nice to meet you, Tammy. You have a good guy here in Trayvon."

"That's what I told my dad. I like him, too."

Leo cleared his throat.

"Since we're all in love and like and stuff, can we get out of here?" he snickered.

"We're ready. Miss Mallory said thank you for sending me and Tammy to help her with the food. Are we taking the train or calling a car?" Trayvon asked.

"Oh, I brought my car," Raquel chimed in.

"I forgot to tell him that," Leo said. "I thought after the museum, we would go out to dinner, get out of the city and it's my treat."

"Does that mean burgers at the diner?" Trayvon asked.

"Of course."

Trayvon turned to Tammy.

"My brother loves this diner and the food is good. Once a month, he takes me and Major there. You'll love it and, in the back, they have an arcade room where all the games are a quarter. We spend hours there."

"Sounds like fun. My dad said to thank you for including me in your day and I wanted to say thanks myself," Tammy said and Leo shook his head acknowledging her thanks.

"What kind of car do you drive, Raquel?" Trayvon asked

Raquel handed him the key.

"Go see for yourself. It's right out in front of the building. It's red."

Trayvon took the keys and headed toward the door.

"Do not start that car up, Tray. I'm warning you," Leo noted in a serious tone.

"Yeah, I hear you."

"You are going to spoil my brother."

"At least he is grounded. I have seen worse," Raquel said as they headed toward the door to leave.

"I have, too. My brothers are going to be strong, powerful and productive men."

"You're a good brother and the perfect boyfriend. I love that everything you do is from the heart."

"When all you have to give is your heart, you dominate the heart game, baby!" he insisted.

"You definitely are the king of that game! Let's go."

Leo grabbed his keys and turned to lock the door behind him when he remembered he was spending the night at Raquel's place and was about to leave the duffle bag with his change of clothes for work in the morning in it. Racing to his room, he grabbed it along with the new box of condoms from the cabinet in his bathroom. With their amorous activities, he needed to make sure they were always equipped for their all-night sessions.

14

Looking around her condo at the staff she'd hired to cater Tyra's girl's night out lingerie party, everyone moved swiftly making sure every instruction was being carried out. Raquel had been on edge all day. Somehow, she'd let Tyra talk her into being the co-host of the event and not just the owner of the place where the party was being held. If Tyra's new house had been finished already, they would have had it there, but with Tyra temporarily staying with their father, the last place they wanted to host a party with women walking around in skimpy lingerie was in the house where their father lived.

What started out as a small get together with about ten women turned into a full blown-out party of twenty-five. When Tyra began the planning, the idea was to have finger food, but as she looked around at the full buffet of food, this was more than a small gathering. Now that she was knee-deep in the party planning, she exhaled and walked the full length of the table to be sure all the food had been put out. She marveled at the silver, white and pearl decorations that covered the table. Chafing dishes were placed along the long, rented table filled with chicken wingettes that were parmesan garlic baked and teriyaki grilled, slices of grilled salmon, jumbo shrimp stuffed with Maryland crab meat, and a salad station where there were ten different ingredients to build your own salad. Along another wall was a cheese, veggie and wine table and finally a round table filled with fruit of all kind from grapes, strawberries, watermelon, pineapples, kiwi, sliced apples and to top that off, a chocolate fountain.

"Everything looks great, doesn't it?" Tyra asked coming into the room after using the spare bedroom to change for the party.

"It does. Security called from the lobby. The ladies are beginning to arrive. He's sending them up."

"Thanks for letting me have the party here. My house is going to be another month and I may spend a few nights in your spare room. With dad dating, I know he wants some privacy without me hanging around all the time. I will only invade your space when I don't want to drive out to New Rochelle to stay in my apartment."

"Nonsense, dad loves having us at the house and he was the one who offered you your old room while your house was being completed."

"I appreciate his offer. I didn't expect my condo to sell as fast as it did, but that's a good thing."

"What made you decide on a house? You could

have kept your condo, too."

"I know, but I didn't want to have a reason to live between two residences. I like having my own pool and the tennis court out back. I miss having that like we have at dad's house. I fell in love with the house one day while I was helping a friend with decorating ideas for her new house. We went around to open houses to see how they were staged to get ideas and this house had me written all over it. I knew I would have to sink money into it for upgrades and it was worth it. The house looks good."

"I can't wait to see the final product," Raquel said.

"One day, you'll want a house, too. You won't want to raise kids in a condo. They'll need a big back yard to run around and play in and noisy, city living is not for kids, in my opinion."

"Kids? You see me with kids?"

Raquel wasn't sure she saw herself with kids. She was so wrapped up in her career, kids had never really crossed her mind.

"I see you with kids before I see myself with kids. Don't you want a family?"

"I never really thought about it. Once I turned thirty a few years back, I stopped thinking about it."

"That's because you were always hooked up with crazy men and not a good one like Leo. I was waiting to see if the differences in your lifestyles would be a negative impact on your relationship, but it's not. I've never seen you this happy before. Trust me, you're at a good age for having kids and getting married. Dad will kill us if one of us don't give him some grandchildren and my vote is on you!" Tyra laughed.

"Yeah, I'll see. I've never been this happy before. Leo is amazing. Being with him makes everything about life better and you're right, before him, I never really thought much about family, marriage or kids."

"But now?" Tyra asked.

"I know it hasn't been that long that we've been dating, but yeah, I can see it with him. He would be the best father any kid could have. You should hear how he looks after his brothers and how much he loves them. He would do anything for them and he makes sure they know he's there for anything they need. He's not fake or putting on a show for me and that means a lot. That means I get to see the real Leo all the time and he makes me think about forever, though we haven't talked about anything like that. We're enjoying each other."

"You are having the kind of love life all women would like to have. He's a winner. Never let go of that," Tyra said.

Raquel gave her a hug. As sisters, they couldn't be closer to each other. They grew up with parents who told them they were to always have each other's backs. They could have a million friends, but they were to always be each other's best friend and Tyra was that for her as she was for Tyra.

"I love you, Ty. I was going to second guess that

each time the invite list grew for this party, but I digressed. It's going to be a fun night."

"It's going to be great. I just spoke with the consultant and she's about to pull up in a few minutes. She's bringing three female models and one sexy male model. You might be able to find something for Leo."

"Trust me, I'm already all over that, but I have a feeling, he will be most happy with something I buy to put on which in essence will be a gift for him as he rips it off of me," she laughed and then winked.

"In that case, I suggest you get some extras for moments when things are so hot and heavy that he doesn't care about the price tag and ruins your expensive lingerie. That's what's up!" Tyra shouted.

Before she could respond, Raquel heard the door buzzer knowing their first guests had arrived. It was time to get their party started.

**

"Where's your lady tonight?" Walt asked the minute Leo walked into the bar out in Brooklyn. He'd been he'd taken the day off to do some errands with his mother. Having the evening off from work and with Raquel busy with her party, he decided to go out for a few beers with the guys. He nodded at his other friends who were also out with them for the evening.

"She's having a party or a girl's night out or something at her place tonight."

"Cool. I figured when you said you had taken off tonight, you did so for time with her. I know you have been working like crazy."

"I had been taking time off to work on my submission for the contest making sure I fine-tune any loose ends. Now that I've submitted that, I'm picking up extra hours, but not this weekend."

"You're doing it, huh?"

"Yeah, I'm doing it."

"What made you finally do it, especially after knowing about Raquel's ex being a judge?"

"I figured if I didn't do this one with that small challenge by way of her ex, I wouldn't do one where there was no potential for drama. I had been working on that short film for a long time, not knowing what I was going to do with it. With Raquel and Tray in my ears around the clock, I knew it was time to get up and do something for me."

"That Raquel is really something special. My lady and I enjoyed the movie and dinner night with the two of you last week. I see why you like her or should I say why you love her. Any woman who supports and pushes you to be the best you, is a woman after my own heart."

"You have no idea how good this woman is for me and to me. We worked together on the paperwork and she read and re-read my application which included an essay, something I'm not the best at. She's been a big help and my staunchest supporter. I'm feeling good about this."

"About what? The contest or Raquel?" Walt asked.

Leo smiled.

"Both."

"She's the one, huh?"

"She's more than that. She's the only one. I've told you about her and you know she didn't have to choose me. She's dated guys who make seven figures, drive flashy cars and can give her anything she could ever want. She knows I don't have all that, but she still wants to be with me."

"That's because men and women go after some relationships for the wrong reason. I know she's loaded and she knows you're not, but she saw the Leo that I know, the one who has been my best friend for years. She knows the Leo who would give up the shirt on his back if he saw a man out in the streets freezing. When a woman is really looking for a genuine man and not these clowns out here mistreating them in the name of prestige, power and money, they will find him and she found you. I'm happy for you."

"Hey, you guys gonna join us or what? There's a dominoes game in the back," Ron screamed at them.

Leo laughed at Ron as he moved away from the wall.

"I'm playing and ready to show you who's boss around these parts," Leo said.

Leo drank the last of his beer and walked with Walt to the area in the back of the bar where they often sat to play dominoes and sometimes chess. He loved hanging out with the fellas when he could and in the back of his mind, he hoped Raquel was enjoying her ladies night out. They loved their time together, but also knew how important it was to have time away and not forget there are others in the world.

**

Raquel thanked the caterer as they left, leaving the rest of the food and setup behind. She told them she would cover the cost of them coming back the next day to pick up everything since it looks like her party was officially going well into the night. With most of the ladies gone, there were still a few hanging around.

There were her friends, Kelly and Kenya and Tyra's close friends who were also friends of hers, Chloe, Erin and Kim. She wasn't a big fan of Chloe or Kim because they liked to gossip about everybody's business except their own. Tonight, the reason for the get together outweighed the minor issues she had with them. She had an opportunity to do something for her sister and she was more than happy to do it. This was the small group she knew would stay after the party where thousands of dollars were spent on sexy lingerie for men and women. Grabbing another glass of wine, she walked over and got comfortable on the sofa and joined in on the girl talk. Before long, when the conversation turned to men, as it often did when women got together, she found herself as the center of attention.

"So, Raquel, I hear there's a new man in your life that you've been keeping a secret from most of us and

I heard you've come back over to the dark side, if you know what I mean," Kim chuckled.

When Raquel looked her way, the look on Kim's face looked more like a glib glare than real interest. She knew everyone else had to be looking her way, sitting on the edge of their seats waiting to hear the latest gossip about her relationship. Looking at Tyra, who was walking away, she low-keyed threw daggers at her with her eyes knowing Tyra had spilled the information about Leo.

"Yes, his name is Leo and I have not been keeping him a secret. I've been enjoying a nice relationship."

"I guess Leo is a lucky guy because I saw the sexy pieces you bought tonight. I guess Elijah is officially out of the picture and out of luck that he no longer gets to see you in stuff like that, huh, or are you having your cake and eating it, too?" Kim asked, goading her, something she was used to. The one good thing was that she didn't have to see Kim often because she was Tyra's friend. Kim never rubbed her the right way, always walking around with a smug look on her face. Tyra once told her that Kim had eyes for Elijah at one time.

"I'm the lucky one because Leo is great."

"Really? What does he do? Is he richer than Elijah? Is he a rapper or professional ball player? I'm sure he has deep pockets. He would have to have that to snag you, right? Isn't that what drew you to Elijah?"

"Stop it, Kim!" Kelly chimed in from the opposite

end of the sofa from Raquel. "You're being a smartass now."

"Who me? I'm just adding to our girl chat. You know how we do when we get together. I'm just asking because some of us haven't seen Raquel in a minute and I'm wondering what's up with her. You know, just being all friendly and stuff," Kim added.

"Well, Raquel?" Chloe added.

Raquel looked her way.

"No, Leo isn't any of those. He's a good guy who doesn't need all that."

"Oh, I get it. In other words, he's a broke brother. Don't tell me you went from a rich, fine ass man like Elijah to a brother with what? What does he bring to the table? Does he know how well off you are? I'm sure that he's been here and seen your condo and know it costs a pretty penny to live here. I bet his eyes bulged knowing that he's struck it rich."

"Leo isn't like that!" Raquel yelled defensively.

"Why are you guys drilling my sister?" Tyra asked, coming back in the room after going in Raquel's spare bedroom to make a private phone call.

"Chloe and Kim are being mean girls trying to find something wrong with Leo," Kenya said.

"I'm not trying to find anything wrong with Leo, though Raquel hasn't denied that he's another broke brother."

"Why does everything have to be about money and status with you all? None of us have had perfect relationships, yet we look to make a mockery of someone else's," Raquel said.

"Okay ladies, no need for bickering and fighting. Kim, how's Eddie doing? Is he back from London yet?" Tyra asked, diverting the conversation away from Raquel's personal life. She loved her friends, but she loved her sister more and wouldn't settle for anyone picking on her, not caring how old they got.

"Oh, he's great. He's not back yet, but should be back in about a week."

"The business deal is going great then?"

"Yes. If he makes this deal, he'll be the new CEO of his father's architectural firm and he'll go from making seven figures to an easy eight figure salary. I'm expecting an engagement ring any day now."

"Wow, that's great and I'm happy for you." Tyra looked at Raquel and winked before turning back to Kim. "When was the last time you talked to him?"

Kim looked at her and the smug look that had graced her face had now turned down to a frown. She looked around the circle of ladies and stuttered nervously.

"I...I...well, I haven't talked to him in a about two weeks, but that's because he's busy making this deal happen," she smiled, happy with saving herself.

Raquel smiled as she sipped her wine, trying hard to hide her smile. She loved her sister who always had her back.

"There are twenty-four hours in a day and he can't

find a few minutes to check in to say hello or to even text you? All that money and he can't even have someone send you some flowers or a nice card to say he's thinking of you or misses you? Shame on Eddie. I thought he would at least do something sweet considering he didn't have time to see you anytime that last week before he left to go to London because he was busy with the deal then, too. I guess money can't buy attention."

"He's a busy man," Kim explained.

"I get that." Tyra whipped her head from Kim around to Chloe. "Chloe, what's Rivard up to? I heard he signed that multi-million-dollar basketball deal and the two of you were planning to run off to Vegas to get married before his big move. I guess that unexpected baby put a glitch in that plan? Did the blood test come back yet?" she asked snidely.

"What? I...I told you that in confidence," Chloe said shyly.

"You did and yet here you are trying to relationship shame my sister? Look, I love my friends, but I love my sister more. She met a great guy and I told you both that because I thought we would all be supportive of how happy she is with Leo. What are you trying to do here? I didn't tell you anything negative about her or Leo or their relationship. Don't come for my sister because friend or no friend, I will slay you with my knowledge of your own relationships gone bad, the saga."

"My relationship may not be perfect, but the money makes it a lot easier to deal with," Chloe said in a smug-like tone.

"Is that so? Well, from what I hear, Rivard moved into that new house of his in Phoenix and photos are out of him holding his cute little daughter in his arms while her mother sun bathes around his swimming pool, naked, at least that was the last picture I saw of them on social media. Have you been to the house yet?" Tyra asked, really going in for the attack. "I didn't plan to spend this night making digs on any of your relationships, but as you can see, no one is perfect."

Raquel stood and exhaled.

"You know, Leo isn't perfect. He's not rich or even close to well off. He's an average guy, the best man I've ever met. He doesn't ignore me and every day, even if it's just a quick text, he lets me know he's thinking about me. He likes to call me at night to tell me he wanted his voice to tuck me in. I love that he may not be rich, but he spends money on flowers he sends to my office, including those two large, lovely arrangements you saw on my entry tables when you arrived. You haven't seen much of me, as you claimed because I work a lot as an executive and not sitting at home waiting for a man with deep pockets to take care of me and yes, my man knows I'm well off and no he isn't taking advantage of that. I do for him, he does for me and for us, it comes naturally. He lets me know how important I am to him and how hearing my voice on a day when he's running crazy is what mellows him out. When we're together, he gives the best massages, especially when he rubs my feet knowing I've been in heels all day. We love going out to the movies and sharing a box of popcorn and a soda. I know some of you would never dream of sipping a soda after your man, scared of where his mouth may have been the night before. We talk about our plans for the future and we bounce ideas off of each other. We take time with each other knowing how important that is. How long has Eddie been gone with no contact? Don't answer, I already know. Leo is the kind of guy I know I don't have to worry about stepping out on me for no other reason than he has the utmost respect for me. I love my sister for taking up for me, but I don't need to explain my happiness by having your vulnerabilities pointed out. One day if you ever meet a man as good, kind and loving as Leo, you'll know what I mean. You'll know that deep pockets don't make for a great guy. I didn't chase after Elijah because he had money and I didn't chase after Leo thinking he did. I love his whole life and he loves all of me. I never question it, I never doubt it and I never wonder where it is. Can you say the same thing about your men?" she asked around the room, making sure they all know her question was mean to for Kim and Chloe.

Raquel felt vindicated knowing that none of them would ever again talk down when it comes to her man.

She watched as Kim stood and stared her down. She waited for the argument she assumed would come next. At the same time, she saw her sister stand up, ready. They all watched as Kim looked around the circle of women before her eyes landed on Raquel.

"So, does Leo have any brothers, uncles or cousins you can introduce us to?"

When the room broke out in laughter, Raquel fell backwards on the sofa and could barely contain her own laughter.

"Only younger brothers and they're not old enough, but I'll ask about any uncles or cousins."

"Yeah, ask for me, too. That's the kind of man I'm talking about. Who wouldn't want a Leo!" Chloe said.

"Let's get more food and find a chick flick to watch. It's only midnight and the night is still young!" Kelly hollered. "I don't get out often with a break from my husband and the kids and I'm staying until Raquel throws me out."

"Yeah! Let's eat!" Tyra yelled.

Raquel, still laughing excused herself and went into her bedroom. The hour was late and she knew Leo had the evening off from his part time job. She needed to hear his voice.

"Hey sexy!" she heard the minute Leo answered.

"Hey yourself good-looking."

"How's the party going or is it over?" he asked.

"I think it's going to be an all-nighter."

"You left it to call me?"

"I wanted to say hello and let you know I was thinking about you."

"You know I was thinking about you, too. I hope your party is a success."

"It was and Tyra made a killing. She made a mint off of me alone, that's for sure."

"You and lingerie? I'm so here for that!" Leo chimed.

"I know you are or you will be. I didn't mean to call you so late."

"You know you can call me anytime. I'm out with Walt and a few of the fellas having a few beers. What are you doing tomorrow?"

"Nothing that I know of. Knowing the party would run late, I'm not going in the office on Saturday. What are you up to tomorrow?"

"I'm off all day and evening and thought we could do a movie out and check out the new Kevin Hart movie."

"Yes, he's one of my favorites. I'd love to. I better get back out there and snatch up car keys with all the wine drinking going on. I'll see you tomorrow?"

"Yes, you will. Have a good night, baby and get some good sleep tomorrow because I think you're going to be out late with your man!" he exclaimed.

"I'm glad about that."

Hanging up, Raquel went back to the party, proud of herself for loving a man from her heart and loving everything about him.

15

Leo made his way down the stairs to the subway train not rushing because he was actually early for work. After spending the weekend at Raquel's, he woke up early and headed out to be sure he wasn't late getting to the advertisement firm. Slowing to a casual stroll as he reached the subway platform, he was about to plug in his earbuds to listen to music while he waited when his eyes locked with a man who seemed to be staring at him. It wouldn't have been noticeable if he hadn't caught the man watching him without looking away. He didn't look familiar, but in a kind gesture, he smiled and went back to his music as the platform began to fill with others waiting on the train.

Over the sounds of the music playing he could hear the train coming and hoped it was the one he needed. As it neared, he was elated to see it was his train. As he moved closer to where he would board, he again felt eyes peering at him and when he turned, the same man was still focused on him and now, he felt uncomfortable. Before looking away, he realized there was something a little familiar about the man. Something within him felt uncomfortable as if he should be afraid, but didn't know why. Was the man mentally ill, planning something harmful? Was the man someone that he'd had a run-in with before and couldn't remember? He didn't have an evil or ill-will look on his face, but one of recognition. Who was he?

Not making the connection, Leo boarded the train as the doors opened. Unable to focus without checking, he saw the man enter the train and watched as he sat in direct line of sight to where he could keep his eyes on him and now Leo's weirdo radar was at full attention.

As the train moved from station to station, Leo tried to find a link to the mysterious stranger and became frustrated with himself when his mind couldn't recall a connection. Again, their eyes met and locked and this time Leo didn't look away. The man lacked any facial expression, which in itself, was alarming because he wouldn't look away even when Leo met his stare. Unexpectedly, the man sneezed and when he looked down to where his hand searched the inside of his jacket for a tissue, the hair on Leo's skin stood on edge. Familiarity set in as he looked at the man from the side and there was no mistaking who the man could be and now, he was the one unable to take his eyes away. It had to be him. There was no mistaking that the man from the side looked exactly like Trayvon whom their mom always said looked exactly like their father. Could that be him?

When their eyes locked once again, he was sure it was him. He was looking into the face of his father, a man he hadn't seen in twelve years. He was looking at Roland Westmoreland, a ghost from his past. There then came the moment he knew his father sensed Leo knew who he was looking at. Leo couldn't move. He was never sure that his father was still living since none of them had seen him since the day he was thrown out of their house and then disappeared. Their mother never tried to find their father. She was glad he was gone and that the abuse was over she never had to lose sleep wondering about him ever again.

The train finally pulled into the station where he would get off and not knowing if he should say or do anything, Leo stood and moved in the opposite direction of his father and prayed the doors would open and he could move quickly out of the station. He didn't want a scene with his father.

As soon as the doors opened, he rushed to the stairs and was halfway up when he heard his name being called. As much as he wanted to keep moving, he stopped and stood still without turning around as people moved hurriedly up the steps on either side of him. He knew that voice and where at one time in his life, the voice birthed a fear in him that made him cower, that wasn't the case anymore. He was no longer that seventeen-year-old boy, he was a grown man and he didn't run from anything.

"Leo? I know it's you and I take it you figured out who I am, too."

"Yeah, I did," he said not turning around.

"If I made you uncomfortable, I didn't mean to. You look pretty much the same except your features are no longer those of a boy, but of a man."

Leo turned and looked at the man in front of him and barely knew what else to say. It had been twelve years and Roland Westmoreland looked nothing like the thin, scrawny man he remembered. This man was bigger, with a lot more weight and he now had a full beard and mustache. Because he'd changed so much, that was why Leo didn't immediately make the connection.

"That's because I am a man," he said.

"I see that and a good looking one. I take it you're doing well?" Roland asked.

"I am," Leo said with little to no emotion in his voice. He looked from person to person as they passed by him standing on the steps to the subway. He felt awkward standing there, but he found it hard to move away. He'd thought about his father over the years, wondering if he was even still alive.

"I don't mean to intrude, but the day I first saw you, I haven't been able to stop thinking about you and for the past few weeks, I've been riding the trains in the morning hoping to run into you again."

"You've been watching me?" he asked. Now, Leo was officially uncomfortable.

"It's more like I've been watching out to see you, trying to get up the nerve to say hello. I moved back to the New York area about six months ago with my wife and two daughters. I've been living in Pennsylvania since I left New York a few weeks after you last saw me, which wasn't one of my best days. I don't have much family, but I had some friends who lived there and they let me bunk with them while I got clean and worked on myself. I was in a bad place back then."

"Yes, you were."

"I'm sorry for that. I wasn't myself doing drugs and drinking. That's no excuse for how I treated your mother and you and your brothers. How are Trayvon and Major?" Roland asked.

"They're fine. In school and doing well. My mother is doing well also," he added.

"That's good to know. I didn't want to upset you by asking about her knowing I don't have a right to inquire."

"You look like you're doing better," Leo said.

"I am. I've put on weight since I'm no longer drinking and doing drugs. It's been a long road, but I'm much better than I was."

"I'm glad you're better. I need to get to work," Leo said.

"Sure, sure. I don't mean to hold you up. If I'm not asking too much, if you think you would ever be okay with talking more, I would like to sit and talk, maybe over lunch or something. Only if you want to. I know I don't deserve anything and you have every right to tell me to go away and you never want to hear from me again. I told my wife I saw you and I tossed between saying something to you if I saw you again or leaving you alone and she reminded me that I'm a changed man and I owe you, your mother and your brothers a huge apology if I got the chance. I'm only asking if that's okay with you. Whatever you decide is what I will do. I don't want to intrude on your lives."

Leo looked around uncomfortably. This wasn't how he planned to start his day and he wasn't ready to answer on the spot.

"Um, let me think about it. I don't think it's a good idea for you to talk to my mom or my brothers, but I'll let you know if I'll have some time for lunch or something," he said.

He watched as his father fumbled around in his pockets.

"I can write my number down for you and if you feel like talking, give me a call. I work evenings at a warehouse, so anytime during the daytime will work. If that's not good, let me know and I can get some time off if an evening works better for you. I'll follow your lead. It's good to see you, Leo. I had hoped that you and your brothers were doing well and from the looks of you as an example, I have no doubt they are doing well, too. Thanks for talking to me. I know you don't have to," Roland said.

"Sure."

Leo took the number and put it in his back pocket.

"Take care," Roland said.

Leo didn't know what else to say. He nodded, turned and continued walking up the stairway to his office. As he walked, he looked behind him several times to see if his father came up the steps, but he didn't see him anywhere. The last person he ever expected to run into was his father, especially after a twelve-year absence. Somehow, he was going to have to tell his mother and brothers and right now, he had no idea what their reaction would be.

**

"Problems with Leo?"

Raquel jumped, startled by the sudden appearance of her sister in the doorway of her office. Once again, she'd been caught in her feelings.

"What? No. Why would you ask me that?" she asked.

"The only time I find you this distracted is when something is wrong and usually it's about a relationship. You were physically in the last meeting of the day, but your mind was someplace else. Anytime we talk about numbers and budget, you're more tuned in than anyone else. Where were you and where is your mind now?" Tyra asked as she walked into the office and made herself comfortable on the blue leather chaise lounge chair and removing her shoes.

Raquel looked down at Tyra rubbing her feet. She grabbed her nose.

"Eww, why are you shoeless in my office and rubbing those crusty dogs in here? I think I can smell them and it's quite rancid," she chuckled. Tyra laughed with her.

"My Spider-Man sense told me you were in distress and I figured I would come find out why. I knew you were working late tonight and I took a chance that you'd be here."

Raquel rolled her eyes.

"Liar. I thought you had a date tonight."

"I do, but my sister and whatever is on her mind is more important than a man. What's up with you?" Tyra questioned.

"Nothing, at least I don't think so."

"Meaning?"

"Don't think I'm crazy or anything, but I get the feeling something's wrong with Leo."

Raquel nervously bit her lip. All day her mind had been distracted by not only good, happy thoughts about Leo, but she had a sense that he was having an off-day. The idea weirded her out and it grew as the day wore on. She tried to shake it and hoped that if Leo needed her for any reason, he would have reached out. Maybe she was thinking too hard on it and causing herself to worry unnecessarily.

"Why? Did something happen?"

"I don't know, it's just a feeling. I've been thinking about him all day."

"Like you always do, in other words," Tyra smiled.

"Right, but this is different. This isn't just the happy in love feeling, but one that he's not the strong, always put together Leo I always encounter."

"If something was wrong, he probably would have called you. The two of you are so in love it sickens me because I want that kind of love with someone."

"He's a great guy."

"It's so nice to see you this happy. Maybe you are overthinking it. Are you still working late tonight? I was going to, but I've been working late a lot lately and I want to give myself a break and go home to relax," Tyra said.

"Yeah, I'll be here late. I thought about leaving early and maybe going over to Leo's place if he didn't have plans since I know he's off tonight. He works so hard."

"Yes, he does and I admire his tenacity with his work ethic and doing what it takes to take care of his family. Too bad he doesn't have any older brothers because I would snatch one right up. I wonder if I can clone him somehow?" Tyra laughed.

"Not on your life! There is only one Leo and he's mine!" Raquel quipped.

"You should get out of here if not early, then on time and go visit your man. Work can wait and you know it. Dad sure has been taking a page from that book lately."

"Dad has been getting his life back and I'm happy for him. I know he loved mommy and showed it every day, but I know he has also questioned the time he could have had with her if he wasn't building his company, spending endless hours in the office."

"That's why I'm telling you not to become like that. You've got a good man, finally, so make the most of all of your time. I think dad would like to retire soon which will leave us at the top with the board and if so, that will require a lot of our time. Enjoy your free time while you have it."

"You're right and I will. Tonight, there is a lot I need to catch up on and besides, I think Leo did mention some plans with friends tonight. Kelly wanted to do a movie and I thought about joining her for that later."

"Well, I hope so. Do something that's not work related."

Raquel started to agree when her cell phone rang. Opening her desk drawer and searching through her purse, she answered it before the ringing stopped and smiled at Tyra.

"Hey! I was just thinking about you," she said to Leo on the other end of the phone. She waved at Tyra who mouthed she was leaving for her last meeting of the day. Sitting down in her office chair, she relaxed.

"I was thinking about you, too. I called because I needed to hear your voice. Thank you for being on the other end of my call considering I know how busy you are at work," he said.

"I'm never too busy for you to hear my voice. You're always a welcomed addition to my day. How are you? Your heart speaks loudly that you're happy to hear my voice, but I sense something in your voice that doesn't sound like your usual jovial self. What gives?" she asked.

"Just a crazy day that has me all out of pocket. Hearing your voice is what I needed to bounce back. I'm heading out of work to go home and chill and thought I'd say hello. I meant to call you earlier to say hello and lost track of my day. My whole day was off and I need a reset button."

"Okay, now you have me worried. I thought you were hanging out with friends tonight."

"I was planning on it, but I don't feel like it. My mind isn't into tonight."

"Leo, what's going on? Talk to me, baby."

"You're at work and you don't want to hear my issues in what has probably been a crazy day for you. I'll be fine once I get home and chill and forget about the day."

"Listen, I know you're used to being that strong, nothing ever bothers you Leo, but you don't have to be that strong around me all the time. You don't have to carry the weight of everything on your shoulders all the time. I am here for you to unload on, relax with and to help you get through anything that bothers or stresses you out. Talk to me and let me take some of your burden away. Don't be the Leo who takes care of every body and all their problems. Come on, tell me what happened. I've been thinking about you all day and I told Tyra I got a feeling that you were troubled. At first, I thought it was weird, but now, hearing your voice and hearing you say you've had a trying day, I know that I was right."

"We're synced like that and yeah, it's been a wild day."

"Tell me about it and don't leave anything out."

"You sure you have time right now?"

"I will always have time for you."

"Okay. I ran into my father today."

Raquel paused. She could have expected a lot of things from Leo when it came to what disrupted his day, but not that he'd seen his father.

"What?"

She knew the story of his father and knew that he and his brothers hadn't seen him in years.

"He was on the subway this morning. He said he'd seen me quite a few times over the past year and today, he got up the nerve to say something when he saw me. Apparently, he's been riding the train that early in the morning for weeks hoping to get a glimpse of me after spotting me about a month ago. I saw him looking at me, but I didn't recognize him at first and then I did and he spoke up."

"Are you alright? What did he say?" she asked.

"Just that he'd seen me a few times and was afraid to say anything and today he decided to speak up. He's married again and I have two younger half-sisters. He wants to meet me for lunch one day to talk. He looks so different. Back then he was always high or drunk and started looking ragged. He said he works the evening shift at a warehouse or something like that. He moved back to New York from Pennsylvania where he's been living since he disappeared from our lives years ago. We only talked for about ten minutes and then I had to get to work. Seeing him didn't sit well with me, yet on the other hand, I want to know where he's been and what he's been doing. I can't say I regret him not being around, but yet, he's still my father."

"Did you agree to meet him?"

"I'm thinking about it. He gave me his number if I'm open to it."

"Did he ask about Trayvon and Major?"

"He did. I told him they were doing fine, but that was about it. Seeing him has me all kinds of messed up right now and I just want to go home and chill. I was unfocused at work and people noticed."

"I'm sure they noticed the always put together Leo wasn't so put together today and that was okay. You know that, right? You don't always have to keep it together. The show of a little weakness doesn't make you weak."

"I know and thank you for listening to me."

"Come see me," she said.

"Tonight?"

"Yes, tonight. I know you spent the night last night and if it's not putting you out when it comes time to get to work, come to my place tonight. I can leave early, make us a nice dinner, draw us a nice hot bath and give you a massage that will make you forget about this day."

"I thought you had to work late tonight," he said.

"I did before you called, but there isn't anything pressing that I can't handle tomorrow. Tonight, my man needs me and some of my attention and that's the priority. Are you already almost home?" Raquel asked checking the time. She knew he got off at four and it was already close to five.

"No, I stayed a little late to work on a campaign and I'm just leaving the office. I took tomorrow off because I needed a day. I hardly ever take time off, but my father has me all shook up with his presence. I need to tell my mother and brothers he's back in New York. I don't want her to run into him on the subway or anything. Look how he just happened to find me, not just once, but several times. She would be devastated and my mom has come a long way since he left years ago."

"Leo, you don't have to fix the world's problems tonight and it's okay to take a night off from worrying. Come let me take care of you for a change. I'm leaving the office right now and I'll meet you at my place."

Raquel grabbed her purse and closed her laptop before placing it in her backpack. She was already heading for the door with no plans of stopping until she reached her condo.

"Are you sure you want to put up with me two nights in a row invading your space?" he asked.

"I would take you every day, all day, baby. An hour?" she asked about the amount of time it would take him to get to her place.

"Yes, baby – an hour. I'll be there. You want me to stop and get us some dinner? Chinese food? Italian?" he asked.

"No. I don't want you to do anything that doesn't include you making your way to me. I'll see you in an hour."

"I love you, Raquel."

"I love you, too and remember, I'm that place you can always come to unwind and let go of your troubles. When I think of you, I want to think of you happy and loving life with no problems or worries on your mind."

"I'm always thinking about you."

"I know and I like that. See you in a few."

As she walked out of her office, Raquel passed by her two assistants who offered to stay late to help her go over the financial records of a new client.

"Why don't both of you take off for the night. I know we were going to stay late, but I'm going to go home and relax for the night. You'll still find the overtime pay on your paychecks because I appreciate you offering to stay around."

"Really?" Malcolm asked as he turned out his desk light and started cleaning up his desk, not waiting for her to change her mind.

"I'm sure and I'll see you in the morning. I may call on you for a late night soon if that's okay?" she asked. She often worked late, but didn't require her team to do so unless they really didn't mind. She never put on the pressure.

"That works for me," Sasha said as she and Malcolm walked with her to the elevator.

"We appreciate you, Raquel. Are you going to be okay getting home? I didn't call for your car service," Malcolm said.

"Don't worry about it. I'll have Jerome get me a car. I'm texting him now."

Raquel knew she could always count on the building security staff to have her back including getting car service when she wasn't expecting it. As they entered the elevator and after texting the head of security that she needed a car, she looked for the number in her phone of one of her favorite restaurants to request a dinner and dessert delivery to her condo which should arrive around the same time as she did. Tonight, she was getting the chance to do for Leo what he always took time to do for her. She was giving him her undivided attention, love, support and if need be, a shoulder for him to lean on because that's what you do when you really love someone.

16

"Good evening, Mr. Westmoreland. Ms. Johnson is expecting you and instructed me to let you right up. Please go ahead to the elevator and use the one on the left. It will take you right to her floor. I'll buzz to let her know you're on your way up."

Leo wasn't sure he'd ever get used to the kind of five-star service Raquel received in her condo building. The closest he came to any kind of greeting at his apartment building was when the kids of his neighbors hung around outside of their building and they would run up to him when they saw him to talk about sports or the latest video game. He had a great rapport with them, just as he did with his own brothers. He thought about them as he walked toward the bank of elevators the building security guy pointed him toward. He was concerned about their reaction to hearing their father was in New York. Both had asked about him over the years and Leo had told them what he could about the few happy times they'd had, but there weren't many. He knew they longed to know more about their father and at one point, they had assumed he was possibly dead because they never again heard from him or knew of anyone who had seen or heard from him.

The elevator doors opened as soon as he walked up to them and he stepped inside, going to the rear and leaning against the back wall for the ride up to Raquel's floor. He was trying hard to not focus too much on his father and his sudden appearance or how he would explain it to his family. Raquel was right that he needed to let go of it for now because the struggle of what to do was weighing heavily on him. He thought about his father's request all day and each time he did, images of his mother bruised and beaten came to mind and he would get angry that he would even give his father the time of day. He felt guilty spending the few minutes talking to him earlier in the day. He needed to shake off the day.

Exiting the elevator, he walked up to Raquel's door when it suddenly swung open.

"You keep doing that!" he laughed and picked her up in his arms, kissing her wildly.

"Mmm, I've missed you," she sighed.

"I was just here last night."

"I know and like I said, I've missed you. How are you?" Raquel asked as Leo walked with her in his arms into the condo while the door closed behind them. He reached back and locked it before walking with her to the sofa where he sat down with her in his lap.

"I'm better now that I'm here with you and you're in my arms. Being with you feels like home," he said and leaned his head forward on her chest. He relaxed the minute Raquel began massaging his head.

"I want you to always feel that way. I am where you come when you need a hug or a kiss, to talk or even not to talk and definitely when you need my lovin'," she whispered in his ear.

"Oh, that's a given, baby. One more kiss and then tell me what is smelling so go around here, besides you."

"Well, I thought about cooking, but decided instead to order dinner. I've got French onion soup, two side salads, smother beef ribs with potatoes and onions, parmesan crusted grilled broccoli and a fresh apple pie. I'm chilling a bottle of win and it will all be ready after we soak in the hot bath I'm running. I know you don't like baths, which is definitely a man thing, but I thought with me in there with you, this would be a bath you'd run to."

"A bath? With you? Of course I'm there! You naked, slipping and sliding around against me? No man in his right mind would say no to that. Dinner sounds great. You take good care of me," he said.

"I'm glad I have a chance to because you're always the one taking good care of me. I've got some soft music playing in the bathroom, candles lit all around, well the battery-operated kind and I even stopped at the store and found bath soap that won't make you smell all girlie after," Raquel joked.

"You mean I don't have to walk around tomorrow explaining the way I smell and telling everyone who looks at me funny that my girlfriend made me take a bath with her and now I smell like flowers and lavender?" he joked.

"How do you know I love lavender?" she asked.

"I've been here before, remember?" he laughed.

Leaving his duffle bag on the floor, Leo stood and carried Raquel with him straight to the bathroom where he walked into the dimly lit room and placed her on her feet.

"I love how excited you are to take a bath."

"Okay, to be very clear, I'm not close to being excited about taking a bath and I do mean me and excitement are not even on the same planet. What I am is excited to be in the tub with you. If there were no you, there would be no Leo in a tub. Now, since you went through all of this trouble to help me relax and I do appreciate it, if you really want me relaxed, you'd be naked already with all of your lusciousness in front of me."

"Show me yours and I'll show you mine," Raquel joked as she removed her tank top and shorts, the only articles of clothing she had on.

After removing his clothes with a quickness and lastly dropping his black boxer briefs, Leo knew there was no way he'd be able to shield his body's reaction to Raquel's naked body and with thoughts of taking a bath slowly drifting away, replaced with images of making love to her until no trace of the day he'd had remained, he moved toward her only to find her moving away from him.

"What?" he questioned.

"What nothing. I'm leading tonight and I say we get in this bath where you can relax and forget about everything except you and me."

"Baby, I'm trying to do that and I have a better idea than a bath together," he said reaching for her again.

"Oh, no you don't. Come on," Raquel said taking him by the hand.

"You know how good you look and you can see how much I need you," Leo said pointing to his manhood which was already long and hard, a sure sign that his mind was only on her.

"I see that and one thing I know about you is that I can look forward to that for the rest of the night – there is never a shortage when it comes to your lovin', so get in the tub with me and relax. You don't know how to relax. That mind of yours is always on something, the next thing or someone else's issues, but not tonight. Let me help you relax."

Raquel got in the large jacuzzi tub and moved toward the back where Leo had no choice but to get in and sit between her legs with his back to her chest.

"Only because I love you am I doing this and you look so damn sexy, I can't deny you anything," he said.

"That's good to know because I will have a need

and since I know you can't deny me of anything, I'll take advantage of that when we get out. Now, lay back against me and relax."

With music by Teddy Pendergrass playing in the background and the candles illuminating the room with a soft, low light, Leo leaned back, closed his eyes and enjoyed the moment, something Raquel was right about, he didn't know how to do. He was always working on his next thing whether it was running to one of his jobs, looking after his brothers or checking in on his mother. Raquel went through great effort to make the night about him and he wouldn't take that away from her.

"This feels good," he uttered.

Leo couldn't deny that the atmosphere was perfect for forgetting about the outside world.

"I told you I could do this for you," Raquel said, rubbing the water across his arms and chest, using a bar of soap to lather up his chest.

"Can I tell you that no woman has ever cared about me as much as you? None has ever gone the extra mile to make my day better. Why is that? Why aren't there more women like you?" he asked.

"Why? You want another one?" she jested.

Leo lightly tapped and then rubbed her legs that wrapped around his waist from the back.

"There is no other woman for me, but you. I never would have thought we'd be here in a million years because our worlds are so far apart."

"That's because you weren't thinking outside the box. What we have in common is more than our worlds be exactly the same. Our hearts are the same and that's all that matters. I love everything about you, but mostly I love how you lead with your heart and that means everything to me."

"You are rare, baby."

"I know and so are you. I'm happy you didn't find the right woman to be involved with because that would mean I wouldn't have you. I didn't know when we met that we'd be here, but I wouldn't want to be anywhere else, but here with you."

"I love you so much. You encourage me, you support me, you listen to me rant and rave and when I'm having a day like the one I had earlier, you're there to let me know you have my back. I could not ask for a more beautiful woman, inside and out."

Leo kissed her arms as Raquel wrapped them around his neck and rubbed his chest lightly as bubbles floated all around them.

"Come here," Leo said and pulled Raquel around so that she was now sitting on him with her legs on either side of him. "I love you for seeing beyond the strong persona I've always felt the need to show everyone. You make me feel vulnerable and I don't have a problem with that."

Holding Leo's face in both of her hands, Raquel locked eyes with him.

"I want to be what you need and want and if that

means a quiet night like this where you can forget about the outside world, then so be it. You can deal with the world and everything else tomorrow. Tonight, it's me and you."

Before he could reply, Raquel kissed him deeply, pouring every bid of what her words meant into the fiery kiss. As he pulled her closer and deepened the kiss even more, Raquel moved around on his lap, unable to ignore the hardness she met there the minute he moved her onto his lap. The moment was as perfect as their love had come to be.

As Leo's hands caressed her body all over, she moaned into his mouth the minute his hands cupped her breasts and rolled her hard nipples between his fingers. She had set out to relax him and in turn, he was doing the same for her.

The kiss went on as if it were life and death for them, getting hotter and wilder as her hips glided around on his hardness as she felt a much larger need growing inside of her, radiating from that place between her legs that longed for him. Without breaking the kiss, Raquel reached for the edges of the tub as she raised her hips up high enough until she felt the head of his penis move across her womanly folds. She exhaled when she knew that Leo's mind was tuned into hers. She waited anxiously as he gripped himself at her entrance and with one hand on his long hard and thick manhood, he used the other to slowly guide her hips down onto him. The feel of him pulled her from the kiss when the need to breathe harder rose in her.

"Yes!" she moaned as she gripped the edge of the tub to brace herself. Closing her eyes and throwing her head back, she moved up and down enjoying the feel of him long and hard going in and out of her body.

"You feel so good, baby. That's it, get what you need," Leo ground out through gritted teeth. The way Raquel felt gripping him like a glove, he had to fight to hold on until she was ready.

Raquel, now bouncing around waywardly enjoying the way Leo filled her leaned her head forward and opened her eyes, encountering his smoldering gaze as she watched his teeth bite down on his lower lip, a sign she knew meant he was getting close.

"I see you, baby," she whispered.

"I see you, too and you look beautifully aroused. More?" he asked, not wanting to break the connection they had, but he also knew she, like him, loved the intensity of their coming together.

"Yes, more."

Raquel leaned forward and down on Leo's shoulder as he held her hips tighter while he now surged harder up into her giving her all of him the way they both loved and needed. As their loving turned wilder and more out of control, water sloshed all around them, even over the edges of the tub, but she didn't care. The only thing that mattered was how he made her feel and how she made him feel.

It wasn't long before Raquel felt that pull between her legs and the tingle that traveled throughout her body that threatened to throw her over the edge and into bliss. She wanted the feeling to last much longer, but the draw to let go was greater, knowing how good her body was about to feel. Holding onto him even tighter, she pumped her hips down to meet his hard upward thrusts and without warning, she climaxed and where she thought she could hold the sound in that wanted to escape, she let her body go and opened to her mouth and let out the scream she hoped wouldn't alert her neighbors to what was going on in her bathroom.

"That's it baby, don't hold back. I'm with you!" Leo shouted and then groaned loudly through his own release while trying his best to hold her hips in place as he pumped wildly for what seemed an eternity. He tried to shake his head from side to side to dispense with the bright, white lights and streaks that shot through his head and across his eyes. His orgasm seemed to go on and on like never before and he was grateful that Raquel was holding on to him as tightly as she was because he was losing all sense of control as his body exploded again and again, joining Raquel in her screams of pleasure.

As their bodies began to calm and the waves they'd made with the water in the tub had finally subsided, Leo leaned back and pulled Raquel with him, tightly in his arms, placing soft kisses across her face and brow. Finding her lips even with his eyes closed, he connected with her, kissing her sweetly as he waited for his body to calm following that powerful detonation.

"See how much fun taking a bath can be?" Raquel asked breathlessly. She had to take in deep gulps to get her body to relax and for her heart to return to its normal beat.

"I do and I also see that you have officially succeeded in completely relaxing me. I'm not sure I want to get out now. You know, I did something I've never done before and I feel the need to apologize," he said.

Opening his eyes, he looked deeply into hers.

"What?" Raquel asked.

"We didn't use protection, baby and I'm sorry. I have never done that before, not one time."

"Neither have I. We're good. I'm on the pill which I use to regulate my out of whack cycle and as far as anything else, I'm good."

"So am I," he said quickly.

"No worries then and for the record, you feel amazing," she said and leaned forward for another kiss, this one turning just as hot as the one that led to their current encounter.

"If you don't stop, we're about to take another ride and I'm thinking we need to get up the water we've already wet the floor up with," he said looking over the edge.

Raquel moved around with him still planted solidly inside of her.

"You can't possibly be rising to the occasion again already? I feel you getting hard while you're still inside of me."

"You do that to me," Leo said in between kisses around her neck as his head drifted down to her breasts.

"Well, since I'm already in position and so are you – I'm glad I was able to take your mind off of your day."

"Yes, you have and now, let's see if we can work on tomorrow's issues, today," he laughed as their body's once again rose into the moment.

17

"Anybody home?" Leo called out the moment he entered the small house his mother and brothers shared. Three weeks had gone by since he'd run into his father in the subway and after talking things through with Raquel, he agreed to meet with him.

After spending that night at her place the day that he'd encountered his father, he woke up the next morning to find himself alone in her condo. He had already taken the day off and he knew Raquel needed to get up early to get to the office. She'd left him a note telling him she loved him and that she'd left breakfast for him in the microwave and she also left a key to the condo and the passcode to the alarm. They had been up most of the night eating, talking and making love and by the time they'd fallen asleep, she had convinced him that he should hear what his father had to say and then decide what to do with the knowledge that he was back in New York. After taking a few weeks to think it over while not running into his father again, he finally decided today was the day to talk to his family.

He also had other news to share with them. In the past few weeks, his life had been crazy after it was announced that he was one of the finalists for the Black Film Festival contest. In that time, he had spent time with Raquel's family a few times, successfully winning over her father and sister. He loved that he and Raquel were also able to hang out with his mother and brothers as well, so that they could get to know more about her. His mother told him on several occasions, having Raquel around was like having the daughter she'd never given birth to. She was already calling Raquel her bonus daughter.

His relationship with Raquel was growing every day and they found new ways to enjoy life together. He was happy that he was able to drop one of his part-time jobs, the overnight one, because he had received a promotion to department head at the marketing firm which came with a significant raise, allowing him more time with his love and with his family.

Today, he was excited to let them know that he was a finalist for the short film contest, something his mother and Raquel already told him they knew he would get. Now, they were at the point of him being one of the last five contestants and the winner would be announced in a few weeks at a banquet being held to celebrate all of the contenders and to finally find out who would win the chance to see their project come to life on the big screen.

"We're back here in the kitchen!"

Leo rushed toward the back of the house after hearing his mother's voice call out. He walked into the kitchen to find her stirring something in a pot on the stove as he dropped the bag with the barbecue chicken in it the he'd called and told them he was bringing over.

"Hey, Ma!" he said excitedly giving her a tight hug.

"I'm glad you're here Leo. I've been excited ever since I found out we were all free tonight. It's been too long since we've spent time like this with all four of us," she said.

"Hey, Leo!" Major said as they embraced.

"Hey, bro!" Trayvon added.

"What's everybody up to?" Leo asked.

"I'm finishing an assignment for class and Tray is finishing his homework. Ma is cooking something that smells good," Major said.

"I'm cooking Leo's favorite macaroni and cheese and string beans. I took off a little early from work to be sure I could have this done by the time you got here with the chicken."

"I had a few things to do before coming over, but I'm here," he said.

"I didn't see you at school today like I usually do," Trayvon said and held his head down as if he was sad to say so.

"I was there. You got my text, right?" he asked.

"Yeah. I was hoping to talk to you, but I guess you were busy."

Leo looked from his mother who shrugged her shoulders to Major who sat with a stoic look on his face as if he was torn between siding with Trayvon about missing the time they spent at the end of the day each Wednesday.

"You can talk to me anytime you need to. What's up?" Leo said sitting at the kitchen table across from him.

"I wanted to tell you that my first game is Friday. I know you can't come because you have to work, but I wanted to tell you about it."

"You're just telling me about your game? Where is my copy of your schedule I usually get? I know you've been going to practices and I'm glad you made varsity baseball this year. You know I'm proud of you, but I don't know why I'm just hearing about your game."

"Well, you've been busy lately and then you have work and now that you're dating Raquel, I didn't want to bother you," he said.

"That's not fair, Tray," there mother said.

Leo looked up at his mother after she spoke.

"It's okay, Ma. I want him to say what he needs to say. I am never too busy for you or Major and you know that. I don't care what else I have going on, you are and will always be a priority. If I'm with Raquel and you need to talk to me, I will always pick up and if you need to see me, I'll always be here or you can come to me. I've never made you feel like you can't come to me, so where is this coming from?" he asked.

He watched as Trayvon looked to Major and then to their mother before making eye contact with him again and not saying anything. He got the message. Trayvon needed a private talk.

"We have some time before the veggies are done," Evelyn said looking at Leo and tilting her head toward Trayvon who was still looking down at his notebook, faking focusing on his school work.

"Cool. I see there's some trash here that needs to go out. Come help me with this, Tray," Leo said as he stood. He grabbed one bag and Trayvon grabbed the other.

"I'll help Ma set the table," Major said.

The minute they were out the back door and walking down the steps to take the trash around to the side of the house, Leo stopped and turned to Trayvon.

"Tray, let me make something very clear. I don't care what I'm in the middle of, if you ever need me, I am always here. You are just as important to me as everything else in my life. If it seems like I've been busy lately and not giving you that brother time you need, I apologize and any time you feel that way, you let me know. Text me, call me or do whatever you need to do. When I sent you that text earlier, all you had to do was tell me you needed to talk to me and I would have stayed around and waited until the end of the day. I had something to do, but it wasn't as important as you. Nothing and no one comes before you, Major and Ma."

"Not even Raquel?" he asked.

"You have an issue with Raquel?" Leo asked.

"No, no, no. I really like her. I mean I like her a lot and I can tell she really cares about you. Are you in love with her?" he asked.

"Yes, I am. She's very special to me and one of the reasons why I love her is because she gets me. She gets how important the three of you are to me. She's not trying to compete with you for my attention. There is enough of me for all of you. She loves the way I care for my family and she knows how important it is that I'm always available to you."

"I'm sorry if I sound selfish – I don't mean to. I'm really happy that you found Raquel after that Misha girl that none of us liked. Raquel is cool and I'm glad she makes you happy."

"Okay, so are you going to tell me what this is all about then?" Leo asked.

Trayvon looked around as he shuffled from one foot to the other while looking up and down the street before finally looking up at Leo.

"It's about Tammy," he said in a quiet voice.

"Tammy? She's not pregnant or anything is she?" Leo asked.

"No! Of course not. We're not doing that and I told you I would tell you if I was doing that and I'm not."

"You sure? I don't want to hear anything about any babies. You and Major know what to do. If I need to hook you up, let me know."

"No, I'm sure. Tammy and I talked about that and we're not ready. I told you she's all about her school work and getting into college."

"Man, I'm so glad you met her. I see she has a hand in you doing better and not just in sports."

"She definitely helps me stay focused. She really wants something in life."

"Okay, so what about Tammy then?"

"She has a birthday coming up in two weeks and her family is having this dinner for her. She asked me to be her date and I want to go. I was hoping I could borrow something nice from your closet. I was thinking all black and maybe your gold Gucci belt and cuff links. Maybe even a pair of your dress shoes? I want to look nice," he said.

"No," Leo quickly said.

"Oh, okay," Trayvon said somberly.

"I didn't say no to you having something nice to wear. I'm saying no to you borrowing something from me. You should have your own gear and not something borrowed. I know Tammy is special to you and this is a special occasion. I say we go out and get you your own fly gear and hook you up. I'm talking about a fresh cut, new kicks and everything. That work?" he asked.

Leo smiled big when he saw the light return to Trayvon's face as his smile spread out throughout his entire body. Before he knew what was happening, Trayvon had wrapped his arms around him and held on tight.

"Thanks."

"I told you I got you, always. Anything you need that I can make happen for you, I'm there. Do you have to wear something in particular? What is she wearing?" he asked.

"She's wearing a gold dress and I thought the all black would go nice. I also have to get her a gift, but I don't know what to get."

"Did you ask Ma?"

"I did and she said something about getting her a nice sweater."

Leo laughed. Only his mother.

"I see, so let's not ask Ma about this. How about you ask Raquel? I know she would help."

"You think she would? She always looks nice and would probably have a good suggestion."

"I know she would. I'll tell her to call you and you can ask her what you should get Tammy. How old is she turning?" Leo asked as they walked back toward the back door.

"She's turning seventeen."

"Seventeen? You're dating an older woman?" Leo joked.

"Funny."

"I won't kid you too much. Raquel is a couple of years older than me and it doesn't mean a thing. Let's get inside for dinner before Ma hollers out the door and alerts the whole neighborhood that we're out here," Leo said as they walked inside.

"Thanks for helping," Trayvon said.

"Always."

"Now, we can focus on your news. I hope it's something really good."

"It is and you may have another opportunity to wear that fly gear we're going to get you. Let's go inside and I'll tell everybody at the same time."

Leo followed Trayvon inside and looked forward to sharing his good news. Win or lose, this was an opportunity he knew his family would throw their full support behind.

**

Leo walked into his apartment and as soon as he shut and locked the door behind him, his cell phone rang. He smiled when he saw Raquel's name.

"Hey, baby!" he said. Seeing her name and hearing his voice always brightened his day.

"Hey yourself. How was your family time?" she asked.

"It was fun. They were excited and happy for me about the contest."

"I still can't believe you're just telling them you won after you've known a while."

"I know and they railed me about that. I wanted to wait until I found out that I was one of the finalists. If I made it that far, then I know they would need to know. The promotion about the contest is about to come out announcing the finalist and the hard push they're making to spread the news about it will have my name and face all over it and I needed to warn them. Even though I was late telling them, they were happy and can't wait for the banquet."

"I'm excited, too. You can have a table of ten for the banquet. Have you decided that yet?"

"My mother and brothers, me and you are all I have so far. That's five. I don't want to extend it too far because there are a lot of family on my mother's side who would want to go and those tickets are expensive. Oh, I also need to include Walt. I asked if he wanted to bring his girlfriend and he said he didn't want to take sand to the beach. Only Walt," he laughed.

"If you don't mind, I know my father and his girlfriend and my sister wanted to go. They were going to sit at a table my dad was going to purchase to support the event, but I know they would love supporting you directly by sitting at your table. Tyrus Hill is one of my father's biggest clients and he wouldn't miss it. I hear Tyrus is also making an appearance at the event. What do you think about my family sitting at your table?" Raquel asked.

"I'm fine with that. In fact, I would love that. I like your dad and your sister already calls me bro!" he jested.

"True. You know she has no boundaries. I'll let them know. That leaves one seat," she said.

"I may check with one of my other buddies or perhaps my uncle. I'll think about it. For now, I want to know how your day went."

"I'm still here at the office," she said.

"What?" Leo checked the time. "It's after ten in the evening. Why are you still there?" he asked.

"Working out some numbers for a new client. I've been checking and rechecking and I'm finally finished and about to head home."

"I'm glad you called. I was thinking about you all the way home on the subway."

"Really? What were you thinking?"

"How much I was going to have to apologize and ask for a rain check for Friday. I know we had plans for me to hang with you at your place Friday night, but I can't. Tray has a home game he failed to tell me about."

"The baseball star is taking to the mound, huh? That's exciting. I was looking forward to our night in, binge watching cable shows and pigging out on pizza. Am I invited to the game?"

"Of course. Are you sure you want to come?"

"I would like to support Trayvon if he doesn't mind me taking part in your family time."

"Don't you have to work Friday? The game is right after school ends."

"No problem. I'm going to take Friday afternoon off and meet you there. I don't want to assume I'm not intruding. Are you sure you don't mind?"

"I don't mind at all and Trayvon won't mind. In fact, he wants to talk to you about something."

"What?"

"I'll let him tell you on Friday. I was going to have you call him, but now that you'll be at the game, you can talk to him then. Can I entice you into spending the night at my place on Friday? We could still go back to your place as we originally planned. I'll leave it up to you."

"I would love staying the night at your place. I wish it was Friday already. I miss you."

"I miss you, too, baby and I can't wait to see you on Friday. Parking is crazy on my block, but we'll find something after the game, though we may need to walk a few blocks."

"I'll be with you and I know I'll be fine. Don't worry. I won't have on any of those high heels you know I love to wear. Wait until you see my baseball game gear. I'm fly for all occasions," she laughed.

"I know you are. Get home safe and text or call me when you get home and locked in for the night."

"I will. I love you, Leo."

"I love you, too."

Leo hung up and as he headed for the shower and to get prepared for work in the morning, he said a silent thanks for how lucky he was to have a supportive family and a girlfriend he could enjoy unconditional love with.

18

Leo paced back and forth waiting to hear from Raquel. Their last conversation had been before she entered the subway station after he explained in detail which trains she needed to take. Usually, when she came into Harlem, she drove her car, but today, she was taking the train and meeting him at Trayvon's school for the baseball game. He knew what life was like taking the train, something that was pretty foreign to Raquel who either drove her own car or secured a car with a driver who took her where she needed to be. He was worried about her as he watched group after group of train riders exit the station.

"Looking for me?"

He turned and when he saw Raquel, he exhaled loudly, releasing his frustration and concern.

"I sure was. I was worried. Where did you come from?"

"About a block away. When I got off the train, I think I went left instead of going right, but I was only a block off. I made it!" she shouted.

"Yes, baby, you did. Give me your bag," Leo said, taking it from her shoulder. "What's in this thing?"

"Everything I need for the weekend. I figured, since I was off, I would hang with you the whole weekend, that is if I'm not intruding on your time and space."

Leo took her hand as they walked toward the school.

"Are you kidding? An entire weekend with you without interruption? I only wish I had taken tomorrow off. I am staging two apartments tomorrow and I'll be gone all day. I was originally scheduled to do it tonight, but with Trayvon's game, I moved it to tomorrow with the open house being Sunday."

"Oh, I forgot about that. I can go home tomorrow when you leave for work."

"You'll do no such thing. Unless you feel unsafe being in my place by yourself, I want you to stay. That'll give me even more reason to get my work done faster and get back to you."

"In that case, there is something special for you in that bag you're now carrying."

"Something special? Are we talking special for me or special on you for me?"

"Something special for you and of course, a few somethings sexy just for me to model for you. Feel free to take them off of me at any time," she whispered in a sexy raspy voice, adding to the image she already was burning into his brain.

"Oh, trust and believe I will be doing that later tonight. For now, let's get to the game. My mom is holding seats for us."

"You never told me what they said when you told them about your father," Raquel said as she placed her hand in Leo's outstretched hand as they walked.

"My mom shocked me by saying she already knew. Her brother told her that he thought he saw him one day and after following him, he realized it was him."

"How did she take the news that he was alive and living in New York again?"

"She said she was fine. It was a long time ago and she was finally over it. Trayvon and Major are still thinking over whether or not they want to meet up with him. They were little boys when he left and neither remember much about him, which is a good thing. I told them that he's working and has cleaned himself up after a stint in rehab years ago and then turning his life around after getting off of drugs and alcohol. I told them that he hasn't done either in a lot of years. I also told them that he remarried five years ago and that he has two daughters, who are our sisters ages three and five. I asked if they thought one day they'd like to meet our sisters and they both said yes without any hesitation. My dad wants to tell the girls about us, but only if we wanted to meet them. From what he's shared, his wife sounds nice. I think my mom is happy that he isn't the man he was a long time ago. She told me she knew it was the drugs and alcohol that had messed him up and she forgave him a long time ago. She had to in order to move on with her own life."

"Sounds like your family is in a good place with your dad, huh?"

"I think so. Talking about meeting up with him and actually doing it are two different things. I've talked to him a few more times and we've been texting. I know what he did back then was wrong, but I can't hold that against him forever and I won't. I can't say we'll ever have that father and son relationship, but I'm glad I was able to see him in a better light. I think Trayvon and Major are going to need some time and I'm going to give them that. When they are ready, I told them to let me know."

"That's good. I'm proud of you. I know how you struggled with what to do and I think you made the right move."

Raquel looked around for Leo's mother and brother as the game was about to start.

"There they are," Leo said. "Don't forget Tray wants to talk to you about something. It's a girlfriend thing about Tammy that he needs help with."

"No problem. I would do anything for him."

"Yeah and he knows it. You're that big sister he never had who spoils him way too much."

"Well, I never had a brother and he and Major are the closest thing to having that, so let me have my moment of spoiling them."

"Only because I love you and they do, too."

"The feeling is mutual. Everyone is wearing a school hat or shirt and I don't have either," she pouted.

"Go over and join my mother and Major and I'll go get you a shirt and a hat from the concession stand. They sell them at each game."

"You're the best boyfriend ever!" Raquel cheered by jumping up and pumping her fist in the air as if she was a cheerleader with a pompom in her hand.

Leo walked away shaking his head.

"You're too much!" he laughed and shouted back.

**

"That was one heck of a win, Tray and you had two homeruns, one being a grand-slam homerun. I didn't realize you played that good," Raquel said as they all walked to the subway to get home.

"I can do a little something," he joked.

As they walked and talked, she noticed how Leo slyly looked at Trayvon with some kind of signal, which reminded her that he'd mentioned Trayvon wanted to talk to her. As Leo walked further ahead, linking arms with his mother giving them time to talk, she linked arms with Trayvon.

"Major's not coming with us?" she asked.

"No, he has a girlfriend and he's going to her house for a while and said he'd be home later. If I know him, he'll be calling to say he'll be out all night."

"Ah, a girlfriend, huh?"

"Yeah. Speaking of girlfriends, you know Tammy is my girlfriend, right?" he asked.

"I do and I enjoyed meeting her and hanging out

with the two of you at the diner."

"It was fun and I hope we can do it again."

"I know Leo would love that and so would I."

"I, um, asked, uh, Leo if I could get your advice on something, if that's okay with you," Trayvon stuttered out.

"You can ask me anything at any time. I'll make sure you have my number to call me whenever you like."

"Are you sure?" Trayvon looked at her and smiled showing all of his pearly whites.

"I am, so what's up?"

"Well, Tammy's family is sort of throwing her this birthday dinner and she asked me to be her date since I'm her boyfriend and all."

"Really? That's nice."

"Yeah, well I was hoping you could help me with what I can get her for a birthday gift. I would ask my mom, but I was hoping to get advice from someone who might know more about what she would want for her seventeenth birthday. I asked Leo, but he thought you would be a better person to ask. What do you think?"

"Sure, I can help with that. Do you know what kinds of things she likes? Don't do the gift card thing that a lot of people like to do these days. They're so impersonal. Do you know her favorite color, music or place to shop?"

"Well, she's wearing a gold dress that night and Leo

is helping me coordinate with what she's wearing. I know she loves that color and also anything blue, white and denim. She loves denim."

"How about getting her a nice denim outfit and maybe a bag to go with it or jewelry."

"A denim jacket would be nice. I think she would like that."

"Do you know if she has one of those charm bracelets, the one's like what I have on my wrist by Pandora?"

Trayvon looked down at her wrist and his eyes bulged.

"Wow, you have a lot of those. I know she loves bracelets, but I haven't seen one like yours."

"Well, I don't recommend buying her as many charms as I have, but maybe you can start her off with a bracelet and one charm."

"They look expensive."

"I'll tell you what, if Leo is okay with it, let me treat you to the gift. You deserve it. Leo tells me you're doing great in school."

"Yeah, I had some problems earlier in the year, but I'm doing much better now and my grades were good enough to get me on the honor roll recently."

"That's sounds like a guy who deserves a treat. You should also get her a corsage to wear on her wrist for the party. That will be a nice touch from you."

"Really? You think so?"

"I know so."

"Leo might say it's too much."

Trayvon looked down not as cheery as he just was.

"He won't say that. He's happy you're happy and doing well and I'll talk to him. I understand you want to make a good impression and we won't go overboard. We'll do just enough. How's that?" Raquel asked.

"You're the best, Raquel. I tell Leo that all the time. He's never been this happy before, ever and I see why. I like you and my brother together all in love and stuff!" he joked.

"That's good because I love your brother very, very much. Now, let's catch up to them and I'll talk to Leo tonight and then we can make plans to go shopping to get what you need. Don't worry, Leo doesn't know how to say no to me," she joked.

**

"You did what?" Leo asked Raquel as they walked into his apartment after walking the four blocks from the subway.

"I told Trayvon that he should get Tammy a nice denim jacket because he said she loves denim and also get her a starter Pandora bracelet with one charm and I want to treat him to it."

"You don't have to do that."

"He also needs to get her a corsage to wear on her wrist for the party. He's her date and he wants to make her feel special. You told me this is his first girlfriend and he seems to really like her."

"True, but you don't have to treat him to that stuff. I can get it for him. I know what those bracelets and charms cost."

Raquel walked inside of the apartment and took her overnight bag to the bedroom before coming back out to join Leo in the kitchen.

"I know I don't have to do this for Trayvon, but he came to me and that felt good. Your family makes me feel so welcomed and like I said, your brothers are the little brothers I never had and I love them very much. I want to do this for him and I'm not saying you can't do it, if that's where you're going with this."

Leo, whose back was to her as he looked in the refrigerator while thinking of what to drink, turned around, giving her his full attention. The one thing they never talk about is money. They were both well aware of how well off she was and that his funds no where matched hers, but what they had was never about money and it never would be.

"I'm not going there at all and you know it. We never talk about money and we're not going to now. It's not about me being able to do or not do something when it comes to finances. I just think it's a lot for you to offer."

"Do you think it's too much for Trayvon to give her for her seventeenth birthday?"

"I don't know. When I was his age I didn't do the birthdays, dances, proms and stuff that Major did and now Trayvon is getting ready to start doing, so I don't know."

"Did you forget you bought me two charms for my bracelet, just because? You know what that meant to me for you to understand my love for Pandora. The charms you gave me have meaning and though Trayvon isn't nearly as serious with her as you and I are, I think a nice friendship charm on a bracelet would be nice."

Leo walked over and pulled Raquel into his arms.

"It is nice and I'm thinking too hard about this. If you want to do that for him, you go ahead and do it. I love you for wanting to."

"You're not going to be mad?"

"Mad? At you? Never, baby. I was really thinking too hard about it. I shouldn't be one to talk because I'm taking him shopping for a new outfit and I'm going all out, so I understand. I know how you feel about him and it's fine. Thank you for helping him with ideas because I didn't know what to do. Major went to a few things, but nothing big like this."

"You do know you're more than enough for me, right? I mean, I need you to know that what we have means more to me than anything and I do mean anything in this world. We are a part of each other's lives and that means your family is my family and my family is your family. We are both a package deal. You've seen how obsessively close my sister and I are and I love how you are with your brothers and I want in on that."

Accepting the kiss that Leo moved toward her to give was all the confirmation she needed.

"I'm all in baby. I may not have a lot, but I love you because all that I am is enough for you and I couldn't ask for more than that."

"You love me like no one ever has. You treat me like a queen every day, all day and I'm happier than I have ever been in my life. When I think of you, it's all love."

"I know how you feel. Now, about that lingerie you mentioned earlier."

"Oh, you didn't forget about that?"

"Be serious! You with this body in sexy lingerie? I'm going to plant myself right on the sofa, put on some fashion show music, turn the lights down and wait for you to change in and out of each one until I can't handle anymore and then I'll be apologizing for ruining something as I'm snatching if off your body."

"Let the show begin!" Raquel declared.

"Yes!" Leo replied as he palmed her behind before she got too far away from him.

"Don't start nothing you aren't willing to finish right this minute."

"Oh, I can finish it, but I've been thinking about lingerie since you mentioned it and the patient man I am, I will make it through as many outfits as I can, but I'm not promising."

"I'll hold you to that," Raquel said and disappeared into the bedroom.

19

Somewhere an alarm was going off in Leo's head and he tried with his might to mentally turn it off. His eyes were closed and, in his arms, he could feel Raquel stirring as he brought her naked body closer to his. The sound of the alarm faded as he remembered their salacious night of loving which lasted well into the early morning hour. He couldn't have gotten more than two hours of sleep, but being tired was well worth it because the best kind of exhaustion is the kind that follows making love to the woman he loved. As the alarm went off again, this time he opened his eyes and reached across Raquel's body to his cell phone that signaled he needed to get up and get to work. Daylight was barely visible through the small window in his bedroom and he would like nothing better than to dismiss his Saturday obligations all together and spend the day in bed. Being a man who could be depended on, he shook off sleep.

"You're woke and moving around," Raquel moaned as she stretched and pulled Leo's arm tighter around her.

"I am and I better get up before I change my mind. You being next to me in bed all naked and sexy is the main cause of my struggle," Leo said kissing her bare shoulder before moving so that he could kiss across her back.

"Don't start anything you can't follow-through and finish before you leave. I may be tired from last night's wonderful night, but I will have no problem finding the energy for you this morning," she moaned out when Leo's kisses began to awaken her body.

"You're tempting me to prove I can take care of my woman and my responsibilities in the same day, but I'll stop so that I'm not late. The sooner I can get there, the sooner I can get back here to you today. What are you going to do stuck here at my place all day?"

Leo got out of bed and cut on a small light instead of the overhead one.

"I'm going back to sleep when you leave. I brought my laptop, so I'll get some things done for work and wait for you to get back. I hope it will be a quick day for you. I'm missing you already."

"Feeling is mutual, baby. I'll do my best. Do you want me to bring us some dinner when I get back? I can stop on the way," Leo said as he walked around his room gathering everything he would need for his shower.

"You're still naked," Raquel said turning over and watching as he walked around. Her body jumped with recognition as she noticed him magnificently aroused and definitely ready for morning fun if he had the time.

"I am and because of you, the shower I was planning to take with some nice hot water will need to be a chilly one so that I'm not freaking people out walking to the subway with a hard-on," he joked.

"You know I could help with that," Raquel said and then purred and stretched like a kitten in heat.

"Is that so? Well, if you're interested in killing two birds with one stone, you could meet me in the shower."

Not waiting for her answer, Leo turned and left the bedroom, walking into the bathroom.

Raquel didn't need any more of an invitation than knowing what was in store for her and seeing him in all of his morning glory.

"Whew! I would never let all that sexiness go to waste," she said and giggled as she ran from the bed, into the bathroom and closed the door behind her.

**

"Raquel, I'm so sorry."

Raquel sat up straight in the bed hearing what sounded like terror in Kelly's voice after answering her cell phone an hour after Leo had left out for work. She had snuggled back into the softness and enjoyed the lingering scent of his cologne left behind.

"Sorry? Sorry for what Kelly?" she said getting up out of the bed and looking for something to put on.

The chill of the morning caused her to shiver in her state of nakedness. She had felt warm the whole time she was wrapped in Leo's arms throughout the night.

"I'm so sorry. I didn't know."

Raquel was now scared. She didn't know what had happened. Had something happened to Leo in the short time that she'd left? Was there danger involving her sister or her father that she was unaware of?

"Kelly, you're scaring me. What are you sorry for? What happened?" she asked again.

"Elijah," was all Kelly said.

"Elijah? What about him?" she asked.

"I said something about you and Leo and I thought he already knew about you, Leo and the contest. By his response, he didn't know and he was pissed off, not out of anger, but clearly in jealousy."

"What?"

Raquel still struggled with comprehending.

"Okay, let me start from the beginning. Clark and I were out last night at an event for his law firm and Elijah was there. He kept talking about you and asking about you and I said something in terms of him not letting his jealousy over your relationship and being in love with Leo impact his vote on the Black Film Festival winner. When we talked the other day, you mentioned Leo was a finalist and how Elijah's firm was judging the contest. You didn't say Elijah didn't know about you and Leo. You did tell me you told him you were seeing someone and I assumed you told him all about Leo and warned him about trying to do anything shady. When he looked confused, I thought he was pulling my leg and so I went in on him about letting you be happy and how in love you and Leo are. I also said he was the same Leo that he was judging for the contest and then I could tell he didn't know. He knew nothing about you and Leo or that the Leo he was judging for the contest was the same Leo. I thought he knew. I really thought he knew. He made some not so nice comments about Leo talking about him not being the guy for you because he doesn't have anything and from what he remembers from Leo's paperwork that he didn't go to college and lives in some apartment in Harlem. He tried to jokingly inquire about what you would be doing with a guy like that and that you were slumming. After I threw my drink in his face and Clark stepped up to flatten Elijah if he tried anything, he walked off talking about Leo should already consider himself a loser not just with you, but for the contest. I am so sorry. I didn't mean to tell your business like that."

Raquel panicked. She wasn't fearful of Elijah knowing about her and Leo because the way she loved him and he loved her, nothing could taint that, especially an ex-boyfriend. What she didn't want was for Elijah to pre-judge Leo and base his decision on Leo's talent and not the fact that she and Leo were involved. That is what she feared from the start.

She could hear Kelly sniffle on the other end.

"Kelly, don't worry about it and I don't want you crying about it either. Eventually, he was going to find out about Leo and me, but I was hoping it was at the banquet where the winner would be announced."

"I know and I'm sorry I had a hand in revealing that ahead of the final vote or at least ahead of the banquet. I don't know what I was thinking, but he was looking so smug talking about you and the life you gave up breaking up with him. I couldn't resist telling him how happily in love you were and instead, I may be the cause of Leo losing the contest. I'm so sorry. Please tell Leo I'm sorry. I guess he'll never want to hang out with Clark and I again and he really likes Leo."

"Leo likes the both of you, too and he's not the kind of guy to hold that kind of grudge. It was an honest mistake and he will realize that. I do fear that Elijah and his black heart will make sure Leo loses for a reason other than his movie wasn't the best of the five."

"I'm sorry," Kelly said again.

"Kelly, stop apologizing. I'm not mad at you and Leo won't be either. I'll tell him to see what he wants to do."

"Maybe you can talk to Elijah and convince him to not take the blue pill and go down that dark path."

Raquel smiled briefly at Kelly's attempt to use the analogy from the Matrix movie to prove her point.

"Elijah will go down that dark path no matter what.

That's who he is and I made the mistake of not recognizing that while I was involved with him. He can now use this contest to get back at me or to try to win me back by making me some kind of proposition, which of course, will never work."

"At one time, I thought Elijah was a good guy, but he was just someone who flashed a lot of money and flashy clothes and cars to hide the fact that he was a despicable person. The look on his face when he walked away said it all. Clark even said that Elijah was already planning on a way to sway the panel against Leo. What can I do to help? This is all my fault," Kelly said.

Raquel didn't know if there was anything anyone could do, but when Leo got home from work, she would tell him and support whatever he wanted to do. If he was anyone other than the person she knew Leo to be, she would say he wouldn't want to go to the banquet knowing he was going to lose, but her Leo was a bigger man. She had a feeling he wouldn't care and would still look forward to sharing that night with his family and friends.

"Don't worry about it. Thanks for calling to let me know. I'll talk to Leo when he gets in and I'll call you later tonight."

"Can I say I'm sorry one more time and I hope you don't hate me for what I did."

"Kelly, stop it. I don't hate you. I love you and Clark and I always will. It was an honest mistake and I know how Elijah can bring out the worse in someone by his smugness. Let it go, don't think about it. Leo already knows all about Elijah and my past with him and the fact that he was going to be a judge for the contest. Ironic, huh? It doesn't matter. Leo once said to me if this contest was meant for him to win, he would win in spite of any outside forces trying to get in the way. Don't worry and go back to your husband and children. We'll talk later," she said.

After hanging up, Raquel paced around Leo's bedroom and wondered how he would take the news. The last thing she wanted was for anything or anyone in her past to come out of a closet and ruin her happiness. It seems she still wasn't able to get away from Elijah and his messiness. The biggest problem was it could impact what could be an accomplishment of a dream for Leo. She wanted every bit of happiness and success that was in store for him. He'd sacrificed so much and she believed now was his time to shine and have something for him where everyone around him could say thank you and congratulate him for a job well done. It's possible Elijah could ruin his moment. Without thinking too hard, she dialed his phone and waited.

"Ah, you must have heard about my encounter last night and couldn't wait to call me to plead for your man, huh?" Elijah said.

Raquel's skin felt prickly the moment Elijah's smug attitude floated through the phone to her ears.

"I'm not calling you to plead for anything, but I will say you shouldn't use your position as a judge to sway the vote of the panel based on anything except the value of the movies you're voting on. I hope you won't let the fact that I'm in love with Leo impact your judgement."

"If you love him so much, why didn't you tell me about him when I called you recently. You knew then that he was a contestant and you didn't say anything other than you have moved on. You aren't proud of who your man is? That's quite a step down for you, huh? Where did you get him from – some guy from the hood? All this time, I assumed you had moved on to some wall street type or some celebrity when all along, he's a thug from Harlem? What is that about? You go from dating a white man, not to a high-powered black man, but a guy who doesn't have anything more than a high school education. I looked up his address on the internet last night and I see he lives in an old apartment building that has seen better days. What are you thinking?"

"Don't try it with me Elijah. You being white, rich and educated doesn't make up for the fact that you're a class act at being a jerk. Why do you care who I see or what his status is? It has nothing to do with you."

"Oh, please, Raquel. I was your first white guy and I exposed you to the finer things in life and you know it."

Raquel felt herself fuming and trying to not be

insulting, though she could think of many things about him she could point out.

"Let me clear something up for you. You didn't expose me to the finer things in life, my parents did a great job of that. You don't have anything nor did you provide anything for me that I couldn't and cannot provide for myself. I didn't date you because you were white or because I had any issues with dating a black man. I do have an issue that you couldn't treat me the way I should have been treated and I settled for that for too long. I didn't call you to plead for anything and I didn't call you to get into a battle of the wits with you. Kelly told me about your conversation and that she revealed my relationship and the fact that Leo was one of the five finalists for the contest, something you wouldn't have known. You may or may not be pissed off, but that has nothing to do with how good Leo's short film is and you know it. If you're planning to do something that could purposely hurt Leo's chances, I am asking that you not do that. Let him win or lose on his own merits and not because you're jealous," Raquel declared.

"Jealous? Jealous! You think I'm jealous of Leo Westmoreland? Sugar, I'm not jealous of him or your relationship with him. I don't understand how you can choose him over being with me, but that's your life of living in the hood you're heading toward. What I do or don't do when it comes to my vote you don't have any say so about – that is unless you'd like to have dinner with me one night and we can talk about it. I may let you try and convince me to help your boyfriend win. Who knows? You may even enjoy yourself and see that you made a mistake in breaking up with me. Perhaps you'll see the error of your ways and find that I'm deeply sorry for my one indiscretion and realize how much better your life would be with someone like me. Think about that and get back to me by tomorrow. I'm a busy man," Elijah said.

Raquel could hear him sneer and it made her stomach turn as if she was going to be sick.

"You are a horrible, horrible person, Elijah Bohner. Absolutely horrible and I would never, ever have dinner with you or try to convince you in any way to have Leo win the contest. Calling you was a mistake on my part for thinking you may have a genuine bone in your body, but I was wrong. Do whatever you want to do, but know that I am not a bargaining chip in your game. You can't scheme for my attention and as far as where my life does or does not go, it's going with a man who knows how to love a woman with all of his heart. He's kind, unique in how he loves deeply and I would take that kind of man over a man rich with things and an ego any day. Oh, and if you ever need to know how to really make a woman happy, figure out how to make her orgasm with your tiny penis inside of her. Maybe, Leo can school you on that. Now, that is how low I can get you dreadful excuse for a man. Have a good life, you snake."

Raquel wished she was on a phone like the one in her office where she could slam it down for the added effect. Instead, she settled for throwing her phone on the bed and walking off the despair she felt over dragging Leo into her mess with Elijah. His future could be impacted and it was her fault.

20

Checking his work, Leo looked around the bedroom he'd just finished setting up for the open house the next day. After doing a double check of the other three bedrooms and the family room, he would be finished this house and off to his second and last for the day.

"Magnificent job, Leo!"

He turned to see the owner of the real estate company who employed him standing in the doorway admiring his work over.

"I'm glad you like it. I made one change in where to place the two chairs that were at the foot of the bed in the draft sketch. I thought it would look better off to the side in front of the fireplace. It looks more inviting and makes the room look larger."

"Great idea."

He smiled at Leah Roberts as she walked around checking out everything else. He had been working for Leah and her husband Earl for four years staging houses and he liked that they treated him like family.

"I'm doing the other house today, too, as soon as I'm done here."

"You're the hardest working person on our team besides all of the agents. I wanted to tell you that Earl and I wanted to buy a table at the event for the contest you entered. We're proud of you and want to celebrate the night with you. Do you know how I can get a table for ten? I figured I'd give the other eight tickets away to our top producers at the firm as a thank you for all of their hard work. I know that event is going to be big and seen advertisement about it everywhere. Are you nervous at all? I know you're typically mister calm, cool and collect, but this has got to be big for you. I know you have dreams of getting into entertainment one day and this could mean something really huge for you."

"Thanks Leah and thank Earl for me. I can put you in touch with the person you need to get your tickets from. They are going on referrals from contestants first to be sure we've reserved enough tables for our guests. I appreciate the support and I look forward to seeing everyone there. Win or lose, it'll be a great night for my family to play dress up and rub elbows with the rich and famous."

"Yeah, I hear Tyrus Hill is going to say a few words himself that night. I'm looking forward to checking out who's who. Send the information to Lily at the office and she'll get the tickets. I'm going to head out. I was nearby so I decided to check this site out. I have no doubt the other will be ready for tomorrow, too."

"It sure will be. I'm heading over there as soon as I

lock up here and good luck with the open house tomorrow."

"Don't forget, if it sells, you get a percentage along with your regular salary. That's how much we appreciate your contribution to the team."

"Every little bit helps."

"I guess when you make it big, we'll be a distant memory. I look forward to following your career. You deserve this and everything else great that will come into your life. I'll have my fingers crossed at the table the night of the banquet."

"Thanks, Leah."

Leo waved as she walked away and he took one last look around before walking into another bedroom. After taking a few pictures of his work, he thought about Raquel and hoped she was able to go back to sleep after he left. Their time in the shower together had gotten pretty wild and if he thought the night before had drained him, Raquel was giving him the kind of workout that reminded him to take his vitamins every day. He sent her a quick text before he headed out.

'Hello beautiful. I hope you were able to get some sleep after I left. In case you want to venture out, I left a key for you near the door. Harlem is beautiful and I think you'll love it. There is a fresh market a few blocks down from my apartment. I know you wanted to pick up some things for dinner. I'll see you tonight. I love you.'

Feeling satisfied that the house was ready and that he'd let Raquel know he was thinking about her, he headed out to the next house and looked forward to being done in order to have a relaxing evening at home.

**

Raquel had spent the morning and afternoon drifting in and out of sleep. Her body was tired, but her mind was still wired from her conversations with Kelly and Elijah. She couldn't stop thinking about what she could do to fix the situation and so far, she'd come up empty. After reading the text message from Leo, she felt even more compelled to do something to be sure Elijah didn't hurt Leo's opportunity of an honest chance at winning. Her man shouldn't have to suffer because her life had been messy at one point. The only person she could confide in besides Leo was her father and right now, she needed his advice. She dialed him at home and hoped he wasn't off playing golf where he never answered his phone.

"Hey, Dad! I'm glad I caught you in."

"It's early for you considering you're off today. Don't tell me you're calling with a work question on your day off," he said.

"No. I'm not doing any work today. Leo and I are having a relaxing weekend in watching movies and doing nothing else."

"That sounds like the kind of perfect evenings your mother and I enjoyed at one time. What's up?" he asked.

"I have an issue and I need your advice."

"I'm all ears, baby girl."

"Elijah's firm has the contract to select the winning short film for the contest Leo entered. Before yesterday, Leo was just another contestant. Last night, Kelly told Elijah who Leo was not knowing I hadn't already told him or that he hadn't figured it out somehow. I told you Elijah had been spending the time since we broke up trying to get me to take him back."

"Not in my lifetime!" Melvin yelled.

"Don't blow a gasket, daddy. I love Leo and I'm not willing to give what I have with him up for anything or anyone. Trust me, being with Elijah again isn't going to happen in my lifetime either. That's not the problem. Elijah is going to purposely make sure Leo doesn't win and it won't have anything to do with the film he submitted. He's going to influence the rest of the judges to his way of thinking to spite me and because he's jealous of my relationship with Leo."

Raquel paused before telling him about Elijah's proposition knowing he would be out of the house and in his car hunting Elijah down. He may be an executive, but the Compton in him would remind Elijah not to mess with his daughter.

"He's doing what? All this because he wants you back? Why would Kelly say anything?" he asked.

"It slipped. Elijah was being his usual arrogant self,

talking about me saying I would never be happy without him and more like that. She was mad and told him how happy I was with Leo and from there, the conversation went downhill. She called me to warn me this morning and then I made an even bigger mistake by calling Elijah, not to beg and plead or anything, but to tell him to be professional and judge on the merit of the submissions. The conversation ended up turning nasty and I'm sure I made things worse."

"What did Leo say?"

Raquel groaned as she walked back and forth nervously.

"I haven't told him yet. He's at work and we're hanging out later. I do plan to tell him to warn him that his submission may be for naught. I can't tell you how bad I feel for dragging Leo into the middle of drama. He doesn't deserve that."

"He doesn't, but Leo is a big boy and from what I've learned about him, he won't let it bother him and he shouldn't. On the other hand, Elijah is wrong if he tries to hurt Leo's chances in order to get back at you. I guess money can't buy common sense and decency. I would say let me give Elijah a call and straighten him out, but I don't think that's the answer. Instead, I'll give Tyrus Hill a call since the contest is for Sky High Hill Entertainment. He'd want to know if things weren't on the up and up. I don't want to cause any trouble for Elijah, but perhaps he can make sure Elijah doesn't go through with his threat. I've been managing Tyrus' millions for many years and he trusts me. I may not like his personal life, but I respect him as a business man and he wouldn't want anything to tarnish his good business name. Don't worry about this another second. I'll take care of this and you focus on your relaxing evening with Leo."

"Thanks, daddy. I've never felt this way about anyone before. I've always wanted to have a guy look at me the way you always looked at mommy. There was no mistaking your love for her just by a look. Leo does that for me. He sees me – not around me or through me, but he sees me. I wanted this moment in his life to be a happy one to celebrate, whether he wins or loses. I don't want to be the cause of this being ruined for him. I love him, daddy."

"I know you do and it's going to be fine. We're all going to be there that night to celebrate with Leo, win or lose, but what I won't allow is for Elijah to taint what would be a bright star in Leo's life for any malicious reason. I'll take care of it. Tell Leo I said hello and I'll see you in the office on Monday."

"Thanks. I love you."

"I would do anything for you and your sister and dealing with a clown is top on my list of things to do to make sure no one disrupts your lives. I love you, too. No worries," Melvin said.

Raquel already felt better the minute she ended the call. Her father was right – she would not allow Elijah to ruin what is a time to celebrate Leo, win or lose as long as if he loses, it's an honest lost.

**

"Hey, baby!"

Raquel jumped up from the sofa the minute Leo entered the apartment.

"Hey, you," she said leaping into his arms and received the spicy kiss she knew was on the agenda. She loved his lips and the way he used them drove her body crazy.

"How was your day?" he asked.

"Relaxing like never before. I've never had so much downtime in my life and I love it. I see that I used to spend to much time being unnecessarily busy. Being with you is good for me," she said, now kissing his face all over.

"I'm happy to hear my impact on you is a good thing!"

"It is and my day was also a little crazy."

"Crazy? Let's talk about it and the craziness. Did you venture out around Harlem? I can tell you went to the market because this place is smelling good like a restaurant."

"I've cooked us something delicious and yes I walked around a little bit today. I had some things I needed to clear my mind about."

"Sounds like something's bothering you. Come sit and talk to me. What's going on?"

Raquel sat on the sofa and braced herself for the conversation about Elijah and the contest.

"The day started with a call from Kelly and it went downhill," she explained.

"You had a fight with Kelly?"

"No, not a fight. She ran into Elijah last night at some function and in the heat of a conversation with him, she not only told him about you and me, but she said enough that he knows you're the Leo who is a finalist in the contest he's judging. He told her he was going to make sure you didn't win and he's doing it out of malice. Then I really messed up by calling him to make sure he didn't do anything stupid, but he's intent on doing that very thing and I'm sorry that my past drama with him is impacting your dream right now. I'm so, so sorry, baby."

Leo didn't immediately respond and seeing the worry on Raquel's face, he hoped she hadn't let that mess up her whole day.

"Come here," he said and pulled her onto his lap.

"I'm sorry, Leo," she said again.

"You have nothing to be sorry for. I don't stress over unhappy people who want to tear someone else down to make themselves look and feel better. If the entire judging panel agrees with anything he says that could tarnish my submission, then it's not a contest I want to win. If things aren't on the up and up, I don't want to be a part of it. This guy is off the chain and I'm good keeping my distance. I'm a nice guy, but I'm not a sucker, far from it. I don't appreciate him taking anything out on you. This contest is one of many contests out here."

"I know, but you put in a lot of hard work on this one."

"I did and no matter what, it was worth it. Now, I feel empowered to check out other contests. Before this one, I had never submitted for any which means this is only the beginning."

"I wanted you to have this. I wanted this so bad for you."

Raquel laid her head on Leo's shoulder, feeling like she wanted to cry.

"I wanted this for me, but this isn't the only thing for me. My life isn't unhappy and I'm not worried about making a million dollars this year. I know that's an exaggeration, but you get my point. I was happy to submit, but it's not a make or break thing for me. The only thing I need to work out for me right now is what's happening between us. This guy wants to ruin things for us because he wants you back and I get it. You're an incredible woman and I love being with you. My mom is doing good, my brothers are good and I'm happy. If not this contest, then maybe the next one or the next one. Either way, don't worry yourself over this."

"Are you still going to the banquet?" she asked.

"Damn right I am and so are you and the rest of my family. They get to enjoy a free night with glitz and glamour and I want to get that for them. I'm looking forward to getting dressed in my finest and seeing you looking all sexy in whatever you wear. I already know it's going to be something that will blow my mind. I can't let an old guy come between what we have. Let's focus on you and me and leave Elijah to his petty scheme. If it works, the contest wasn't meant for me to win. Did you say this guy was forty years old?"

"Yeah, forty and childish."

"He's too old for these teenage games and I'm not here for that and neither should you be. I'm good and I want you to be, too."

"Are you sure?"

Raquel had been worried that Leo would be upset, but her sadness turned to jubilance knowing he had no plans to worry.

"Baby, I'm more than sure," Leo admitted.

"Are you always this calm? I'm still waiting to see the out of control Leo," she joked.

"Not always, but things like dealing with people like your ex doesn't get to me. Apparently, he didn't treat you right and you moved on. Too bad he didn't or he wouldn't set out to make you regret leaving him. Stop worrying because if there is anything or anyone in this apartment besides me and you tonight and that means on our minds too, then I'm going to have to hold out on you and you know what that means. The only time I want you to see me out of control is when I'm making love to you."

Raquel turned so that instead of sitting sideways on his lap, she now straddled his legs.

"Is that so? You think you can resist me?"

Testing her theory that he was lying, she kissed him and not one of those soft pecks on the lips either. This kiss was laced with delicious images of other things her lips could do to his body. Leaning further into the kiss, she suddenly leaned back when she felt Leo's hands grip her behind. She laughed as she reached and moved his hands back to his side.

"What?" he asked.

"You're supposed to be proving to me that you can resist me. You lasted a whole one second, a new record for you, so no touching."

"Listen, I know this situation bothers you and I'm sorry you spent the day worrying about my reaction or what impact this would have on my chances. I love how much you care, but as of this moment, I don't want you thinking about this anymore. I'm going to get a shower and spend the night loving and appreciating you. I smell a good meal and I can't wait to taste everything. I had a busy day and the only thing I thought about was holding you in my arms all evening and then all night long. With our busy work schedules, we don't get enough time where it's just you and me. I worked hard and faster than I usually do because I knew you were here waiting for me."

Raquel kissed him swiftly on the lips with a soft and meaningful peck.

"You are one in a million. I've never met anyone like you who doesn't let things that destroys other people's confidence and self-worth bother him. The world is cruel and anyone who sets out to purposely hurt another person has their own self-esteem issues they need to work out. You're right that I've been worried about your reaction all day and I should have known better. Worry gets us no place."

Leo grinned.

"Well, I wouldn't say no place. It has you in my arms, sitting on my lap with my body is trying to decide if it needs food or you right this moment."

When another kiss landed on his lips, this time longer and deeper, Leo knew his body was winning out over his stomach,

"You've been working all day and we have all night for loving. Get your shower and I'll heat dinner up. You're going to love everything including the pie, I didn't make, but I did buy it the fresh market. The woman behind the counter said they used all organic ingredients and people were ordering them, three and four pies at a time hot out of their oven. I was lucky to get us one. I also picked one up for neighbor, Ms. Mallory. I didn't want to knock on her door since she doesn't know me. Can you take it to her after your shower?"

"See? That's what I'm talking about. What did I do to deserve a woman as good as you are?"

"You asked for my number!" Raquel quipped.

"Yes, I did and that was one of the best days of my life. Mmm, I can smell those fresh apples. I'll get a shower while you heat up the food and then I'm going to come out and fix our plates after running the pie upstairs," he said.

"I can heat the food up and fix our plates."

"Baby, you cooked all day. I want the chance to take care of you. I won't be long," Leo said standing with Raquel in his arms as he walked toward the bathroom.

Raquel giggled.

"Uh, you know you still have me in your arms, right? I'm all for taking a shower with you, but then I doubt we'll ever get to the food. In just a flash, my mind took me through how that would play out and you're tempting me," she said.

"Noted."

Leo placed her on her feet and before turning to walk into the bathroom, he got the one last kiss he needed.

"I love you," Raquel said.

"When I think of you, every thought is love," he said and rushed to shower.

**

"By the way you're rubbing your stomach, I would say you enjoyed dinner."

Leo looked at Raquel with a questionable look as if she shouldn't even have to ask him that. He left no traces of the meal on his plate and he was glad his mother taught him manners because he wanted to lift the plate and lick the last of the tasty gravy from it.

"That was one of the best meals I've ever eaten. You

are a master with seasonings. Now, is when I would go out and get a run on because I know I've gained a few pounds after that, but it's all good. That was absolutely delicious. Who taught you to cook like that? Your mom?" he asked.

"Actually, it was my dad. He was the cook in the family. One day when I was a teenager, I remember asking him why we didn't have a cook or a chef who made our meals like a lot of our neighbors did. Even back then, I knew we were well off, but even the simple things like cooking, my dad did himself. This was even before my mother got sick. She did some cooking, but big tasty dinners and extravagant large breakfast meals were all him. He said his mother had taught him and his brother how to cook in case they either never married or if they met women who didn't know how to cook. When he went off to college and moved into his fraternity house, he became the cook and those guys didn't have to eat noodles and take-out food every night. He taught my sister and me everything he knew and those ended up being the best father-daughter bonding moments ever."

"I'll have to tell your father thanks for what he taught you. A brother could get use to this."

"Did you want to go out for a walk and walk some of this meal off? It's a chilly evening, but I brought a jacket," Raquel asked.

"No, I'm good, unless you do. I think a night here and there of big eating is okay. I'd rather cuddle up with you on the sofa watching one of those chick-flicks you like."

"I vote for cuddling and movies and then dessert later."

They finished washing and putting the dishes away together.

"You go ahead and get comfortable and I'll finish up here," Leo offered.

"How did I get so lucky to have a man like you?"

"You said yes when I asked for your number," he said turning the tables on her response earlier.

Raquel walked over to the sofa and turned on the flat screen television and searched for a movie they could enjoy together.

"I've never been treated this well. I know that probably sounds crazy, but I've never dated anyone whose love I can feel from the heart."

"You haven't been dating the right man – now you are. That's not to slight any other man because that's not who I am, but I told you, I watched a lot with my parents and to hear my mom cry, to see the look on her face and to watch her cringe when he demeaned her, chastised her and hit her remains with me. I teach my brothers better and I made sure I always did better," Leo explained as he turned out the lights, sending the room into darkness except for the glow from the television. He walked over and joined Raquel on the sofa.

"One day, I'd like to thank your ex-girlfriend for

walking away. I'm not sure I would have ever met a man like you. I hadn't before you and now I know what I've been missing. So many things I thought were important aren't at all."

Leo moved so that he laid behind her on the sofa and pulled her back, snug into his embrace.

"We both have people to thank. When I think of you, I think of moments like this where we've shut the outside world out and concentrate on cherishing every moment together. Nothing bad, no issues and no drama from the outside world."

Leo nuzzled her neck as he caressed her arm while they settled in with each other.

"I'm all for that," Raquel agreed.

"Love rules, it rocks and you've made me feel more loved than any time in my life. I know you feel my love and I feel yours, too. This is what love is supposed to be."

Raquel pulled Leo's arm even tighter around her as they stretched out comfortably.

"Even though you had no intention to, you've taught me a lot and I want to make sure I say thank you," she said.

"It's all love, baby. I have as much love as you need. You'll always be able to find it in my arms. Anytime you need it, it's yours."

"I never want to be without it. Never," Raquel said.

She knew there were times when she sounded like a broken record, repeating her gratitude and her love for Leo, but what they shared overwhelmed her in a good way. For too many years, she'd been focused on the wrong things in relationships when the number one focus should have been love. Now she knows and nothing will ever compare."

"It's yours," Leo added.

21

Elijah paced back and forth across the brightly striped carpet of the secure conference room at the Marriott Marquis Hotel in New York City where he and the other judges of the short film contest were gathering for their final decision on the winner. This is the last night before the big gala
banquet and they agreed to make the choice this late in the game to be sure nothing about the selection got out ahead of time. The closer to the event they decided, the less there was a chance that any information would get out. They had a team ready to provide the winning statue and the large version of the winning check with the name of the winner on it sometime in the afternoon of the day of the gala.

A secure room was reserved for them in a place no one expected so that prying ears and eyes couldn't leak any information about the winner of the contest. This was one of the biggest contests held by Sky High Hill Entertainment and it took a lot of kissing up to Tyrus and hooking him up with some of the hottest women in New York for him to get the contract to oversee the contest. His plan, in the beginning, had been to run a contest that was on the up and up, but to his dismay, he had to make a change to that plan.

"How dare she!" he said to himself. As in she, he was speaking of Raquel, the only woman who had ever broken up with him before. He was Elijah Bohner and women didn't leave him. They put up with his mess because he was good looking, sexy and rich, three things that paid his way into many lives and beds and Raquel's life and bed were two places he wanted to be again. It wasn't that she was all that special, but no woman had ever gotten the best of him and he looked forward to having her back in his life so that you could dump her like he should have done before she had the chance to dump him and have it well known that she had done so. That pissed him off and he had an image to protect.

As he waited for the other judges to show up, he set the room for an all-day meeting believing it would take that long for him to convince them to see things his way. He looked across the small conference room at the beverage cart that had been delivered with coffee, tea, water and sodas and knew that a light continental breakfast would be delivered soon. He retrieved the score sheets from his backpack and placed one in front of each seat at the table just as the door opened and everyone else on the panel filed in.

"You're here already? We thought we were early!"

Marjorie said.

Elijah smiled as they all entered.

"I was up early and I wanted some extra time to think things through," he lied.

"That's good because our last meeting was pretty intense with the way you had a complete change of heart after pushing for one person for weeks and then changing your mind to someone none of us thought would be first. I agree that Amara Evans presentation was good and was a good fit for second place, but first place, I'm not so sure of."

"I agree with Marjorie," Wilson, another judge chimed in. "I liked Leo Westmoreland's presentation better than them all. His graphics and design created some of the best imagery I've ever seen. The story leaped off of the screen. Everything about it was five-star, everything. I enjoyed Amara's work as well and hers was just as good, but we're thinking long term the way the guidelines were designed to be followed and I can imagine his movie short turned into a full feature movie. That's what we're looking for as the end result, isn't that right?" he said taking a seat at the table after grabbing a bottle of water.

Elijah knew he was in for an uphill battle and he was ready for their objections.

"I see where you're both coming from, but I have to disagree with you. I've been over and over my initial assessment a few times and Leo comes in a close second, but definitely not first. I'm not so sure the quality is up to the standards that Sky High Hill is used to having. We're not doing them justice by going second rate," Elijah explained.

"Elijah, what are you saying? Are you insinuating that me, Wilson, Stanley and Bobbett are all wrong? We were in agreeance with Leo Westmoreland and we thought we were finished and then you had a change of heart. What gives?" Marjorie asked.

"I'm saying, I think the submission by Amara Evans is the best of the batch. We've talked until we're all tired at meeting after meeting and I still believe hers is the best."

He looked around the room to see if he could see signs of changing the minds of the rest of the judges. He selected the team knowing that when things came down to the wire, they would side with him because he was the boss. He didn't want to throw his position around, but he would if it meant he would get his way. He wouldn't give Raquel or her new man the satisfaction of winning the contest and watching their smug faces the night of the gala. He didn't really believe Amara's submission was better, but the things she did to him when he invited himself to her hotel room the other night was her ticket to the winning seat. He'd never been with a woman with a more talented tongue before.

"I'm not sure I agree," Wilson, one of the other judges said.

"What did we get from Tyrus Hill?" Marjorie asked.

She looked around the room at everyone else and wondered if anyone else was questioning why Elijah chose them. Was it because he was expecting them to side with him even if he was wrong? Something was wrong, yet she couldn't figure out what. She usually trusted Elijah and she had until he suddenly changed his mind without good reason.

Elijah turned, not allowing them to see his snicker as he pulled copies of the fake letter from Tyrus Hill from his backpack. He'd been up all-night working in his office to replicate the letterhead from Sky High Hill in order to change Tyrus' recommendation. The minute he opened the envelope, he had a feeling Tyrus was going to recommend Leo Westmoreland because the truth was, Leo's was the best. If he allowed Leo to win, that meant that Raquel would win and he couldn't have that. He wanted Raquel to know that since she left him, she was now in the loser's circle.

"I had my assistant make copies and you all can take a look. Tyrus and I are on the same page. He also recommended Amara Evans, not that we have to vote for her because he wants us to go with what we agree on. He would respect any choice we made. I think we can make a case for Amara at the gala when I announce the winner."

"Hmm, I find it hard to believe that a man like Tyrus wouldn't see the benefit of selecting Mr. Westmoreland. His submission would be on the level of Avatar, one of the best movies, visually, ever made.

I was caught up from the first frame until the last and came away hoping for a sequel. I didn't get that from Amara's film," Wilson said.

The room was quiet as everyone scanned the letter from Tyrus. Elijah waited patiently through silence that seemed to go on forever as he watched them all read the letter.

"It seems Mr. Hill gave rave reviews of Amara's presentation though some of his justification doesn't seem to refer to her short film. Isn't that odd?" Marjorie asked.

"Are you really questioning Mr. Hill right now?" Elijah asked, further throwing Marjorie's reservations to the wolves. "That's what we're doing now?"

"We don't' have to go with his recommendation," Wilson added.

"Very true and I've said that, but wouldn't it be nice to know we're on the same page? He knows what he wants and, again, I think we can do a great write-up announcing Amara as the winner. Tyrus could mean great things for the company in the long run. We need to think about that, too," Elijah pleaded.

"He makes a good point," Stanley said. "Think of the other work he could throw our way knowing we're with him on this. Let's sit down and see how we can make some good points about her submission and get this over with. This has been a long process and it's time for it to end. Can we all agree on that?" he asked.

"Yeah," everyone added.

Elijah walked away to make a cup of coffee and inwardly cheered that he was able to kill two birds with one stone. He would throw the loss in Raquel's face and also see her boyfriend go back to his pathetic life in Harlem with his dreams officially killed.

"Ah, satisfaction," Elijah said to himself.

"Did you say something?" Marjorie said joining him at the cart.

"Oh, I was saying how a hot cup of coffee is so satisfying."

Elijah took his cup and headed back to the table for the discussion. He gloated knowing this was pretty much in the bag.

**

Tyrus Hill rolled off of his latest conquest, not even sure he remembered her name. In the past five days that he'd been in New York visiting his offices there and getting ready for the gala where the winner of his contest would be announced, he grabbed his chest, feeling a tightness there he'd never felt before. He stretched left and right to try and make it go away, but the quick sting was still there. He shook he shoulders, trying to shake it off and soon felt a little better. Lately he hadn't been feeling his best and for sixty-four, he felt like he was in the best of health. The reason could be attributed to the young women he couldn't seem to get enough of. The blue pills were working, but he needed to make sure nothing else was being negatively impacted when it came to his health.

This latest bed warmer was a wild one and the aches and pains he was feeling was all her.

"Are we finished?" the nameless woman asked.

Tyrus looked across the bed as she sat up with her large enhanced breast barely moving caught his eye. Enhanced or not, he loved all of the things she could do with them and all the things she allowed him to do to them. He had to give it to Elijah for knowing the kind of young thing he liked. This one looked so young, he had to have a quick background check done on her to make sure she was legal and he wasn't crossing a line. Thankfully, information came back that she was actually a very young looking twenty-four-year-old, just his type. She'd been everything Elijah said she would be and he barely had to do anything. At his age, he didn't want to do much other than enjoy the attention.

He loved his wife who was back in Los Angeles where they lived, but he had never been faithful to her and he would leave the earth one day still not being faithful. He was happy that he had enough people on his payroll to help keep all of his indiscretions secret enough that after over forty years of marriage, Audrey had never called him to the table over his roving eye.

"Not as long as that blue pill is still working. Give me a few minutes and get your sexy ass back in bed. I have all night with you and I intend to use it," he said.

Tyrus was about to add more when he heard his cell phone vibrating. Thinking it was his assistant calling to check on him before the end of the night, he grabbed it out of the nightstand where he'd placed it when he entered his hotel room a few hours earlier.

"Melvin Johnson? This is a surprise. It's good to hear from you brother! I was going to give you a call tomorrow to let you know I was in town. I wanted to sit and talk money while I'm here. You have any time for me in the next five days, which is how long I'll be in New York?" Tyrus asked.

He stood, grabbed his robe and left the bedroom, closing the door behind him. He never liked talking about money with women around who he only had an interest in what they could do for him naked. He kept anything business from them.

"I do have time and I'll have my assistant set up something for us. I'm actually calling for another reason. Do you have a minute to chat or are you busy? I know what your visits to New York include and I figured you were entangled with someone's daughter," he said.

Melvin chuckled knowing one of the richest men in the country had no moral compass whatsoever and used his money and power to conquer those who had the weakest character, especially women and from what he heard, he liked them legal, but young.

"I have a few minutes though the twenty-four-year-old in the bedroom will be calling for me in a minute. New York sure has some wild women."

"Is that so?" Melvin asked, not really interested in

knowing, but tolerating the conversation.

"You mean you don't indulge?" Tyrus asked while fixing himself a drink at the full bar located in the living room.

"I have a beautiful woman who is closer to my age. I have no business with women my daughters' ages."

"You don't know what you're missing. Let me hook you up. I know the right people."

"I'm good, but you go ahead and do you. Listen, I wanted to talk to you about the contest. I don't usually get involved in your work like this, but something has been brought to my attention that I'd like to talk to you about."

"Okay, I'm all ears. What's this about?" Tyrus asked.

"Elijah Bohner."

"Good ol' Elijah. What about him?"

Melvin gave Tyrus the short version of the conversation he'd had with Raquel about Elijah rigging the contest away from Leo. He didn't want to seem like he wanted Tyrus to lean in Leo's direction, but he wanted to be sure the contest was fair and that Elijah couldn't taint the results.

"He did what? He's using my contest for some personal vendetta? I would never have that and you know it. I already sent my recommendation to the panel of judges and though they can make their own decision, I had recommended Leo Westmoreland. His short film was incredible. I know you won't divulge that so I have no problem sharing with you. The storyline and the visual are going to make me millions when we turn it from a short film into a full movie. Now, I can't say who the panel will go with, but I will check with one of the other judges to see what's been going on with the discussions. Trust me, whoever the winner is, it will be done fair and square. You can trust me on that. We've been in business together for thirty-years and if I trust you to manage my money, I trust your concern. I hope I'll see you at the event," Tyrus said.

He turned when the bedroom door opened and his guest stood in the doorway naked and proving that though her hair on her head was blond, she was a true brunette as his eyes traveled down her body to that area she flashed at him along with a big smile.

"That's good to know and yes, I'll be there. Raquel, Tyra and I are looking forward to it."

"How are your girls? I haven't seen them in long time."

"They're good. Both are executives in my firm and I'm hoping to leave it to them when I retire in a few years."

"I know they've learned from the best," Tyrus said, gulping down his drink and dropping his robe.

"I hope when I retire, you won't find another money management firm," Melvin said.

"Not on your life. Your firm has made me the kind of money from investments I never thought I'd see.

I'm a client for life and even when I'm gone, as long as you're in business, your company will have my company's business as well. Listen, I'll see you at the gala and no worries about Elijah. Consider that taken care of."

"Good to hear."

Melvin hung up the phone and thought about calling Raquel to ease her worry, but decided against it. He would wait to see what Tyrus would do to rectify any wrongdoing Elijah had planned.

22

Raquel cringed the moment her eyes landed on Elijah walking across the room with that power, self-confident posture in his stride that she now hated. The last thing she wanted was to get into another battle of the wits with him over her choice of Leo over him. Their last conversation had turned into a shouting match. She allowed him to take her there and she still regretted, not what she said, but the fact that she felt she needed to say it.

Shuffling in her seat, she caught her sister's gaze which had also caught sight of Elijah heading their way.

"What's wrong, beautiful?" Leo asked, sensing her discomfort.

Raquel turned and faced him.

"Elijah is heading this way and I'm trying to brace myself in this public place. He tends to bring out the worst in me especially after what he tried to do."

"Baby, you look beautiful and this is our night. Whatever happens, we are celebrating and nothing or no one can change that. You good?" he asked and looked beyond her to see Elijah getting closer.

"Yes, I'm fine."

Raquel turned as Elijah approached the table.

"Raquel, Tyra," he said greeting them and then turned toward Leo. "You must be Leo Westmoreland," Elijah said and extended his hand, making sure he used the hand with the expensive watch on it.

Leo stood and exchanged the handshake already annoyed because there was no way Elijah didn't know who he was. His company was responsible not just for the judging, but for the promotional campaign that has his picture all over it. He let it go and faked a smile.

"Yes, I am."

"Well, well, well. It's nice to finally meet you," Elijah said snidely.

"Raquel told me she knew one of the contestants. Did she tell you that we were involved before?" Elijah asked.

"She did and she also told me that she's never been happier than she is right now, which is the only thing that matters to me."

Elijah donned a fake smile and held it.

"Oh, okay, I see where you're coming from. No hate and I'm glad she's happy. Did she also tell you that I'm on the committee to select the winner of the contest you entered that could be the next movie to compete with the largest superhero movie ever made? The team and I were looking over the final applicants earlier today. I hope you know there's some stiff competition for the top prize including four others who have not only completed undergraduate school, but who have post-graduate degrees in multi-media arts, animation, visual and digital special effects and arts and design. I didn't see anything like that in your paperwork. Perhaps it was missing," Elijah said and turned his attention to Raquel, smiling and then back to him.

Leo was keen to Elijah's attempt at mockery over his lack of a college degree, but he wasn't falling for it. He may not have the degrees under his belt, but he knew how talented he was and he'd already been told by Raquel of Elijah's involvement in the selection process.

"Nothing was missing. What you saw is what you got and what you did get was talent in all of those areas from me. I'm happy to have made the first cut and I look forward to celebrating whoever wins, especially if it's me."

Elijah reached up and rubbed the light stubble on his chin and looked Leo up and down. He hated men who exuded more confidence than him and he was taken back by how Leo wasn't bothered by the way he struggled to make ends meet while dating a woman who was worth a few million dollars.

"I guess we will see. We looked at everything, especially someone who values how important post education is when it comes to making it in that field.

Did Raquel tell you I have two master's degrees and a doctorate in marketing and promotion and I know that I wouldn't be as successful as I am today if I didn't value the importance of going to college and working day and night on my craft. That kind of hustle means something."

Leo held steady. He wasn't intimidated by an educated guy who didn't know his worth without it.

"I agree, but I also think that any hustle should be respected. We may not all walk the same path, but there's enough room for all types of backgrounds when you're confident enough to know what you bring to the table. Studios and producers are looking for that when it comes to having the right talent to get movie goers in the seats and hitting that multi-million dollar or billion-dollar mark. I know the importance of a college education and trust me, I plan to go that route no matter what, but right now, I have priorities like family and two brothers who I plan to make sure get their piece of the American dream and when it's my time, it will be my time," he said.

"That's noble of you. I see your hustle and respect it. I hope that works out for you."

"Leo and I were about to go dance. It was nice seeing and talking to you, Elijah," Raquel said putting her hand in Leo's at her side.

"Well, you and I haven't talked at all. I was hoping to talk to you about a project that may benefit your father's company, sort of a partnership," he said.

"Sounds good. My dad is here tonight, though I know he doesn't want to talk business and neither do I. I'm here to celebrate Leo's achievement in being in the final group of possible contest winners and that's my only focus for tonight. Why don't you make an appointment with my father's assistant and I'll let him decide who you'll give your pitch to."

"Well, I was hoping to have that meeting one day this week and getting on your father's calendar could take weeks if not months. Maybe I can call you this week and your assistant can set up a meeting," Elijah said, pleading.

"No can do. I'm going on vacation this week and the last thing I'm interested in is anything work related. I've been dying to get to the beach and I'm finally going," she said.

"Really? The beach? Where? The French Riviera or another luxury beach somewhere else in the world? You and Tyra and your girls Kenya and Kelly are finally getting away?"

Raquel knew Elijah was prying. She smiled when Leo gave her hand a small grasp letting her know he was okay with her laying it out for Elijah so that there was no room for misunderstanding on his part to what was going on between her and Leo.

"No, Leo is taking me away to a place I've never been and I'm excited."

"Oh really? You're going to a public beach? Have you ever been to any?"

"Don't be coy, Elijah. It's not a good look for you. I don't care if he was taking me to our favorite diner to eat pancakes and burgers because the only thing that matters is time alone enjoying each other with no talk of work at all. You should try that. Perhaps you would be a lot less stuck-up. Now, if you'll excuse us, I need to get my dance on."

Leo took her hand to guide her around Elijah who stood before them turning white as a ghost.

"After you, baby," Leo said. "It was nice to meet you Elijah," he said and placed his hand out for another friendly handshake. He watched as Elijah looked down at it, but not before seeing a look of defeat on his face.

"Likewise," Elijah said and watched them walk away.

Tyra stood from her seat after listening to the exchange and stood beside Elijah.

"You tried it, didn't you? When will you learn what my sister is all about? I use to have my doubts when she was with you, but she is in love with Leo and I've never seen her happier or stronger, so move on. Any attempt you're going to try to mess up what they have, you can forget about it. You can't intimidate Leo with your style or status and it no longer impresses my sister. She's discovered what it means to really love someone and to have someone love her back with honesty and respect, those areas you lack. Give it up, bruh. No matter how you want to play this, you lost"

Tyra said and patted him on the back.

"I don't know what you mean," Elijah said, not realizing his face no longer bared a smile but a grimace.

"Let me put it this way, if you try and sabotage Leo in any way, you'll have to deal with the wrath of Melvin Johnson and you don't want to see that side of my dad. I'm not saying you should give him any unfair positive treatment, but don't try to disparage his chance at winning because you and I both know that he is more talented than anyone you've come across in years. If it wasn't for his allegiance to making sure his family is good first, he would be living the high life in Hollywood right now, but the limelight isn't his priority; family is and so is his love for my sister. Look at them," Tyra said and watched them sway to the sweet sounds of Anthony Hamilton who was the musical guest for the night. "That, right there, is pure love. Don't even try it, so back of. You messed up by not loving her right, so like I said, move on. Okay, bruh? Good, it was nice having this chat with you or it wasn't."

Tyra took one last sip of her drink before walking away from the table, leaving Elijah standing, admiring what she knew his eyes were taking in. Elijah had to see that any chance he had of getting Raquel back was gone because the love in their eyes for each other could never be tested by anyone.

Elijah didn't immediately walk away as he tried to

not let on that he was watching Raquel and Leo. He fumed even more when he watched how free and happy Raquel looked in Leo's arms. He didn't know what she saw in a man who had no money and nothing going for himself. It was true the winner of the contest would most likely end up being the next Steven Spielberg or Stan Lee, but if it was up to him and in a way, it was, Leo would remain that 'could have been' from Harlem that he already was. He would make sure Leo came in last place and then when Raquel saw that Leo would always be a nobody, she may think twice and give him a second chance.

In another thirty minutes, Leo's night would be ruined and Raquel will see that she's with a man who isn't going anywhere in life and she'd come running back to him. He straightened his tie and walked back to his table to wait. Before he reached it, he felt a tap on his shoulder and turned to find Tyrus Hill standing behind him.

"Tyrus! It's good to see you. Are you ready for tonight's announcement?" he asked.

"I'd like to talk to you about that. Let's step out into the hall," Tyrus said.

"You know we're close to beginning the award phase and I want to take the last twenty-minutes to go over what I'm going to say."

"I want to talk to you about that. This will only take a few minutes," Tyrus said escorting Elijah through the side doors to the hallway.

"Is everything okay?" Elijah asked when he saw no hint of happiness on Tyrus' face. "How was Jenae that I hooked you up with last night? She was good, right?" he asked.

"That's what her name was? I couldn't seem to remember that, but for now, let's keep the personal and professional separate. I want to talk to you about the contest. What did you think you would achieve by cheating?" Tyrus asked getting straight to the issue at hand.

Elijah opened his mouth to play ignorant to what he was talking about and then remembered this was Tyrus Hill, a scoundrel of men, the most sinister he'd ever encountered. No matter what he had to say, Tyrus would know it was a lie.

"I know why you're upset," he said nervously.

"You do? So, there's one brain thinking for both of us? You tried to sabotage the contest. I'm not sure what to think about that. I don't take kindly to people being more scandalous than me. Not only that, you're doing this to hurt a woman whose father manages all of my money? Are you out of your mind? All of this over a dude? Really? You have enough money to buy any woman you want and instead, you want one that doesn't want you and to try and get her back, you use my contest in a vengeful way. Before you try to justify anything, I've already checked with one of the other judges and I understand my letter of recommendation wasn't the letter I sent to you. I won't even get into how you could have manipulated that because I don't have time to do that, but I will deal with you after the announcement, which I will be making tonight. I was up for the rest of the night fixing what you messed up. I had to have everything changed over to the true winner and do you know what it took to have that done at the last minute? I trusted you to do the right thing, yet here we are. Believe me when I tell you, no piece of tail that you can possibly hook me up with will ever match up to the good name I've established over the years with the business world and believe me the world is watching. You were about to give my one hundred-thousand-dollar prize to a woman no one thought should have been in first place and yes, I talked with each of the judges separately and I know how they were planning to vote before you used your position as owner of your company to sway them your way. You have a lot to learn when it comes to business. One thing I've learned is that business and personal should never live in the same space. You have a seat at your table and learn from the master. I am always in charge and I don't care how many women you hook me up with, business comes before a young snatch any day – remember that."

"Mr. Hill, I'm really sorry. I don't know what I was thinking," Elijah admitted. He knew that Tyrus could make or break his business.

"You can kiss my ass later. There's business to be done. Go up and introduce me and I'll take it from there."

"But..."

"Conversation over, Elijah," Tyrus said and walked away.

Elijah fumed, but he had to show face in front of the crowd. Gathering himself, he went back into the ballroom and before taking his seat, he looked toward Raquel and Leo who were still dancing. Some would call what he was feeling, jealousy, but he was Elijah Bohner and he didn't get jealous. He hated how happy they looked.

23

"It looks like we're about to begin the best part of the night," Raquel said nervously twitching in her seat. To calm her anxiety, she reached for the single red rose that sat on the table, the only red rose in the entire room, courtesy of Leo. He never ceased to amaze her with his surprises.

"It is a good evening, no matter what, right?" Leo asked.

"I just hate that Elijah is in a position to control how the night ends, but yes, it's a good night and I'm having the time of my life."

"And you look amazing doing it in your royal and silver gown and you look extra sexy with your hair pinned up. Remember that Elijah doesn't control how our night ends, baby. This contest isn't the end of the world. We already know what he has planned and we're not going to worry about it."

"More contests, right?" she asked and kissed him sweetly.

"No doubt. As soon as we get back from the beach,

I'm going to check into more. I'm on a mission now," Leo said as the lights in the room dimmed and they watched Elijah walk across the stage to the podium.

"This is it, bro," Trayvon said from the other side of him.

Leo turned to him and Major as both gave him a thumbs up and crossed their fingers. He looked around the table at his mother, Walt and Raquel's family and knew he was already the luckiest man in the room. He'd tried looking around for another invitee, but didn't see him. He didn't have room for him at their table and wouldn't invite him to sit there, but he wanted him in the room. There were three other tables near his that were full of supporters, one with family that included his uncles, aunt and cousins. He couldn't believe it when he received a check in the mail from his uncle who had purchased an entire table. Another table had employees of the real estate company he worked for and the last was a surprise, full of employees from the marketing firm where he worked full-time. They had also purchased an entire table to support him. Throughout the room, he'd seen others he wasn't expecting, including employees of the museum where he worked as well as some of the teachers from Trayvon's school where he volunteered his time. Not everyone got the chance to be as lucky as him to have people who cared about him and win or lose, he was the luckiest man in the room.

Holding onto Raquel's hand a little tighter as she

gripped his with her two hands, he listened as Elijah spoke. He may be up there with power over the night, but Leo knew Elijah had no power over his life.

"Good evening everyone and thank you for being here tonight for the announcement of the winner of the Short Film Festival contest. For those who don't know me, my name is Elijah Bohner and I'm the owner of Bohner Marketing and Promotion, the firm responsible for the judging and promotion of the contest. I welcome you to the gala tonight and hope that everyone is having a great time so far. There is a little change up from what you see on the agenda. I'm listed to make the announcement of the winner tonight, but I'm happy to report that Tyrus Hill, CEO of Sky High Hill Entertainment is here tonight and he'll be announcing the winner. Help me welcome to the stage, Tyrus Hill."

The audience went wild and everyone stood to clap and cheer. Raquel turned to Leo with a questionable look on her face.

"I wonder what happened? I can't imagine Elijah willingly giving up an opportunity to have the spotlight on himself," she whispered.

"I guess we're about to find out."

Raquel looked around the table at everyone as her eyes landed on her father, the only person whose eyes were on her. He winked and she smiled while turning her attention back to the stage as everyone quieted down.

"Wow, he's actually here. Usually he's too busy to attend things like this and he often sends representatives," Raquel said as she leaned over to whisper in Leo's ear again.

"I heard he might be here and before he showed up, I wasn't nervous. Now, I am," he said.

"Don't be. I'm here for you, boo. I love you."

"I know and that means everything. I hear he's pretty ruthless in how he runs his company," he whispered.

"I'm sure he has to be with a billion-dollar empire in the movie, television and music fields. No one is doing things as big as he is. Can you imagine working for him?"

"I may not get the opportunity."

"Win or lose, we're winners," she exclaimed.

"No doubt," Leo said.

On the other side of him, his mother leaned over past Trayvon.

"I'm proud of you. No matter what happens tonight, I have always been proud of you and I always will be," she said.

"Thank you, Ma. That means everything and again, you look amazing tonight."

"Thank your lovely girlfriend because she helped me pick this gown out. I feel beautiful," she said.

"You are beautiful," he said.

Turning his attention to the stage, he watched as Elijah tried to hand an envelope to Tyrus, but Tyrus didn't take it. Instead, he took the microphone in his hand and thanked Elijah who turned and walked off of the stage.

"You all look beautiful tonight and I want to thank you for supporting Sky High Hill Entertainment every time to go see our movies, watch our television shows and listen to our musical artists. I am because of you and I appreciate it. I'm happy to be in the place tonight to make the announcement of the winner of the film contest. I don't usually make the winning announcement, but tonight I felt empowered because this winning short film is one of the best I've ever seen in my career. I've put out films that have made millions and millions and I'm a believer that this winning short will make an incredible full feature that I can't wait to have my studio get behind. I want to thank Elijah and his team for all of their hard work on picking this year's winner and believe me, from what I hear, it was a tough decision. Throughout the night, we were able to see short five-minute plugs from each submission and I'm sure I don't have to tell you how hard it was to choose just one. I don't want to delay the announcement any longer."

Tyrus reached into the inside jacket pocket of his suit and pulled out an envelope.

"In my hand is the name of tonight's third and second place runners up. Let's start with those. Our third-place winner is Justin Towers who submitted a short film titled, "The Delirious Planet.""

The crowd went wild as Justin stood, hugged a few people around his table and headed toward the stage.

Raquel's nervousness was on a level that had her whole body shaking. Even though she knew that Elijah had played dirty, she was still remained hopeful.

"You're more nervous than me," Leo whispered in her ear.

"I love you and I wanted this so much for you," she said.

"I know and it's okay. You know that, right? It's okay?"

"Yes, I know because that's the kind of man I fell in love with."

"You better believe it," he smiled.

"Next, we have our second runner up. That honor goes to Amara Evans for her short film submission of, "Shasta Island.""

Raquel and Leo clapped along with everyone else and some in the crowd, like them noticed something odd about Amara. Though she won second place, she wasn't happy as if she expected to win the top prize. When her eyes turned and landed on Elijah who avoided returning her gaze, Raquel had a feeling more was going on than even she was clued in on.

"Did you see that?" she asked Leo.

"I did. I wonder what that was about?"

"Knowing Elijah, he did something and made her think she was going to win. I can't believe I ever dated him."

"We all have our pasts and thank goodness, he's in yours and not your present or future. I'm the only future you will ever have to worry about," Leo said confidently.

"Oh, yes!" Raquel shouted quietly and then turned back to the stage.

"And now for our winner - I'm happy to announce that the winner of the annual Sky High Hill Short Film Festival Contest is...Leo Westmoreland for his short film submission of "Korinth: They Live Among Us!" Tyrus announced.

The crowd went wild and Leo didn't move. While Raquel and his mother jumped up along with everyone at his table and in the room, he sat stoic still trying to wrap his head around the fact that he thought one of the most powerful men in the world had just called his name. Raquel wrapped her arms around his neck while his mother held her face in her hands as she cried tears of joy.

He'd won. Did he hear Tyrus Hill correctly? Did he just win? He thought Elijah had sealed his fate as a loser, but he'd won. His name had been called and his face now graced the large jumbotron screen over the stage along with the words winner in large, bold letters. Balloons and confetti fell from the rafters as the room went wild. He was stunned and still hadn't moved yet.

"You won!" Trayvon and Major shouted and

jumped around.

Leo stood, still dazed and turned to Raquel.

"I won," he said softly.

Raquel took his face in her hands and kissed him.

"Yes, baby, you won. Get up there and have your moment. This night is all about you. We're proud of you. Go up there and be celebrated," she said.

As the words that he'd won finally sunk in, Leo walked to the stage through the throngs of well-wishers. He'd never known what it felt like to be the center of attention. The feeling was overwhelming. He'd won. As many times as he'd said the words in his head, he still couldn't believe it as he walked up the steps to the stage and Tyrus Hill pulled him into a tight hug.

"Congratulations. You deserved this!" Tyrus told him.

"Thank you, sir. Thank you very much."

"I know what happened and trust me, you were the pick from the start. Go ahead and take this stage like a winner."

Leo shook his head, took the golden statue from the woman who had walked out on the stage and handed the large oval-shaped glass statue to him.

As he walked up to the microphone, he reached inside of his jacket for the speech he'd been up all-night working on just in case he won. He was a true believer that if something were meant for him, it would be and if nothing else, he needed to be prepared just in case. He believed in a power much higher than Elijah and that power proved once again that he was worthy to be a winner. He smiled and waved as the crowd got louder and louder and over them all, he could hear his brothers cheering and hollering. He looked around the room and let his eyes briefly land on Elijah. He didn't snicker or send any negative vibes his way. He hoped Elijah could see that what is meant to be, was. He then turned back to the microphone as everyone quieted down, but stood standing around their tables.

"Thank you, thank you, thank you. I want to thank God, the author and finisher of my life story and who gets all the honor for guiding my footsteps and allowing me to be here in this moment accepting this honor tonight. I'm thankful and humble that the panel took a chance on me and saw every bit of me that I poured into my short film, "Korinth: They Live Among Us". I've been writing that film for a few years and I'm glad that they saw the value in what a movie audience would be able to get out of it once it's turned into a full feature movie. I'm excited about seeing my vision come to life for the big screen. I want to thank Mr. Tyrus Hill and everyone at Sky High Hill Entertainment for this opportunity and I won't let you down. I'd like to thank the judges who had the hardest decision to make. I'm bringing my best to the project. I want to thank my family and friends who are here with me tonight. I don't want to take up too much of your time, but I need to thank them individually. First, to mister Melvin Johnson and Tyra, you've been in my corner from day one and your support is invaluable. I appreciate you welcoming me into your lives with open arms. Your acceptance from day one has enriched my life. To my best friend Walt, we've been boys our whole lives and I share this moment with you, my friend, who has always been in my corner. You are my brother from another mother and I thank you for always being there. To my aunt, uncles and cousins who are here tonight lending their support, you've been there for me all of my life pushing me and letting me know that you had my back and I'm the man I am today because of your love and support. To my brothers Trayvon and Major, this win tonight isn't just a win for me, it's a win for all of us. There are great things in store for me and as a result of that, there are even greater things in store for you. Remember this day and understand when I tell you how much hard work does pay off. Don't stray from the path of greatness you're already on. I love you! To the love of my life, Raquel, you are the light that shines in my life every single day. With your love and support, I applied for this contest and put faith in God and the talent He gave me and not once have you ever let me fall back from being great. I've told you this before and I'll say it again publicly that every man in the world should have a woman as wonderful, magnificent and loving as you are in his corner. You are my rock and tonight wouldn't mean the same if you were not here to share it with me. I am an even better man because you are that great woman in my life who loves me, pushes me, supports me and lets me know that through the good, bad and the ugly, you're with me and your steps have never faltered. I love you, baby, always. I love you. To my mother, Evelyn, I know life hasn't always been easy, but I hope and pray that my love for you has made it a little easier. Throughout my life, you've shown Trayvon, Major and me love, grace and kindness and because of that, we are better, strong and more determined than ever to make you proud of the men we are. I remember when I was younger, you told me that I could be anything in this life that I wanted to be with hard work and I've always believed that. Even tonight, before the announcement, you whispered to me that you were proud of me and it makes me happy to see you smile and also, you look amazing! Doesn't my mom look beautiful, y'all?" he asked the crowd. When they cheered again, he smiled harder.

"Thank you, Ma, for being the kind of mother we needed and a win for me, is a win for you. You know how I feel about family and family comes first. This award is for you the real, true winner in my life. We're going to place this prominently in your house so that every time you look at it, you know that I have this all because of you and your love."

Leo paused before continuing. He was about to

reveal something that his mother nor his brothers knew, but it was time.

"One more thing and then I'll take my seat. Throughout my adult life, I didn't have a relationship with my father. Our paths separated many years ago and life took him in a different direction. Recently, I saw my father on the subway and I had a chance to talk to him about my life and the lives of my brothers. I won't go into the conversation, but let me just say that I, like anyone else, would have loved having my father in my life as I grew up and became a man, but God had another plan in mind and it was one that brought my father back into my life, maybe not when I would have wanted him to, but more like when he was ready to. Many years have passed and a long time ago, he made some bad choices, but tonight, I see him standing over by the door because I invited him to be here. He was hesitant because he told me he was unworthy, but I'm glad he made it to see this night. I believe that everyone should have a chance at redemption and it may not make up for the bad times in the past, we can look to the future and be thankful that God provides time for healing and forgiveness. Thanks dad for showing up tonight and being a part of my night."

Leo knew the night was extra special because old wounds were healed and a few days ago, his brothers were able to sit down and talk to their father, a man they didn't remember. They were also able to meet their little sisters who asked a million questions. There was instant love between the five siblings. Though he knew his mother and father would never be able to communicate again, he was okay with that, but he had to open his heart in order for him to live a happy life. He no longer wanted to carry the burden of the past. He looked from his father who waved. He then turned back to the audience.

"It's never too late to follow a dream or repair a broken relationship. Everything takes time, just as me winning this contest and being on a path many wondered why I wasn't on before today. That wasn't my time, but now is. It's time for forgiveness and goal chasing. I look forward to you all, one day, seeing my movie on the big screen and getting as much enjoyment out of watching it as I have had writing it. Stay tuned!" he shouted and held the award up to the crowd who again went wild.

He looked toward the table where his brothers stood, clapping and both crying looking in the direction of where their father stood. He also looked toward his mother and hoped he hadn't ruined her night, but what he saw was love as she also turned toward where his father stood and clapped in his direction. Leo knew she was thanking him for being there for their son for his big night.

"Thank you again for this honor tonight and I will make you proud. Thank you!" Leo said and took his award and walked backstage. When he reached the wings, Tyrus walked back up to him.

"I look forward to having you in California soon to talk about how we can get your film to the big screen. I see not only that one movie, but several sequels. I hope you're ready for that," he said.

"Yes, I am and I have some great ideas."

"Be ready for big changes in your life."

Leo shook his hand again and headed back to his seat with his award in hand as he watched Elijah take the stage from the other side.

As he took the long way around to his table, Leo thought about Tyrus' comment about the big changes that were in store for him. He was comfortable and happy with his life in Harlem and now he was about to be thrown into the spotlight and for the first time, he wondered if he was ready. The moment his family came into view, he put all reservations to the side and walked into his destiny.

24

With the time well after midnight, Leo couldn't be wider awake as the town car drove him and Raquel to his apartment. The original plan was for him to get dressed and use the town car to then pick her up at her condo, but the night before, after going back and forth about where to get dressed, he let Raquel win and they agreed to get dressed at his place and let him show off a little for his neighborhood.

After the gala, the whole family had gone out to the diner for celebratory desserts where they sat, talked and laughed until after one in the morning. Leo thought he would be tired, but he wasn't. He stared at the glass statue in his hands and smiled as the car headed toward his place.

"You did it!" Raquel said leaning back in his arms as they rode in the back of the car.

"It still doesn't feel real. I don't want to think too hard about what happened because that would mean giving your ex space in my head and I don't want that," he said.

"I spoke with my father and he told me he reached

out to Tyrus Hill and explained everything. Tyrus told him that he had already recommended you and that after he talked to each of the judges, they had all voted on you also until Elijah turned the tables. Tyrus approached Elijah about it tonight and he let him know that he would take things over and handle it. He didn't appreciate what Elijah tried to do. I don't want you to think that my father did anything to push things in your favor."

"That is some shady mess. He went to great lengths to mess this up and I'm glad he didn't succeed. I know I won, but I cannot believe what that means. My whole life is about to change."

"It is and that also means you'll be away from me often as you head to Los Angeles in a few months to begin working with a team on the movie idea."

Leo kissed the back of her hand and Raquel felt the closeness she always felt when he was near.

"Nothing is going to keep me from you. I haven't had a chance to think through what going out to Los Angeles is going to mean."

"You'll have to quit your jobs, but with the prize money, you won't have to worry about bills or anything and that's good. You'll also sign your contract and see more money than you ever have."

"I won't let that change me," he said.

"I know you won't. I may second guess that with some people, but not with you. You'll be down to one job, but that one job will take you to the other coast. I wish I could go with you."

"I would love it if you could. We have a lot to talk about, but we don't have to talk about all of it tonight. I want to go back to my place and hold you all night long. I'm so wide awake and happy and I don't want to think of anything else, but you."

"I feel the same way."

"Good. We can talk about what's next another time as long as it's not tonight. Besides, we're still going to the beach tomorrow for an entire week. I have to do press, which is part of the contest rules, but that's doesn't start for another week. There's a person from Tyrus' office here in New York who is setting up talk shows, radio shows, internet interviews. So much is tied to this that I'm looking forward to our down time before that all jumps off."

"I'm so proud of you."

"This is a win for us, not just me. I am now a 'we' and every decision I make, I don't want to consider only what it means for me, my brothers and my mom, but you also. You're a big part of my life. You have become my life and I don't want that to change. I don't want anything to change when it comes to us."

"Neither do I. Whatever support you need from me, I'm here for you."

"That's why I love you," Leo said, pulling her closer into his arms for a deeper kiss.

"I love you, too."

"Did I tell you within the last few minutes how

gorgeous you look in this gown tonight. I couldn't stop imagining taking it off of you."

"It's a good thing we're close to your place or the driver would get an eyeful. I'm ready to attack you in this back seat the way you look in that tuxedo. You dress up nice and sexy," she said, purring in his ear.

Leo was about to respond when the town car came to a stop in front of his building. He exited and came around to help her out. When Raquel exited the car and stood before him, he leaned in and kissed her deeply before they moved away from the car.

After tipping their driver, they walked toward the entrance of his building where they were greeted by some of the kids who lived in his building.

"Leo! You sure clean up nice, man!" one shouted.

"Yeah and your lady is fine. We were waiting for you to get back and tell us how the party was. Did you rub elbows with a lot of rich people? We already heard that you won! It's been all over social media," another kid said.

"I did, but I still prefer to be here hanging with you dudes when I can. It's kind of late for you to be out," Leo said.

"We know, but we wanted to congratulate you when you got home and we were watching your lady's car making sure no one messed with it. We were ready to go toe-to-toe with any fool who wanted to try anything, but nothing jumped off."

"Kenny, ain't nobody gonna mess with Leo's

woman's car. They know better!" Mikey, the youngest of the crew said.

"Well, I appreciate you looking out for my lady and holding things down around here. Get inside before your mothers come hollering for you," he advised.

"We good. They told us we could wait out here until one for you and then we had to go inside. It's a good thing you came home when you did or we would have missed you."

"You guys are the best and yes, I had a really good time with my beautiful lady by my side."

"Alright, Leo. You representing us good," Kenny said.

Leo gave them the thumbs up as they entered the building and walked toward his apartment.

"I love how people love you. It's a sincere love for you and I don't even have to wonder or question why. You are an incredible man," Raquel said as they entered his apartment.

Leo locked the door behind them and pulled her snug against him, finally happy that they were alone.

"Am I?" he said, lowering his voice an octave as he leaned in and kissed her neck, planting open mouth kisses from one side of her neck to the other, taking her purse from her hand and tossing it to the sofa.

"Oh, yes you are and you're all mine mister incredible."

Leo leaned back and looked her in the eyes, marveling at the love he found in them for him.

"This night was perfect," he said.

"It was pretty perfect. Joining me?" Raquel asked as she walked toward the bedroom.

"You think you have to ask?" he laughed. "Do you want anything to eat or drink?"

"Is there any fruit?"

"Yes. I have grapes and mixed fruit or I can bring you an apple I can slice up."

"You're so good to me. Grapes are good and a bottle of water. I'm going into the bedroom to change and make sure you finished packing for our trip."

"I may not have three big suit cases like you, but I have one filled with everything I'll need for a week on the beach. I'm ready for this road trip."

"So am I. I can't wait," Raquel said.

"I'll be right in."

Leo was still flying above the clouds as he looked over at his award now sitting on the kitchen counter. He'll need to find something special to keep it in and prominently display it at his mother's house. He wouldn't be where he was without the love she never wavered in showing him.

Life was going to change for them all. First, he had a lot of paperwork to read through which he will print out and take with him on their trip. He already knew he needed to find a good lawyer to look over everything and was thankful for the recommendation of a good one he'd received from Raquel's father. Not far from his mind was the cash prize that would hit his bank account in a few days. After the press junket he would be on, he needed to plan his first trip to the west coast to visit Sky High Hill Entertainment studios in Hollywood, California. He'd never been before and wondered how the trip would change his life. He would soon see.

Grabbing the water and bowl of grapes, he turned out the lights in the apartment and joined Raquel in the bedroom where he encountered her removing her jewelry as she stared at the single red rose she'd brought back with her from the gala event.

"I love my rose," Raquel said the minute he entered the room. "You have a way of surprising me with the unexpected. Walking into the ballroom and finding that rose sitting on my plate was everything."

Leo laughed lightly.

"You know Trayvon asked me if I'd spent so much on this tuxedo tonight that I didn't have enough money to buy you more than one rose. He had me laughing so hard and then I had to school him."

"What did you say?"

"I told him that a single rose had meaning that a full bouquet didn't hold. I explained that you are the *One*, the only *One* for me. I told him that you are the *One* singularity in my life that has me waking up smiling in the morning and going to bed with that same smile at night. I explained that you are my *One* love and though I can buy you many flowers, I really can now, that's not what's important. What mattered to me most was going to that event tonight knowing that no one else in the room was able to bribe one of the set up crew to place a single red rose for his woman so that when she entered, she would look around and see that the one red rose stood out in a room decorated in other colors."

"I had a lot of people come over and ask me where the rose came from since only my plate had a rose on it. I told them the love of my life always finds new ways to amaze me with his love for me. I even saw one woman punch her husband on the shoulder and ask why he never did little things like that for her. He shrugged and walked off. You, my love, are extra special and I am in awe by your thoughtfulness."

"Anything for you. I don't know if I'll ever be able to thank you enough for being in my corner."

Raquel turned toward Leo as he walked closer to her.

"Baby, loving me the way you do is thanks enough. I don't need more than that. I've waited a long time for a man like you and you being who you are is everything to me and I do mean everything."

Raquel turned back to the dresser to remove the rest of her jewelry.

"Did I remark about your beauty tonight? I mean you're always beautiful, but you, in this gown adorned with rhinestones had you looking even more like a queen. You are incredibly beautiful."

Placing the water and fruit on the one-night stand,

Leo pressed closed to Raquel allowing her to feel his desire for her, that same constant state of arousal he always seemed to be in around her.

"Thank you and you know you always make me feel extra beautiful."

Leo wrapped his arms around her from behind and let his eyes roam over her from head to toe in the mirror.

"I will always remember this night and how big of a role you played in everything. This night is because you had faith in me."

"Baby, this night was always meant to be for you and so I knew to have faith, though for a minute I was scared that I had ruined everything."

"You couldn't have because this was meant to be and not just the award, but you and me."

Leo watched himself in the mirror and waited for Raquel's erotic reaction to the kiss he planted first on one of her bare shoulders and then the other. When she leaned back into him and closed her eyes, he kissed up and down the length of her neck.

"Don't close your eyes. Look in the mirror at us. I can't stop looking at how stunningly beautiful you are and I'm still in a haze that you love me. I never want to forget this moment."

He reached for the thin straps of her gown and pulled them slowly from her shoulders, still kissing every piece of exposed skin as the dress disappeared from her body and dropped to the floor. He could see

Raquel's pulse quicken as her breaths increased. He then kissed his way around to her back as he reached for the snap to the navy blue strapless bra that kept his hands and eyes from her beautiful breasts. The minute the lacy fabric fell into his hands, he placed it on the dresser and immediately cupped her waiting mounds.

"Ohhhh," Raquel uttered.

"You feel good in my hands all heavy and plump."

Leo couldn't resist caressing not only the large mounds, but also the hard peaks of her nipples that came out to greet his touch. As he rolled the harden tips between his fingers, he caressed the part of her neck that was open for his admiration.

"Nothing with you is more relaxing than when you touch me like this."

"Really? Nothing? I can think of a few more relaxing things and I'd like to show you some tonight. Come here, baby," he said turning her around in his arms. He was more than ready for the kiss that he knew would electrify the room and send waves of desire through his body. As they kissed, he turned and walked her backwards toward the bed. With Raquel in panties and heels only, he felt overdressed and quickly dispensed with all of clothes, barely able to contain his need for her.

"I'm always ready for you," Raquel whispered.

"Yes, you are and I'm always ready for you."

Testing his theory, Raquel reached out and tested

the weight of his readiness by holding his manhood in her hands, stroking him while feeling his need growing in length and width as she drew as much pleasure from pleasing him as she saw him getting by the look on his face.

"Yes, you are. I need to get these panties and heels off," she said, breathlessly.

"Mmm, panties yes, heels, not on our life. I like the heels and I like them on you. I look forward to seeing them in the air over my shoulders."

Barely holding on, Raquel reached down and drew the navy thong down her legs, kicked them off and moved backwards up and onto the bed.

"I love that we enjoy lots and lots of foreplay, but not tonight. All I need right now is you inside of me."

To prove her point, she reached up and caressed her own breasts playing around with the hardened tips as she watched Leo reach down to stroke his already hard as steel erection.

"I aim to please," he groaned out with heated desire.

"Something I know all too well. Are you just going to stand there and tease me or are you going to join me?"

"I don't need to be told more than once."

With no more words, Leo moved onto the bed and in between her already opened legs. As her arms came up to bring him closer to her lips, he spread her legs a little wider and entered her at the exact moment that their lips met and his tongue slipped into her mouth, mimicking the action his penis took as he entered her body, going into her slipperiness until he was fully seated inside. Moving his arms until they were nestled under her knees, Leo lifted her legs up and over his shoulder for a much deeper penetration. He wanted to scream his pleasure, but any sound was muffled by the intensely erotic kiss they were sharing as their tongues dueled trying to get as close as they possibly could.

With her legs high up so that he could plunge into her body deep and penetrating they way they loved their lovemaking.

"Yes, baby!"

"Hold on," he said and increased the pace. He loved how Raquel met him stroke for stroke, raising her hips up to meet his downward strokes. As Raquel quickened her thrusts, he knew she was close and wanted her to get everything from him that she wanted and needed. Her pleasure was always his priority when they were together.

As her breathing sped up, matching the speed of her pumps, he watched as Raquel opened her mouth as if she was about to say something, but instead, he watched her mouth form the letter 'O' and at that moment, he knew what was coming next, causing him to give her more as his hips coursed forward again and again as Raquel's orgasm surged, sending her over the edge, screaming out her release, riding him as he rode her. Seeing her in a haze of ecstasy was all he could stand when it came to holding on any longer. He let go as his body convulsed through one tumultuous wave after another, causing him to literally lose control of his body. He surged into her, releasing her legs, letting them down as he grabbed a hold of her hips while continuing his motion in and out of her, feeling the walls of her body grip him in desire.

As their bodies began to calm, Leo slowed his strokes as their eyes locked.

"This is only the beginning for us. You know that right. The world is ours!" Raquel proclaimed.

"Yes, it is and it's only getting better because you're with me for the ride."

"As long as you want me, I'm here," she said.

"I'll always want you. That will never change."

"Then yes, I'm here for that ride and I don't care where it takes us."

"I never knew love like this before," Leo said.

His mind went back to a time when he put all women in the same category because one woman made him think that he wasn't enough. He smiled, happy that he never gave up on the idea that there were women who meant it when they said they wanted a good man who treated like a queen in all aspects of life and love and not just from the wallet.

"I'm glad we're experiencing it together."

Raquel pulled Leo closer for an even deeper kiss,

sealing her words with action.

Epilogue

One Year Later

"Are you ready, babe?" Raquel asked.

Being in California was everything she thought it would be and now with a possible permanent move to the west coast because opportunities were pouring in since Leo won the contest, she couldn't be more excited. Of course, there was the beginning of their happy ending with the engagement ring that sat bright and sparkling on her ring finger.

"Almost, but we don't have to rush. I think Tyrus is going to be late anyway. I got a text from his assistant who said instead of meeting him for dinner at seven, it looks like the time is going to be closer to eight."

"That's good. Are you excited about the dinner with him?"

"Not really. Tyrus is a lot to take in. Until I began working with his studio on the final ideas for the movie, I hadn't really spent any time with him. Then he shows up one day and has a few other projects in the making that he wants me on and in Tyrus Hill fashion, he pushes the ideas followed by dollar signs and then is shocked when I tell him my interest is in the final outcome of the project and not just the dollar value of what he's offering. I think he's used to buying people and not really caring what they think."

"Yeah, my dad gave me several warnings about Tyrus when I told him about our move to Los Angeles. They're on the same page when it comes to money matters, but on a personal level, my dad doesn't care for him. He can be a lot to take in."

"Whew! That's an understatement. I've read, like everyone else, about his personal life and it wasn't until recently that I saw a lot of it for myself. I think he was testing me to see if I was that type of guy to step out on his lady, but he soon learned I wasn't and he backed off. He's always trying to show me off at his private parties and then when I tell him let me reach out to be sure you're free to come, he looks at me wondering why I would bring you when he's insinuated the kind of party it would be. I'm happy to no longer get invited. I want to keep everything about business and that's it."

"Babe, you know I don't worry about you when it comes to that, but I don't know how Tyrus' wife deals with his mess. I know his money goes a long way to keeping people silent, but from what I hear, he has a lot of skeletons in his closet and one day if that ever blows up, it will be one of the biggest scandals Hollywood has ever heard of."

Raquel continued getting ready as they talked.

There was a lot about Tyrus that she'd have to share with Leo even though she knew, like her, her father had schooled Leo on being cautious when Tyrus tries to get closer than just business associates.

"I'm not looking to be anywhere near Tyrus and his scandals and besides, with that ring on your finger, pledging my life and love to you, the last thing I want to do is to become all Hollywood and jeopardize what we have. You know me," Leo said and looked at her, smiling with every tooth in his mouth.

"Goodness, you are so handsome, so sexy. Are you sure we need to go to this dinner? I can think of other things I'd like to do with my night."

She laughed when Leo looked at her side-eyed. All he had to do was look her way to know what was on her mind.

"I promise we won't stay too late. He's bringing some big wigs with him and they want to talk about me joining a writing team for a new television show. It sounds like it's right up my alley. I'm glad you're with me. I couldn't be where I am without you. I'm going to grab my phone and call to check on Trayvon. He called me and I promised to call him back."

"I'll be ready in a minute."

Raquel watched Leo leave the bedroom of the beach house they were renting while in Los Angeles. She turned and looked out of the bedroom window which overlooked the Pacific Ocean and thought about the road their lives had taken since Leo had won the contest.

After winning and working out the deal around his contract, Leo was able to quit all three of his jobs because of the amount of time he would have to spend going back and forth to Los Angeles. With the winning cash prize, he was able to pay for Major to attend a four-year college for his last two years and they were all happy when he chose Florida A&M. He was able to pay his and his mother's bills up for a few months so that he wouldn't have to worry about them while focused on the movie.

Raquel smiled thinking about how her life had also changed in the year since he'd won the contest. Her father had decided to officially retire and spend more time traveling and playing golf and no time in the office. The plan was for her and Tyra to sit at the top of the company with the blessing of the board, but she decided to give up her position in order to support Leo. He was going to need a money manager and since that was her specialty, she gave up her position in the company and decided to live off of her savings and her trust fun so that she could be what Leo needed her to be.

Tyra had also made a change by deciding to open up a clothing boutique, something she'd talked about for years and now was able to do. Once they talked about their decisions with their father, he sold the company and gave her and Tyra a large chunk of the financial settlement to make sure they were financially secure. Knowing she was and money wasn't an issue, she traveled back and forth when Leo needed to travel.

They had recently begun talking about moving to Los Angeles to cut down on some of the time in the air, but the struggle was being away from his mother and brothers. To compromise, she suggested if they decided to move, that he bring his mother with them to California and let Trayvon decide what he wanted to do once it was time for college. Until then, he would move in with their uncle Max who had already agreed to look after Trayvon.

In the midst of that, Leo had proposed to her on his thirtieth birthday at a party she threw for him at her condo and in front of their family and friends, he shared with them how much she meant to him and how everything he needed in life could be found in her arms. If he was having a bad day, all he needed to do was think of her and his day would begin to look brighter. She was looking forward to being his wife, the mother of his children and his partner in business.

Waiting for Leo to finish his call, she turned on the television and before she could get comfortable, the sight of Tyrus Hill's face on the screen caught her attention as she turned up the volume. Within seconds, the remote control hit the floor as she covered her mouth to stifle a scream.

"Leo!" she hollered causing Leo to come running into the bedroom looking startled. She knew she scared him with her shriek, but she couldn't contain it as she watched the headline across the television screen.

"Baby, what's wrong?" he asked, walking toward her and looking her over for something wrong, an injury or something.

"The television – look!" she shouted. All Leo could see on her face was fright.

He turned to the television and saw what she saw. The headline scrolling across the television said, *"Tyrus Hill, billionaire mogul dead at sixty-four."*

"What happened?" Raquel asked.

"I don't know, but it can't be good and all hell is about to break loose. I hate to say it, but that fortune of his is about to make people crazy."

"Not only that. I have a feeling, we're about to get a glimpse into that closet where all of Tyrus' secrets will soon be released. Years of philandering, scheming, and I'm sure a crime or two are about to be unleased. Whatever happened to Tyrus Hill won't be the last word. We won't be able to count the number of secrets that have remained hidden all these years. Let the scandals commence!" Raquel declared.

"I agree baby. Scandalous!"

**

Tyrus Hill's entire life was built on one scandal after another. There were hints of illegitimate children, back room business dealings, illegal gambling and possibly murder as Tyrus Hill built his empire and now family, friends and foes are determined to take back what Tyrus stole from them and bring out the claws to get what is rightfully theirs.

Tyrus' legacy after his death begins with daughters no one else knew he had, but he put a plan in place, in case of his death, to be sure they not only found each other, but that they ran his empire together, keeping his heritage alive. Little did he know that his offspring were as treacherous, conniving and evil as he was. The world isn't ready for the Divas of High Hill. Don't even think of coming for them because they're too busy coming for each other. The fourteen-book series, "The Divas of High Hill" kicks off with "Secrets", launching in August 2020 and boy are there plenty of them!

Join the discussion on Facebook and get to know these Divas. They may be sisters, but the rivalry may have you thinking otherwise!
https://www.facebook.com/DivasOfHighHill/

Now Available

"And Then There Was You"

Book 1 of the "Malibu Hearts" Series

"And Then There Was You," is a steamy love story, set in Malibu, California. Diezel Wilder is a sexy corporate attorney from New York who recently moved to California after a bitter divorce from a woman he married on a whim after going through a tragedy that caused him to act out. In need of a break from the drama that surrounded him in New York, he hoped for a new start in sunny California.

Brooklyn Hunter, a sexy Armenian bombshell, is a late-night, on-air radio talk show host who woos men all over the country with her sexy, sultry, seductive voice. She's coming off of a divorce from a movie studio executive who is twenty years older. When they met, she saw him as her escape from a dismal life in Nebraska, but found herself thrust into the Hollywood spotlight, revealing a marriage clouded by adultery and out of wedlock children in a scandal that was broadcast worldwide.

Seeking a new lease on life, Diezel and Brooklyn are in search of the kind of connection with a mate that leaves them breathless. Little did they know they would find it right next door.

Bring on the ice-cold water because you're about to go on one very steamy ride to love in, *"And Then There Was You."*

I Can't Let Go

Carter Garrison vowed to love, honor and cherish his wife, Sienna, forsaking all others, something he forgot to do during a weekend of fun, bad company and poor judgement.

Sienna Garrison never dreamed her college sweetheart, Carter, whom she pledged her life to, would break her heart and when he did, she moved out and moved on - or tried to.

What better occasion is there than a friend's wedding to stir up old feelings and memories of love, intense passion and nights of sensual titillation. Gazes from across a room after almost two years apart revealed depths of love that had never died.

Seeing Sienna again reminded Carter of what he'd lost and he vowed to never let go by doing whatever he could to get his wife back even if it included begging and pleading. Is Sienna ready to forgive and take a chance on life again with the only man she'd ever really loved?

When Carter brings on the charm and turns up the heat, no woman is immune, especially Sienna.

Bossy – Now Available

Cassidy 'Bossy' Bostic came from nothing, but knew she would be something. Pregnant and alone, she was forced to run from her past in order to have a future. Her rise to the top as the owner of a fashion dynasty is what dreams are made of, but her hard, icy persona could have her living a lonely existence.

Drake Montgomery, a rising attorney heading toward the political arena, has fallen in love with the 'Bossy' mogul only to discover it's 'Cassidy' he loves, but 'Bossy', not so much.

Can their hot, steamy romance melt even her cold, icy heart? Only time and love will tell.

His Halloween Promise – Now Available

Dylan Kennedy and Savannah Eaton-Kennedy may be divorced, but that doesn't stop them from indulging in some pretty hot and sexy encounters.

A divorce decree may mean that their life together is over, but Dylan has a promise to keep that could bring his wife back where she belongs; in his life permanently.

Heartthrob – Now Available

Cade Weston, Hollywood's most eligible bachelor and named the world's sexiest man of the year, lives life at the top with a bevy of beauties at his beck and call, people providing his every desire and more money than any one person should have.

Callie Hurston struggles to make it as a stylist to the

stars in a world where women are intimidated by her beauty and men are interested in her body and not her talent.

Cade thought he had it all until he has a chance meeting with Callie and decides to take a chance on her talent and ends up taking an even bigger chance with his heart.

Can the playboy turn in his player's card and give in to love?

Home for Thanksgiving – Now Available

Firefighter Nicholas Sullivan is going home for the holiday after he was sidelined due to an injury on the job. Guilt over a life lost has kept him away from his family's ranch in Montana and now he's forced to face his past demons and deal with a self-imposed life of regret.

Veterinarian Parker Wingate's first encounter with the handsome firefighter was less than pleasurable. She sympathized with his hurt, understood his pain and before long, felt his love.

Knowing the holiday season is ending soon, can Nick go from living in love for the moment to allowing himself to finally live in love forever?

A Better Man – Now Available

Phoenix Graham is living her best life with the best man, her fiancé, Carson Stone, heir to the Stone Tower Hotel Empire. Her perfect life is shaken up when a handsome, rugged and extremely sexy mysterious man moves in across the hall and she begins to see that the rose-colored glasses she had been seeing life through were blinders. She soon discovers that Carson was the best man for her until she takes notice of a better man and his name is Gavin Black.

What's a girl to do when the best doesn't get better and better is what she craves?

Take a Knee – Now Available

Professional football player, Kenrick Wilson, never thought twice about taking a knee in solidarity with his team to show support for a cause that was near and dear to his heart. He was applauded for wearing his heart on his sleeve. His greatest love was for Justine Banks, the woman who stole his heart years ago, the mother of his children and his biggest supporter. Even though he loves Justine with everything in him, Kenrick has secrets and deep-seated hurt that has kept him from taking a knee for the most important purpose in life, making Justine his wife. Can he let go of the hurt from his past to secure his family for the future?

The Lake House – Now Available

Summers together at their families' lake houses as teenagers are what Danielle Fenton and the boy next door, Gannon Wilcox, loved about being on the lake in North Carolina. They fell in love at a young age and then one day it was over after Danielle ended their relationship with no explanation. The only thing Gannon remembered was seeing the woman he loved in the arms of another man.

Years later, Danielle and Gannon find themselves back at the lake, in their families' lake houses, both divorced after unhappy marriages and trying to find their next moves. They now have a chance to get this thing called love right as long as they believe in the history and power of love found at the lake that was always meant to be everlasting.

My First Love – Now Available

Ethan Bennett has what everyone wished they had, money, power and respect. When his first love, Valencia, walks back into his life, the love they shared as teenagers resurfaces and reminds him that there is no love like that first love.

Valencia Ramos never forgot the first person who loved her unconditionally. Now all grown up, Ethan is still everything she ever wanted and the love she still feels for him is a love she's never been able to forget.

Discover their path to finding out if first love is truly real love.

About the Author

Cheryl Barton lives in Maryland and in her spare time she loves to read espionage, crime and romance novels, cook, watch Sci-fi movies, spend time with family and friends and enjoy Maryland steamed crabs. Cheryl is celebrating 30 years as a government employee and loves writing romance novels when she's not working. Cheryl is the author of 31 romance novels, 3 inspirational novels and is proud of 4 book compilation projects with several other incredible women called, "One Sister Away: Encouraging Words from One Sister to Another" – a series of books meant to encourage, empower and inspire other women. People often ask Cheryl which book is her favorite of all of those she's written. While she finds it hard to select one favorite, Cheryl still looks to her first novel, Bachelor Not for Sale, if she had to pick a favorite because it was her first novel and the one that inspired her to continue writing.

Cheryl was a 2018 Finalist of the Literary Trailblazer of the Year award, given by the Indie Author Legacy Awards' yearly event. Cheryl is a member of the Romance Writers of America – National Chapter and the Maryland Romance Writers. She is also a member of the Black Writers' Guild of Maryland and a member of the International Women Writers Guild.

Indulge in more romance and inspirational novels by visiting her website at www.cherylbarton.net and connect with Cheryl on social media at:

Facebook
https://www.facebook.com/authorcherylbarton/
Twitter
https://twitter.com/AuthorCBarton
Instagram
https://www.instagram.com/authorcherylbarton/

www.ingramcontent.com/pod-product-compliance
Lightning Source LLC
Chambersburg PA
CBHW021217260626
47172CB00002B/472